Brunching with Ophelia

Brunching with Ophelia

Angshukanta Chakraborty

Vitasta

Vitasta Publishing Pvt. Ltd.
New Delhi

Published by
Renu Kaul Verma for
Vitasta Publishing Pvt. Ltd.
2/15 Ansari Road, Daryaganj,
New Delhi - 110 002

ISBN 81-89766-48-1

Typeset by Vitasta Publishing Pvt. Ltd.
Printed at Saurabh Printers Pvt. Ltd., New Delhi
Cover design by SREEDEEP

To
Subbu Ma'am

Contents

Acknowledgement

Perhaps I should 'thank' the fever foremost that had descended on me on one particularly unbecoming late-April afternoon in 2005, so as to completely dissuade me from taking four of the remaining MA (Previous) Eng Lit. papers and actually use the suddenly proffered time to 'get *it* out at last'. Gratitude then would also be directed to the benevolent rules of Delhi University which allowed me a promotion to MA (Final) despite the partial absconding on my part. Balloonfuls of thank yous and thankgoodnesses to Bonu, Dada, Baba and Ma for seeing me through that prolonged feverishness (when they solemnly agreed to overlook my disingenuous disregard for Crocin and other such miracles of pharmacy that could have delivered me from the fetters of that ferocious fever to the doors of room number 22, Arts Block, the venue of our MA English examinations).

Thanks to Sreedeep for the incredible cover-design. To Rashika, Amit, Vaibhav, Dhamini, Rahul and Pawas for giving me usable insights into college life as such, although they remain blissfully unaware of this passive osmosis. Sincere thanks to Brinda Ma'am, Dua Sir, Suroopa Ma'am, Tapan Sir, PK Sir for inspiring me at uncertain times, for getting me addicted to academia with its long-drawn queernesses and flashes of brilliance.

Really big thank you to Renu, who made *Brunching with C* see the light of day, in spite of my stubbornness with the title. Th Renu for bearing with me.

Thank you Namita and Ila for going through the pain-stak ordeal of proof-reading; Namita, thanks for withstanding my relen less onslaughts on punctuation and penchant for *italicization*.

Thank you Bonu for your intermittent FOs and bloody-hells; they kept me going.

Thanks Doc for finding *scope* in it.

Finally, thank you Subbu Ma'am for everything. This is for you.

One
Acknowledgement Screen

[illegible]

ONE

Screen

N.Y.C.!

There, real, live N.Y.C.

She called out, "Shoi, Shoooooiiii, come here, take a looook, dammit, I've got N.Y.C.!"

Shoiiii looked up from her Constitutional Law and sighed. *Foolish stuff,* she didn't say, just meant.

"En Why See, Shoiiii!"

-- Ennui Sea, Shoiiii...

New York City floated around vertically pasted on the computer screen. The Times Square Cam.

WebCameraObscura, WebCameraIndica, WebCameraLucida.

She appropriated those names, suitably.

Please leave a message, it said, the page. Then begged on behalf of its begging bowl, the yellow bars meant for name and email ID [for confirmation later] and the white blank square space for Comments.

Comments were special. They were personal. They indicated intimacy. Intimacy with distant farflung beauties. The beauties were pots of uncommonness in the Ennui Sea's bosom. Those pots grew bigger each day collecting comments like souls. Ennui Sea was an endless heaven with glasshousehotels that reflected Ennui Sea and yourpunyunfitface back. She didn't notice that because it was the image of En Why See she was looking at and dismissed the inherent question that lurked within. She gawked, happy for prattle.

"Shoiiii, you're soooo boring!" Prattle rose.

"And you're sooooo dumb." Shoiiii didn't say, but meant, *You, like all the apers, gawkers, gazegobblers, are suffering from a Historical Dumbing Down. You take any and all the givens for eyecandies. You don't 'distinguish', not even Now.*

Shoiiii didn't say, just meant. Didn't see, just went. Away. To their bedroom. Which had the cooler. Desert, it said. Oasis, it could have been. Names on coolers.

Aye, Aye, Aye, Aye. She replaced the i's in Shoiiii's phoneme with her own affirmatives. That was the way she showed her allegiance to Ant-Aye-Ennui-Sea camp which Shoiiii led. Only showed, never meant.

Suddenly the page said, the page is not available. She Refreshed it, upon which it said, ReLoad Macro Flash Player. Commanded, actually. She guessed the order, sinking within. The Ennui Sea meanwhile had stopped churning and had frozen, as if it was the Ice Age once again. The frozen image was dumb and deaf, like her, metaphorically, implicitly, as Shoiiii would qualify.

Macro Flash Player re-loaded itself like Flash Gordon who used to zigzag through colourful cartoon candystickers [stickers were for free, always] when she was younger. That implied deafer and dumber, as Shoiii would mean, not say.

The frozen image-sea moved a bit. Flashed a bit. Poured its waters a bit into her eyepits. Sockets. Sockets found a black man, in grey overcoat and blue jeans bending to collect something. An EnnuiSea comment that he had misplaced? She couldn't guess. Black man was hefty and was folded onto himself and he looked like a zebracrossed Use Me in the middle of the broad pavement. She didn't know if it was correct to call it [in the middle of which the black man folded onto himself, involuted, as Shoiii would say, and mean] footpath or pavement. She stuck to pavement. The greyblack Use Me collected pinkfaced *Can I Use You*? s around it. They all didn't move. Just flashed a bit. They all were steadied by the Macro Flash Player which was re-loading itself. Their sandwichwrappers, Pepsicans, tissuepapers, facewipes, drinkstraws, doodledscrips waited to be used up in the greyblack Use Me. Collected. But she couldn't have the collection until Gordon had re-loaded himself. The Wait said, you're being awfully, stereotypically, Literaturally, uncritically slaveapish in Recasting Fanon. Recasting Fanon was a job she had to do as a part of her college curriculum which had *Othello*. She also had *Hamlet* but *Hamlet* didn't need Recasting Fanon. She realized that she wasn't good enough yet in Recasting Fanon and brushed off the imaginary sandwichpapers et al as one brushes off a filthy streeturchin flattening its nose on a spotless car window.

That was before marriage. After marriage she means, doesn't say, for there's no Shoiii to say to, I've got London. Trafalgar Square Cam. Which shows her a perpetually grey sky. Teary eyed Trafalgar Square Sky cries often to make her very feelgood. Once she had seen it dawning on the TS Cam. Teary eyed TS Sky changed from blackcottony to violetvelvetty to skybluegreybladdered LondonUranus who peed in no time. And peed copiously making puddles at a little distance from the twin fountains at TSquare. She saw pee-rain rainpeeing merging with fountaineering glistening globules of H_2O. She remembered Gargantua who drenched Par ris, playfully.

And the neat division that was enforced, brought into practice, persisted. En Why See EnnuiSea premarriage, LondonUranus postmarriage.

Such was a neat division that arose only to breed its inmates in the jail of her soul. More 'Still Neater Divisions'.

Neat division arose because En Why See had reincarnated itself into another thing. A Man's something. Big Apple had metamorphosed into Her Adam's apple and insisted on staying stuck in her throat, pulsating like a haughty heart. Throwing tantrums like a stubborn kid when the electricity went off just before Tom & Jerry was about to begin. Making itself conspicuous and omnipresent in Her Adam's apple, making itself transmittable as airwaves or cablewaves or the expectation of it.

Her Adam was Shumonto Roy. Microbiologist. Dr. S. Roy.

Shoiiii was Shoili Sengupta. Miss Shoili Sengupta.

She was Ivy Sengupta. Mrs. Ivy Roy. Now.

Of course Trafalgar Square Cam was on and the enlarge.php flashed, blueblackedout, then reflashed TSq every two seconds. Or something like that.

That was her way of looking through the glass. She saw clouds, rains, greysky, greybuildings, fountaineering and a tall half-cut column which she thought was the lower portion of the Big Ben! She saw all that and considered herself a Clarissa Dalloway. A touristically virgin she-wolf that she was, her eyes sat in ambush behind the concrete shrubs of a far away place, its clouds haunting her through textbooks of time. Its mysterious rain, the all time rain, kissed her from the screen. *The vapoury leaden circles dissolved in the peedupon air.*

Later when she had realized that the Big Ben was at Westminster, (another famous somewhere else, amid galaxies of them) she had immersed herself in an imploding cry of misrecognition. She had invested in TSq. In that half-cut pillar which was suddenly not Big Ben. In that rectangle of livecam she had believed, in a story of gaze she had faith. TSq was her Londonesque Cannaught Place. Exactly the same feeling she used to get when she used to walk in the CP rain. Seepeerain. White and grey were interchangeable colours where it rained often, or during the rainy season where it didn't rain that often. In August for example.

[And then on such a fine August evening, Ivy Roy rummaging through the old archives on Yahoo Messenger came upon a rather unusual looking message from her husband Shumonto Roy, asking her to try logging into one of his relatively unused Yahoo accounts and check for mails. It also mentioned that for some weird reason Shumonto was not able to open his mail account from his computer in a microbiology lab of John Hopkins University where he was a PhD research scholar. The message was dated 16th October 2001, a time when Ivy and Shumonto were merely good chat-friends, and had never seen each other in person. The message was also marked unread which implied that somehow she had overlooked it when she received Shumonto's offliners.]

Shoiiii wasn't the literary kind. She was the legaliteral kind. She didn't like very twisted sentences. She preferred Clarity. Another neat division that Ayevee had concocted to ratify Shoiiii's calling her deaf and dumb. Shoiiii was a ssshh-ed set of four 'i's and Ayevee was its affirmative. That indicated, metaphorically, implicitly, that Shoiiii was egotistical while Ayevee was her egoless yeswoman. One was centripetal, another, centrifugal, and she rechecked the dictionary.com to refind out which was which.

But it was then, when she confused the two centri words. Now only one remained. Centripetal.

Her Adam's apple insisted on staying centripetalled. The World, she read EnnuiSea, converged into that ticking tool.

[And on such a fine August dusk it became increasingly difficult for Ivy to decide on the next move. She knew that her much loving hubby had an unshakeable trust in her and wouldn't mind Ivy's granting him a much delayed favour. However, she was unsure of a few things. Firstly, she didn't know the password to that particular Yahoo account. Apparently, Shumonto never used it or had newly created it just before it got blocked. Shumonto, otherwise almost insanely patient a person, was rather snappy and short-tempered when faced with technical failures of any kind. Therefore, it's more than obvious that he had bidden this troublesome account goodbye forever and had shifted to more reliable mail servers. Precisely why Ivy Roy never had an inkling of this weird sounding mail account, <blacksabbath75@yahoo.com>.

Secondly, Ivy found herself unnecessarily tormented by marital ethics. She didn't know if a wife ought to have unconditional access to her husband's accounts; accounts of all sorts viz., of the bank, the credit card number, emails or personal diaries. Of course, Shumonto had no time to harbour secrets from her; he was an extremely busy man, working even on Sundays, occasionally. Also he was never inclined to pour out his heart into a silly notebook with a page for each of the 365 days of a year. Shumonto was therefore as secretless as water was odourless and colourless and Ivy was more than convinced that branching out into secret lives would be an interesting alternative for both of them.]

But secret lives existed. For instance, that they were Ayevee the affirmative and Shoiiii the egotistical Shumonto didn't know. He wasn't intimated. He wasn't a part of the sisterly charmcharmis circle. That was the circle that they had drawn with the distance between them serving as the diameter. The circle expanded, contracted. A bit geophysics experimentalishly.

Ayevee the affirmative had tumbled into the world two years after Shoiiii the setoffour-i's had. One year, 10 months, 13 days to be precise. They didn't count the hours minutes seconds. Such nanomalies were permissible preservatives in their mixedfruitjam of a sisterhood. Their postnatally conjoint lives unfolded in parentheses that they kept from him, and most of the rest, sometimes even from Ma-Baba. What was in brackets was patented implicitly, with a mutual understanding of unbroken vow. That was their way of keeping it theirs, the deepest well of secrecies, their secret lives in first second third brackets, always just theirs. Trespassing was not allowed. For a trespasser's offence one of them had to be penalized. Shoiiii and Ayevee, one of them, who voluntarily or involuntarily, became the betrayer. For each trespassing, there would develop a chink in the secretwalled charmcharmis circle which oozed out a bit of secret. For each oozing out, the circle would become a bit imperfect, flagging at points.

Shumonto was instrumental in imperfecting the circle, at lot of points.

[Nevertheless, Ivy decided to go ahead and bring that dead account back to life. She wasn't sure how to do it though, for she had no password. She wasn't even sure if the unchecked mails were already deleted from the account because of the long neglect. However, she had tinkered enough with online messengers and small-time softwares to know of the little tricks of the big trade. She ventured into cracking it with the shaky thrill of a schoolgirl fed on the Adventures of Nancy Drew.

She opened the Welcome to Yahoo Mail page and typed the ID. In her excitement, she pressed the caps lock key accidentally, deleted the faulty typo and then typed it once again. B L A C K S A B B A T H 7 5. All in small case, without space. Then she clicked the link:

Forgot Your Password?

She filled out the requisite tabs on the next page under the Confirm Your Identity section. She mentioned Shumonto's date of birth, 22 May 1975, the zip code of JHU, 21218, (only the first five digits) and mentioned the country Shumonto was then living in, United States. Then she re-entered the Yahoo-ID in the tab in the section headed 'Forgot Your Password?' and pressed the 'Get New Password' Button. In a second she was transferred to another page that said in bold red fonts:

Congratulations! You have successfully created a new password.
Your current password is: devilface666

Ivy gave out a triumphant little shriek of exultation. So Shumonto should not be ashamed of his rather technophobic wife anymore, she had managed enough skills to pass off as a moderately all right techie. She mentally gave herself kudos and gleefully went on to sign in to the account.]

Neat division cracked at places. Premarriage, postmarriage. Chaste haste of testy knot made the circle get protrusions and involutions which then became tubular tunnels that ferried out secrets to him. At first, at times, then often.

Together they had been parenting the thesis for a very long time. 26 years. Until the knot was constructed. Until he came in with a vengeance once again and turned her mind inside out. She then began keeping secrets from her.

[Username: blacksabbath75
Password: devilface666]

Their one-studyroomed, one-doublebedroomed bookish life had transformed itself into an electronically facilitated life. They stayed in touch through sms-es, emails, and phonecalls. That was because Shoiiii, vintage Shoiiii, unlike vintage Ayevee, had chosen a mobile life. She moved around the country on sponsored missions of Jaagaran. She had been to Western India quite often, centring at Bombay. Er, Mumbai. Shoiiii, therefore, saw the world As It Is, unlike Ayevee who saw the world As On Cam. The real versus the phenomenal. Ideal versus shadow.

The computer-room was the studyroom wherein the computer came much later but managed to rechristen the room. Computer was the wonder-wander glass that reflected the World As on Cam. Reflected EnWhySee-EnnuiSea. Reflected the rainpeeing London-Uranus. Reflected glasshousehotels and greysobbingskies. Reflected the twin points of reference that built up the Worlds eyes.

They saw through the World's eyes. She saw, more truly. Saw what the eyes shone with. Manhattan miracle, Trafalgar twinkle.

They hugged each other tight the night she discovered EnWhySee. In the joint semivirgin bed their legs wrapped around each others' to fight the cooler's chill. Already it was pleasant. The chill crept up their moist inner calves and inner thighs and something in between sweat and cold trickled down into the crumpled flowerprinted bedsheet. She whispered into Shoiiii's coldblocked ears, "Hey, do you think we will ever stay there? You and me together though?"

Elder sister smiled, "Aye you're such a li'l sow. You learnt nothing from all those harangues at D-school."

Aye frowny-ed, for frowning was a childhood thingy, a thingy of the pastry-past, for frowny-ing had its geometry displayed on every chat-screen, for frowny-ing was easier to prove and demonstrate, for a yellow fullmoon with an upturned semicircle conveyed the universal electronic frown, with which AyeVee identified: "C'mon, we can meet Ash there, and Groggy, Poppy, Gory, and the rest. They all stay there, don't they? And you got Sejomama too, and Munipishi! What 'bout 'em?"

Elder sister became all the more elderly, "That is not the point, *shona*. On principle it is. I can't go and live in a country the policies of which I so firmly oppose. Don't you think that I would be a spoilt hypocrite if I live on US money and blabber against it?"

"Sooo whattt? All the intellectuals do that!"

Thus they made pillowblankets of each other, thinking at once that perhaps they should turn the Desert cooler off and put on the All Out mosquito repellent instead. But no one moved. Endured the little chillpricks here and there, pulling up the legs in order to do the occasional scratching. And when Ma opened their bedroom door to check she saw the usual stuff. She wished they really had been the twins if they behaved so much like a psycholocked pair.

[And in that postrain August twilight, Mrs Ivy Roy, in her newfound sleuthsituation, was then delivered to the next page which welcomed Shumonto and said there were seven unread messages in the Inbox. She heaved a sigh of relief; so the mails had not been deleted after all! Thank Goodness for that. However, she hovered on the page for a while devouring the word 'Shumonto' written in bold blue fonts at the top of the page. She was in love with the name itself. She would keep chattering it to herself and would break it up into smaller parts, each conferring a new meaning to her understanding of her husband's character. Ivy Roy, as a matter of fact, was obsessed with names of every creed and size and loved to rechristen herself after a character from English or Bengali literature at every possible instance. She became Isabel Archer, Anna Karenina, Bonolota Sen or Emma Bovary every now and then. As far as Shumonto was concerned, she would call him Shumon, meaning Good Heart or Flower in Bengali, or Shuto, meaning Thread, (rather ill-fitting considering his gargantuan stature) or would alter it to Ghumonto, meaning Sleeping, for the man would do anything to get some nap virtually anytime anywhere.

Her eyes inadvertently shifted to the pretty female face in the ad space on the right. The regular shaadi.com virtual poster featuring wannabe brides in search of grooms and vice-versa. Very Indian, very customary. The speaking cloud emanating from the girl's dreamy eyes said: Hi I'm Gayatri. I'm 25, 5'6", MBA, now Junior Executive in an MNC. I'm looking for a sensible and sensitive man who would share my passions of books, travel, music and dogs! Ivy remembered the last time she had logged into her personal account the same woman was there posing as a prospective bride but had a different speaking cloud: Hello, this is Ekta. I'm 22, 5'3", a Music Teacher in a Public School in Delhi. I want someone with an appreciation of classical Indian music and traditional cuisine. I'm a homely cultured girl and looking for a sensitive and encouraging partner.]

"Gudevens!! You're marrying him?! Him??"

Shoiiii was evidently exasperated.

Aye was nonplussed, outwardly. "Who else to marry?"

"Yeah, that's there. But can't you wait? Why just now? What's the Big Hurry??!"

Big Hurry was a Big Joe from a Big Country who had a Big Baton in his hand. Their *Boromama* was BigJoeish always with aplomb, throwing around his humungous weight everywhere. Ex-merchant navy man, he was only used to hurryingscrurrying and to precise execution of His orders. Mintu and Rintu, his sons would blankly obey the "Keep it there!"s, "Walk tall and straight without fail!"s, "Eat your dinner fast and take ten rounds of the colony after that!"s with the silent grudge of simpering labourers who are made to work in preposterous postfeudal fiefdoms. Shoiiii had found something BigJoeish about Shumonto as well, hence the exasperation, hence the I-have-to-save-my-Aye desperation.

"Aye you're making a Big Mistake!"

Aye realized that Big Mistake was the first kin of BigJoe, and that the entire extended family of BigHurryJoe was waiting in ambush in Shoiiii's mouth to Charrrrgeeee! *On a Poet's lips I slept...*

"Has he proposed you?"

Aye smiled slyly. "He said, it's a difficult proposition, so he'd pass."

"Pass? Pass my ass! Tell him to pass or bypass or trespass somewhere else! Pass my foot!"

When u temme u love me
I wonder with glee

Why can't ur love be
ten per cent free
like our energizing Glucon D!!

Aye got slier. "Shooiiiiiiiii...." She was pleading.

"Don't even try! A damn EmSeePee you're courting who treats you like shit always. You know what's your problem? You just fell for the always bit of it. He makes his shittery so persistent that you think it's his everlasting love for you merely appearing inverted!"

EmSeePee. MCP. Male Chauvinistic Pig. A perfectly okay way to describe a prospective groom, or an unwanted suitor, or a narcissistic male boar who doesn't yield to a woman's subtle invites. MCP was a fit-all term, an umbrella term to indicate the inscrutable males.

"He half-loves me, I'm sure of that. We won't have any adjustment problems."

"He told you that? He gave you that crap?"

"Nope."

"Shucks, not even that?"

[She took the cursor on the Inbox link but stopped herself awhile. Was it really right for her to thus open Shumonto's account? After all, he hadn't asked her to open his Inbox, only to check if it was a server problem or a problem with the account. It must have been the latter for that was why it was never really accessed after that day. 16th October 2001. Those were the days when their relationship was exponentially growing although it took them almost three and a half years to actually meet each other in person. Shumonto rested all his faith in her, for some unfathomable reason, and even she trusted him deeply. Every single online information, credit card dealing, software installation, hardware problems, net connection, webcam image modulation, sound card set-up was first surveyed and sanctioned by him and then only would she go on to do as instructed. Moreover, never did she access his accounts in his absence or unscrupulously fidget with his JHU online bookbank number, which was given to her for anytime use. Presently Ivy, wondering what to do next, took refuge in old Miltonic lessons. Virtue cloistered is no virtue at all. It must stand the test of evil. So would their rather neoconventional bond. She wondered if there was a talking serpent in that Gayatri of shaadi.com, whether it had crept in as a black mist inside her, making her perform unmentionable deeds. No way, she told herself, she would definitely tell him everything over dinner tonight, he would be amused for sure. She wouldn't keep anything from him. Not anymore, not after 10 months of their marriage.]

They would giggletalk in Hingali and discuss in Seminar English. Nightlychats were of lispysugary sisterhood, daily conversations were crisp and to-the-point. Dinnertable talks, before Baba-Ma, were in Benglish. Precise Bengali and Precise English.

Now, postmarriage, conversations were electronic. They now lived Inboxing Outboxing. They talked in lowercase, and occasionally, to display surprise, happiness or sorrow, they turned the Caps Lock on. Smileys were rare. But none had a folder called Shoiiii or Ayevee to give each other the special sisterly privilege. Mutual Interest was a secret pact that they hadn't bothered making electronic yet.

E-convos informed them of whereabouts, upcoming seminars, latest books, cinemas (never movies, movies were for the uninitiateds), boozeparties, who's been the sickest dog/bitch lately, what each took for comfort binging this time around, launches, screenings, others' life/annual/monthly/weekly partners. Their e-convos could be mistaken for a PR brochure or a supplementary tabloid of a middlebrow newspaper.

[Seven unread messages, the Inbox said. To Ivy's mild surprise, the first six out of those seven were from one Irene Scott and the last and latest one from a certain Richa Arora. Ivy had no inkling as to who these women were. Ivy hesitated for a while and then clicked Next on the Inbox list. Those turned out to be junk mails from shabby sources and Ivy selected all and deleted them in one go.

Having cleansed the Inbox thus, she pondered whether she should actually read those seven mails. They looked a bit fishy. Six unanswered mails from the same woman. Ah! why of course, she knew now! The account got blocked and turned inaccessible. Either this Irene didn't receive a reply, or perhaps, and more obviously, got notified of Shumonto's new account. She looked at the dates. All of them were posted around October/November and the latest one was dated 18 February 2002. The pattern looked slightly uncanny.]

They both suffered from frequent simultaneous stomachaches. Usual monthlies, unusual bi/tri/tetrayearlies. They would recite psalms to ward off evil. To Pyricontin, the painkiller.

Hymn to Pyricontin in Our Sickness
pyrrhic pyres of pain
scrounging scavenges scalping scrapes of scum
enter Thou
amid eyes of base acid
alkaline alter
churning chunks of chum
tissues torn, templates tossed
around ample ache

At that, cramps would redouble. They increased the pitch.

do dissolve
parts pronouncing pain
mingle 'mongst my moulds
knead knowledges of knaves
in inner intestinal instincts
innate interstices infringing
solid souls' solace
enter Thou

Ma would hastily bring the hot water bottle. Hot water's heat soothed somewhat. Shoiii's was purple and hers red. The leathery hot water bottles with a stopper in the tapering mouth, similar to an airpillow, could be made into a waterpillow for babyheads. The final outburst before the storm slowly ceased.

crossing crass crocinated cramps
stubborn stomach's stalls
ur-Ophelian uterus
through throngs threatened thebes
climes clanking clues
enter Thou
calming calls
Amen!

Baalaishaat! Komechhe byatha?

Godsaveyou! Has it come down? Ma would anxiously want to know.

Twin twinkles told her, *komechhe*.

[She uttered an Alright, here we GO! and clicked the oldest mail. After having read that, she didn't wait a second to go on to the next and then the next to finally reach the one posted by Richa Arora. The mails read as follows:

From: Irene Scott <ishq_75@hotmail.com>

To: Shumonto Roy <blacksabbath75@yahoo.com>
Date: 7 October 2001
Subject: None

Dear Shumi,

I know it is crazy of me to write to u after so long but u know dammit why I never wrote before. I needed time and so did u so I did what I thot wud be best for both of us. But needless to say that I've missed u and am missing u right now, especially now.

Shumi, it's terrible. I'm dying. Really. I've been tested HIV+ and I dunno if I got AIDS for that's immaterial now. I dunno how I got it, but I did have some injections taken when I developed the chest pain again. It was bad but now it's worse. I'm alone here and I can't fight my last battle all by myself.

I need u. Please can u come to Dallas for once? Just for a li'l while. Please. I won't even touch u. AIDS isn't contagious anyway. Heck whom am I telling? A Microbiologist there!

Shumi won't u come and see me?

Love as always,
Ishq

******

From: Irene Scott <ishq_75@hotmail.com>
To: Shumonto Roy <blacksabbath75@yahoo.com>
Date: 16 October 2001
Subject: None

Dear Shumi,

I know why u didn't reply. You thot it was a sick joke of mine again, nope? But really Shumi, I'm not lying. Who lies about dying Shumi?

Will u ever take me seriously?

Love,
Ishq

P.S.
Do Reply!!

******

From: Irene Scott <ishq_75@hotmail.com>
To: Shumonto Roy <blacksabbath75@yahoo.com>
Date: 18 October 2001
Subject: None

What on earth is your problem dammit? Shit you won't even talk to me when I dunno till how long am gonna be alive you fucker. You think it's a big farce right? Just fuck off !

******

From: Irene Scott <ishq_75@hotmail.com>
To: Shumonto Roy <blacksabbath75@yahoo.com>
Date: 20 November 2001
Subject: None

Dearest Shumi,

I've no clue why haven't u replied. There must be something wrong for I know u too well and u can't do this shit to me.

Whatever, I'm off everything. You should see your plump Ishq now, as thin as a stick. LOL

Crap, yeah, I oughtta be modelling for those drug-awareness campaigns. Here, posting u a recent sexbomb pic of mine.

Smooch,
Ishq
Attachment: Ishq19112001.jpg
Total Size: 80K

******

From: Irene Scott <ishq_75@hotmail.com>
To: Shumonto Roy <blacksabbath75@yahoo.com>
Date: 22 November 2001
Subject: None

Shumiiiiiiiii,

I refused a blood transfusion yesterday! I'm loving it.
Hugzy,
Ishq

******

From: Irene Scott <ishq_75@hotmail.com>
To: Shumonto Roy <blacksabbath75@yahoo.com>
Date: 29 November 2001
Subject: None

I will never ever write to you again.
Adios Amigo

******

From: Richa Arora <arora_richa2000@indiatimes.com>
To: Shumonto Roy <blacksabbath75@yahoo.com>
Date: 18 February 2002
Subject: Irene no more

Hello Shumonto,

I'm a friend of Irene. She had told me of you but had forbidden me from establishing any correspondence for she was extremely hurt because of your callous and negligent behaviour towards her.

It's important I think that I let you know that she's no more. She left us on the 27th of last month for another world.

May God make her soul rest in peace.

You should be sorry for what you've done.

Richa

******

Ivy Roy, Lecturer of English, MH College, wife of Dr. Shumonto Roy, Research Analyst, Department of Microbiology, All India Institute of Medical Sciences, New Delhi, sat stunned, glued to her chair, in front of the computer screen, till she felt a cringe rising, till the worldtimeserver.com recorded 10:42 p.m. IST, and smiled, Happy Time Check!]

TWO

Slash

Exactly at 10:42 p.m., the doorbell rang and Ivy Roy figured that she was alive and confronting a brand new world. That was none other than her workaholic husband Shumonto Roy back home after a hard day's labour. Often he would turn on the Beatles soundtrack and listen to it until Ivy got fed up of him and yelled loud enough to make him do a CD transplant.

Tonight things were already different. Tonight Difference sat on the window grill and hawked on them. Ivy, quiet as stone, observed her husband come in with that selfsame worn-out look, keep his bag on the sofa casually and sit down exhaling a lot of tired air. She turned on the fan and offered him water without even asking how his day was. If Shumonto felt this was out of ordinary, he was self-combative enough and didn't appear to have noticed.

He sat there for a while and then was compelled to say a word,

'Remote?'

Ivy looked around and fetched the thing asked for from under a sofa cushion. It had slid under when she was watching her share of late afternoon sitcoms after returning from college. She would unwind a bit during that mundane hour, watching NDTV or Zee English, or if lucky, catch a decent movie on Star or HBO. Both of them had long stopped watching Hindi flicks unless it was just released or coming on the local cable channel; the regular ones on the Hindi movie channels were old wine they had had an overdose of.

Ivy felt that both of them had already watched all the possible old Hindi flicks and there was rarely anything new waiting to be unveiled. She would regularly watch the regional films on Doordarshan, the afternoon telecast on Sundays especially. Most of them had been nominated for national awards or screened somewhere abroad, respectable enough for her to sit through the two hours or more, of course with intermittent jaunts to the kitchen, the bedroom to see if anyone was online, or simply to the balcony to get a glimpse of the desiccated Delhi's afternoon surroundings.

She had devised a perfect way to tell if the film was worth watching or not. Subtitles. The magic word that cast a spell on the cinema aficionados, national or international. English subtitles seemed to grant that aura of perfect poise, grandeur and intellectualism to the 'local' flavours. It was here that narrow particularities merged with broader elegance, where the strange became believable, understandable. Oh, but for the utility of English, her own country-people's art would remain a question mark to her. But for the magnanimity of English subtitles, the regional films—the homegrown exotic, the neighbouring unknown—would never see the bright lights at Locarno, Venice or Cannes, would never unfold on gigantic screens that would transmogrify the vernacular to the cosmopolitan, that would dissolve the antonymity between the two. She had her regular fills of Baangla films though, of course those were the ones for which, thankfully enough, she didn't need a linguistic intermediary. The old ones, the certified-by-time ones, starring Uttam-Suchitra, or Shoumitro-Aparna, or occasionally those directed by Goutam Ghose, Rituporno or Aparna Sen. As far as Satyajit Ray and Ritwik Ghatak were concerned, she had them earlier devoured during her university-time film festivals, and would refresh her experience of those visual treats as often as the Alpha Baangla channel would permit, internally fighting that Great Bengali Battle of who was better than whom.

Presently Ivy sat with her knees joined together on the sofa next to the big one, where Shumonto had stretched himself out. He was flipping channels in a frenzy, as if that was the way to elicit an answer from her. Why the deuce was she in one of her black moods, he thought, mentally computing all the possible sources of her complaints and not really arriving at a conclusion. Finally, he settled for the Richard Gere starrer *Autumn in New York* rejecting Tom Hanks-Meg Ryan's *You've Got Mail* which he was forced to watch a good three-four times over, thanks to his rather senti wife.

Ivy Roy, sitting at about a meter's length from her husband Shumonto Roy, slipped into that bad habit of speculating while appearing to watch the snowclad New York on the TV screen. She embarked on an elaborate project of mythmaking, thought of him as a living fossil of a heroic age, an age that still prized calculated orthodoxy, that still measured glory in martial terms. He was a fighter, a warrior almost quixotic in spirit, worshipping an image of something and condemning the live specimens of that ideal as unworthy and degraded. As he divided the world neatly into angels and whores, he failed to realize how deep he had sunk in the quicksand of illusion. His was not a capacity to delineate, but an obstinacy not to see, and it was an artistic failure that he refused to accept himself. He could not or chose not to see the overlap that whores were the real angels and the ethereal beings that masqueraded as angels before him were bloodsuckers of a staggering rate. He called himself Ash, yet he looked out for a clear divide between black and white, for in his digitized world even the shades of ash were a permutation of certain units of black and white, the original shades, the shades that were given to him in the womb and that he could never part with. It was the folly of his digitized world that sought to measure everything.

But 'orthodoxy' was a rather vague term: how could he possibly belong to that moribund creed when he could cook, clean, compute and have unbridled copulatory fantasies at once! Surely, he had made a clean break; his ancestors last breathed that poisoned air of coercive extravagance when they had 'exploited' on the basis of gender, class, caste, territory, headships, schooling, and other such 'issues'. Things were different now: he was that perfect combination of liberality and protectiveness that a woman would lap up at the first instance—more so, her grateful middle class educated parents. Yet he was afraid, he had a lurking fear of contamination, he loathed pollution of his mind, though he was aware of his already polluted soul. Nevertheless, that was something to be kept at bay: that pollution, that perversion of mind. It should be ritually expelled from his system by a regular indulgence in pornography, knowing that it was a 'sin' that he was committing, for anything culturally endorsed and shunned at the same time must be copiously sinful, precisely because it was unconcluded, still debatable. Such an indulgence made him feel suitably criminal and comfortable, for then at least he stood the chance of a certain confession. By admitting his guilt to the only receptacle of his molten phantasms, he would feel a sense of relief. His self-exculpation would ensure that any 'perversion' on his part got recorded strictly as perversion and vice, that those entries in his register of sin got properly marked so that once he had them expunged they could be struck out for permanent erasure and sent off to the trashbin of time.

His remorse-bug would bite him periodically, he would neatly empty the recycle bin of his mental C-drive, defragment his system once more, run an antivirus auto scan, and there! It would all be clean and clear and admirably debugged. His was a strange lot, though his type was more common than apparently acknowledged, for these bugs bury their corpses deep beneath their graveyards of souls. But like living fossils, they have their charms and fatal attractions. His was a magnetic one; his vulnerability was his best tool. He was rigid, yet not brittle, something granite-like had entered his heart, it was impenetrable. Yet one only had to deploy X-rays, alright a mental version of them, to see through him, those high-frequency beams which snatch off the privacy of the remotest heart. So he was seen through too, though obviously by the time a general impression had been arrived at, the inferences from the observation made, he had already changed his internal constitution, staying grey still but just outwardly. His soul was an electrolytic battery, with the charged ions of his thoughts accumulating at shifting ends at different times, so that a neat deduction was impossible. However, those charged ions had a backward pull, and belonged to a bygone time when ions actually separated, or perhaps shapeless thoughts were at all compared to units of fixed positive or negative charge. Though in his digitized world that metaphor not only held good, but actively patterned his system of thought, and convinced him of the divisibility of every action, thought, emotion, feeling into constitutive minutiae of digits. 0 or 1, everything was either 0 or 1, or a certain combination of it. It was a world of binaries, of exclusion, of a sign corresponding to just one signified, in which even his trilinguality was a matter of fact.

Whose fault was it? Perhaps it was ridiculous to call it a fault at all, and obviously Ivy was being hideously judgmental. Can a longing for staying happy the ordinary way be a fault at any rate? Can regularity be a crime? Have we reached such an exalted state wherein every being in itself is a miracle of creation contributing to the onward march of history? Theoretically, yes, but theatrically no. Uniqueness in every nook and cranny wasn't spectacular. His dispassionate nature wasn't devoid of passions, but they were as transient as a whiff of fresh air.

His wasn't even a dilettantish kind of a mental bent, for he was far too religious to be capricious about something he believed in, but a kind of unwillingness to bring about a revolution. He was the typical upholder of status quo, though he was slightly more fortunate than his forefathers to be born in less unfortunate times. The solution for all woes was a play of digits for him, merely a recombination, a reshuffling was all that was needed, without hampering the delicacy of the exquisite fabric called life. He could be a later day Achilles, if warring was equivalent to lab-testing, and if the focus was kept merely on the broodings of the solitary Greek man on the banks of Thetis. For him, too, glory was concrete, in the efficacy of the lately purchased GPS for example, or in the installation of an instant messaging program with camming, VOIPing and AV tagged in. Glory still, could also be discovered in his silencing his online detractors by a generous use of tongue, often so copiously and fetishistically that others would be daunted in no time. He was a terrible beauty in that sense, his heroism was sublime in the subtlest way, so fine that almost invisible to the unaided eye.

For amid his meeker cohorts he stood out as distinctly as a blot would on a newspaper sheet. He was a blot, for he wasn't a well-intended bit of reformist writing. He didn't ooze from the pens or appear from the keys of the existent thinktank. His origin wasn't a mystery, wasn't anything special. He came into this world as blots often do, to indicate the writtenness of the world around. Yet he wasn't a piece of writing, he was the product of years of involuntary intellectual inertia, that became a knot in the mind and from an off guard jerk of hand manifested as a blot on a sheet of paper. Precisely that was his difference; amid the herd of scribblers he was the one who dared to stay clear of the tendency.

Was it a lack of adaptability? Wasn't he the one who would advocate the policy: 'blend in'? The belief in assimilation, in integration was unshakable. Wasn't he constructed to be the quintessential patriarch, the protective father-figure? Was this because of the primordial lack, the uprooting he had undergone when he could barely utter Pa? His desire to penetrate and impregnate, a psychic offshoot of the departed father?

Yet would these illuminations (she would like to see them so, her mind trained in the gruels of Literary Theory would never stop short of adding another into the sea of definitions or metaphors) be enough to explain what meant those seven mails from two different women, one now extinct. Was she seeking an explanation altogether? Did she, Ivy Roy, who liked to think of herself as a rather enlightened and open person, at least open to twists and turns of life, in an accommodating way, enriching way, need an apologia of some kind from her weary husband to cleanse and reform their relationship? Can a dead letter from coffins of time actually bring about a difference in the way they would perceive each other from now on? Were there more 'mysteries' to dig out? Would they be worth digging out? And what then once they're out in the open? And then, would the buried notebooks of her past too be read aloud that day? Was she going to rewind time, run backwards?

It was the problem of intellectual affluence, lost in translation. Here was Ivy Roy, armed with the theoretical rockets of self-defence, all too guarded, all too removed for any real injury. Here she was ready to lap up an iota of pain to consign it to the museum of analysis, and when that ache was suitably dissected, when its carcass was disfigured with the scissors and forceps of understanding, she would be ready to mummify it with pen and paper, or preferably on the MS Word document she would hastily create to save the aestheticized feeling. T.S. Eliot had affected her in more than casual way:

> From wrong to wrong the exasperated spirit
> Proceeds, unless restored by that refining fire
> Where you must move in measure, like a dancer.
> The day was breaking. In the disfigured street
> He left me, with a kind of valediction,
> And faded on the blowing of the horn.

******

After 45 minutes of Richard Gere prancing about an ailing Winona Ryder, Shumonto got up and made a beeline for the bath. He spent 10 minutes there freshening up, slipped into his XL white Children of Bodom T-shirt, came back to find his wife sitting in exactly the same position as he had left her. He made a quizzical expression and lightly patted her left shoulder. She glanced up, in a way too calm to grasp. It was as if she was studying him, watching his every move, grading him silently. Generally he liked being watched, he liked it when she would keep staring at him for several minutes over without looking away even for once while he would be watching a flick on DVD or just working overtime on the daily residue.

But today, it felt weird. First, she hadn't even bothered asking him a single question since he'd stepped in, and second, she was making no move to lay the table and set the dinner. Not that it was her prerogative to do those chores; they had, at the very outset of their conjugal life, reached a mutual understanding, to be co-operative. Shumonto was a far better cook than she was, he would gloat over that mockingly at every opportunity and she too would join in the mutual admiration society. Shumonto liked her basically for her ability to take things in good spirit, not to make a fuss over smaller things of life, to be able to distance herself when he would feel her way too near than he would like her to be. She was flexible, almost unbelievably flexible which made him wonder if she really did love him at all.

She did, of course, he would conclude after some retrospection. She had undeniably been there, been there when he needed her the most, during his rather lonely stay at JHU, while doing his doctoral. It was a strange situation; he was amid a crowd but forever out of place. He was without a woman for a good length of time; his mother was staying in Benares with a cousin then, his elder brother lived in Boston with wife and child. He missed his family, the idea of family. The idea of regularity, of a unit, of being knitted together so that when one feels like it one can always go away from something to feel free. However, he needed that something to come back to. To define his sentimental freedom, his cultivated nonchalance, he needed something to periodically distance himself from. But over there, that something was missing; he was confined to a draconian solitude doing everything by himself for himself. It roughened him but also softened him.

Then one day he talked to a chat-nick called Ophelia. He recognized that name, the female from Shakespeare. Which one was it, he tried to remember. Oh yes, *Hamlet*. He was Ash of course, the notorious Ash of Kolkata Online. Others often thought he was a female, some similar adventitious extras on the virtual stage proclaimed him a cross-dresser, a dragqueen, but he was unmoved. He was lightening quick with effective repartees that would leave his opponents panting for breath. So it began with her too, a war of wit, a play with words, a battle of sexes, a quibbling with roles, just anything to ward off that monster pain.

They had hit off instantly, and the attraction proved stable and resilient to the onslaughts of time and space. It began with a semi-romantic infatuation, went on to become a strong bond of understanding and secret sharing. Without knowing, the two were spending more than five to six hours a day talking to each other. She was Ivy, an MA student of English Literature in Delhi. She was erratic in her schedules, and differed from him a lot. Yet, they held on to each other. For what exactly they didn't know. He did for he was too tired to ever forge ahead into a real relationship again, though he longed for female breath near him. The difference between the real and virtual had blurred for him; the real was fantastic with scores of White, Chinese, and African faces fleeting past. Knowing them wasn't difficult; it was a matter of time mostly. Time and interest. Interest and patience. Patience and self-effacement. Then assimilation, before blending in, becoming American, becoming standardized and becoming universalized.

There was Gary, his colleague on the project, there were Timothy, Raymond, Hugh, Shin Lee, Joe Nbaku., and his supervisor, Professor Adolph Benjamin. For six years, he had shared his laboratories with them, shared information, exchanged databanks, and tossed around with the genepools of the minute inhabitants of the world. Gradually, he realized that he could be more at ease with the microbes breeding in the petridish, than with other human individuals. People here wouldn't understand his college-time Hinglish jokes; it was his job to comprehend and get acculturated to American humor. Yes, with the 'u' missing. Was it any different? Didn't matter though; it was a systematic levelling happening all around. A global cloning of types. Of psyches, of emotions, of jokes. Acclimatization: the simple term in his Record Folders assumed mammoth proportions of significance.

Just within a few days of talking to Ophelia on Yahoo Messenger and Kolkata Online, he had ventured on to declare:

"I don't care about anything, nor do I care if anyone gives a damn about me. I'm beyond repair: difficult, arrogant and frustratingly self-centred. I dispose off women as fast as I acquire them. With men, I rarely form bonds, and when I do I give them their due."

Ophelia had answered,

"Never mind. I like challenges."

He had smiled and said,

"But I'm a tough one. A really tough one."

She had coolly replied,

"All the better."

Now standing besides her, gazing at her upturned face, he tried finding that Ophelia once again. For some reason, Ash and Ophelia were still alive in them; they would poke fun by calling each other Iishh and Ooops during intimate moments. Earlier, he used to wonder what made her log on to the net, come online, talk to him, no matter how mundane it would get. They were the wits of the chat-rooms but during private conversations would become dependably predictable and then gradually dependent on each other. Once he stumbled on to the idea that she could be awfully unattractive in person, but then he had phoned her and liked that tinkling, a trifle kiddish voice. What was he trying to be, a father-figure? She was merely four years his junior; could that transform her into a child-woman? Could a child-woman question the very basis of opinion formation: Who the fuck decides whether one's attractive or not? Who determines the categories of attractiveness? Why this crave for a universal attraction?

"Are you alright? Feeling ill?"

She slowly rose from the ice-bluish sofa and stood erect looking at him. Small. She barely reached his shoulders. All good things come in small packets, she'd kid him.

"I'm fine. I'll lay the table. Let's eat."

He sensed something was wrong. Or at least not quite right.

"Periods?" he asked, concerned and ready to lay the table himself.

"Nope, it's nothing. A li'l tired may be."

"Hmm. May be you should rest. I'll get the dinner."

He made her sit down and went to the kitchen to find out what she had cooked for the night. Vegetable rice, heavy *masoor daal* and omelettes. He never liked salads. So she avoided making them for dinners. There was yesterday's chicken left for him in the fridge. He couldn't do without non-veg, a peculiar trait that linked him to the rest of his Bong brethren. She wasn't a meat-buff, in fact, she hardly had a taste bud; omnivorous to the core, she could consume and digest almost anything, albeit in far lesser quantities. A small person like her could hardly stomach in more.

He put the food in the microwave and let it warm for a minute. Then he wiped the dining table with an old wet towel she used as the table-cleaner and poured water from the refrigerated bottles. She loved iced water; she would gnash ice between her teeth in front of him, making odd sounds of cracking ice. If he displayed even a slight sign of irritation she would doubly embark on her 'freezing the moment' enterprise. The typical after-dark banquet would only make him feel more at home.

Today, she was unusually quiet. Not that everyday she would chatter away, but at least small-talk. Or keep smiling and staring in a rather kind way. In other words, he would have her undiluted attention, her entire concentration. It intrigued this much critical man, for he had seen the brigades of firewomen. She would get angry at the very mention of the word though. Again you're typecasting, branding women, she would say. He felt that she had an untouched sanctity of her beliefs, something he could never penetrate. Nor did he want to disturb her over there. For him, the approach was to simplify life. She fiercely believed in complicating it. Problematize it, we need to problematize it all. Everything has to be rethought over, she would mumble on. Yet all she had done with him was to make his life much simpler, graspable and at times blissful.

She was elsewhere today. Far removed.

"Whassamatter?" he pressed her smallish hands.

"Nothing." The voice came from a distance.

"Temme." He insisted. "C'mon, what has happened?"

He always used fork and spoon while she preferred eating with her hands. Bringing up, she would say, unassumingly. My Amro-Bank. Yeah, America-Drop Out, he would add. Baah, she would jerk him hard, America-Jilter.

She was hardly eating anything. He offered her the chicken but she declined. Just don't feel like, she added. There were traces of turmeric in her right hand fingers. The *daal*-water was trickling down her forearm as she rested her hand in her mouth for eternity. He wiped the stain clean and gave her a shrug in the shoulders. Suddenly unguarded tears started rolling down her cheeks. She started sobbing violently and had no idea why. He kept insisting that she tell him what it was but she could hardly speak, squealing like a little mouse newly entrapped.

He held her close while she staggered to the bed. Acting, was she? She wasn't sure. All her life she had been pretty sure of her theatricality at every phase. Now all of a sudden her band of stage-metaphors weren't helping her. It's my unconscious that's doing the role-play now, she thought. A role-play nevertheless.

He tucked her into the bed and covered her with the sheet, putting two pillows to support her throbbing head. It could be the power, he thought; her eyes need a recheck. He went to the kitchen and cleared the dishes from the dining table, swabbed the tiny puddles of *daal* she had scattered while running her fingers through the centre of the plate, then put the empty bowls in the sink. He ran some water to let the stains of grub soak for a while. He put a big mug of milk and water in the microwave meanwhile and let it heat. She would need some coffee, he thought. He washed the dishes at a jet speed and was back to her with the coffee in 20 minutes.

She wasn't in the bed. Instead, she had turned the comp on and was reading a mail. He came to the desk and peered over, placing the coffee on the bedside stool. In that smallish bedroom of theirs, there wasn't much space to walk around, so he would inadvertently sit down the moment he came in, or lie down if he was tired enough.

Presently, he asked her in a mildly chiding tone, "What crap are you doing there? Get back to bed and have the coffee hot. Right now."

She was unflinched, and was sitting on the chair dumb as a doll, scrolling the page down. He came closer to get a better look. Squinted his eyes, sharpened his gaze, then hurriedly scrolled the page up. He read the name of the addressee. Something struck him down, but he still stayed calm. Nerves, he had them in inhuman abundance.

He glanced back on her face and studied it for a while. Then in a self-assured manner, he said, "She's a good friend back in the States. Long lost touch though. But this account I had completely written off from my mind. It is okay, nothing to panic. You know I'm not enthu enough to carry out an extra-marital behind your back. I got no time you know that. So get your tiny head some rest now. Hurry up. I'll just go through the mails, write a decent reply, and join you in a while. Okay?"

She got up and he helped her back into the bed, placed the mug in her hands, and smiled warmly. I'll keep you fine my sugar, it seemed to say. She regretted it at that very instant. Sheeeeit. He didn't even know it. She could have kept it a secret. Or deleted those mails. Or simply blocked the damn account. Why didn't it strike her earlier? An odd little trifle sometime in the past, was that trivial detail going to redirect the course of their lives? Would there be a change? Would he feel guilty? She didn't want him to go through all that. But why, just why did she have to act so stupid? Why couldn't she omit the ill-formed lines from the script of her life? That would shatter the play, or would it? Should she wait and watch his reactions? Could a cached death affect him? Who on earth was that Irene? A prankster? No, since he just acknowledged his having known her. Then, who? A psyched-out junky? On drugs? How did he get to know her? When at all did he ever visit Dallas?

As she was immersed deep in her thoughts, she eventually heard a faint string of words coming from his lips.

"I killed her."

Prelude to Dereliction

[..burrowing into the origins of life or into its detritus
which pardons the paradox—Derek Walcott]
Let the machinated time grin awhile
minutes spent in retrospection of just lost moments
I, like a benumbed blinded bird
Will perch on branches of blank window screens
While you scream or smile or pant in heaves
Or shut life's spring from its animus source
And wait for a benignant second
To pour out my second thoughts.
I'll look for animal signs
Impassioned with fire frames
Blinking on half-lit bluish face
A face to read and left effaced
I'll be there, like an unclaimed arch-priestess.
Minutes will pass in slow penumbra
Under hollow skies of solid strength
Enough to squeeze out your mortal breath
From inherited pneumatic cavities
I'll watch the dim words come out slow
Line up like obedient assembly kids
With smattering of rebellion crushed beneath the stick

And if they disgorge on their own accord
After being well-thought, well-put, well-recited,
well-received
I'll let them be, glad being scattered
They'll make good reflectors of this harrowed time
Glad to be of use, some use of some kind
Tumbling forth like an unwanted birth
From metaphorically cellotaped mouths
Mouth of lust hidden behind
A translucent veil of angelic white
Perhaps you'll know it all
When you drink from the cup of shattered myths
This façade of playing the mute
When words like kisses are bubbling within
You can see even though you can't
See through the separating silent seas
Seas that send across unaccepted invitations
Of open pain and open scars
Seas that fondle in waves of cries and whispers
Seas that trample underneath a weight
But then the hours have to be passed
[How they blow away when you're around and murmuring
murders!]
And tortuous moments closeted and denied
Only half-produced but doubly stored
Complaints that multiply like viruses within
Our restless gonads, anxious devils in mucous sacks.
Should my words be softer 'cause my tissues are?
For there's no tranquillity, only recollection
Unrelenting in spasmodic spurts
Do they unsettle your perfect poise?
Bring in creases on that steadied countenance?
[Flushed out now, after those thoughtless words]
But hours tell you that it's not so
For it is what it ought to be
Just like you'd have it here, suiting,
soothing your grey cells.
I'll be the eager listener you'd need at times
During half-deserted spells to confide a sin
When your mortal flesh gave in
To greeting medusas of cactusland
How your tepid soul tempered at that
Prospects of incipient flirtations with generous deaths
Death of futile needs to feel!
You see them burning on the pyre
Of your collected dreams and memories
of tenderness

Then narrate me the remains in ashes
Grey splendours in your consciousness
Specks of fraudulence on a mundane plain
A suffering virility's toils in vain
Virtual world, balanced on disconnection
That's where we met suddenly on a certain day
And since that time so many times
I've hacked into your water belly's underland
Only to find some weeds of stray
And fell before fuming medusas
Who turned their violent eyes at me
To petrify of course
Turn to stone and stop its flow
Whatever that's protoplasmic here
But I escaped somehow, unnoticed, from their cavernous mouths
Landed back on dirty keys to tease out a word of ease
To comfort your haggard heart
[That's your most cherished part
to act the Knight beneath burrowing darts]
I saw the snake-haired nymphs on the verge of an almost rage
Not yet retiring, anticipating still with persistent gaze.
Time I felt an intractable bond
That flashed past as epiphanies do
Often without recurrence.

******

THREE
Gnaw

The brothel of a sky was full of dark promises the next morning. Ivy woke up with a puffy face, hardly able to get any sleep, couched in the lonely bed for the whole night. It was disparagingly soundless, as mute as a tomb, and he was away, wrenched and self-exiled in the drawing room, sprawled on the big sofa. He had made it clear that he wanted to be left alone and she thought that was the best she could do at that ungodly hour.

She checked with her cell phone timer, 8:36 a.m. Late, already. Had he left? She got up in a panic and came running out. There was an empty bottle of Red Label lying on the small Persian carpet under the teak center table. The Borosil glass had somehow escaped a crash; it was rolling at a deadly edge on the table. The curtains had been drawn aside though, the room was full of light and a cake of sun was warming the southeast corner.

She could hear sounds of running water in the kitchen. Perhaps he was making himself a quick breakfast; he too must have got up late and thought it wouldn't be wise to raise her that early. It was early for her in a way; she was attuned to her afternoon teaching schedules at college, she was never an early morning person. Consequently, she was also a semi-insomniac staying up till late into the nights and sitting up reading, surfing, chatting or simply hooked onto the idiot box. On the contrary, he preferred a well-compartmentalized life, with due respect to everything, and as a result certainly occupied a higher rung in the efficiency scale. Yet they were pretty well-adjusted to each other's ways of life, and only mildly objected to any particularly annoying idiosyncrasy of the spouse.

He was making a toast for himself, and some black coffee. As she came up to him, she seemed to ask the anticipated question. How was he feeling? He averted her gaze and asked her to sit down. Calm. So terribly unflinched, unperturbed he looked.

"Aren't you running late?" she asked meekly.

"Yeah," he answered, while pouring some milk into the remaining liquor, "but I've called up the Lab office. Told them I might get a little late."

"Okay," she said.

She picked up the *Friday Review* to distract herself. Without her glasses she had to strain her eyes to make the letters out. Must get them checked, she mentally noted. There was a function for the promotion of the heritage of North-East India at the India Habitat Centre in the evening. Included a photo exhibition, regional dances, folk songs and ballads and a skit on the invasion of 'urbanity' and cultural abrasion. She would have gone with either Shoili or Kamya, or perhaps with Nalli and Bishakha directly from campus, had she been in the mood. Appreciation of cultures is only a matter of receptive moods, she figured.

He handed her the coffee and seated himself in the next chair. He was in the middle of reading the *Times of India*. Without much sound, without a single word. As quiet as a cat, she thought, or perhaps a jungle beast that moves around in padded feet. A leopard or something like that. There wouldn't be too many leopards left in the course of time. Suddenly she was happy to have one at hand, at home. A precious predator.

"What does it say?" she asked, desperate to release the tension.

"Ugh let me see. Onion prices soaring in Gujarat. Now Kolkata stores can sell liquor. Centre does balancing act on temple. Cerebral Malaria in Mewat. Mars is the limit for Delhi schoolboy. Pak tests nuclear-capable missile. Babri panel: no talks under threat. Right to strike feature at Indian Labour Congress. Interpol meet to focus on fugitives. Gautam Ghose tribute to Satyajit Ray. Lingerie lures them to net. Vampires at work, of course at nights. Animation film on attack. 17 thousand Ram-bhakts leave for Ayodhya. Senegal President gets ceremonial welcome. Nepal Maoists seek rebel base in Bihar. India's sex prowess: 8th in the world. Mother Teresa's beatification."

And now, all this is no more but history. Dead and alive in the archives of time, she thought, struck by the cold taste of his elocution.

"And this, my dear, is what your clan feeds on. News! You'll get a better sense of it if you get Eminem to rap on it."

Was that a jibe at her, or at the morning? Or at the fact that she was Ivy and not Irene? Was he distressed that she could never be anybody but Ivy? Had he always secretly wished her to be Irene?

Weird. She was Ivy Sengupta before marriage. She's Irene Scott. They shared their initials. I.S. Ivy still is, Irene is not. Is that really so? Is she really not?

That scraggy attachment of a pic was absolutely useless. Horribly unclear, bad resolution, a bit too dark to make anything out. Apparently taken inside an ill-lit room. Must be one of those cheap digicams sold on the footpath. *Recent sexbomb pic of mine*, that's what she'd said, hadn't she? Humouring death, well, sort of. A joke is a pretty antidote to human immunodeficiency virus, perhaps. Irene Scott was determined to remain a mystery to Ivy Sengupta. No, Ivy Roy.

He left about an hour later than his usual time. She had barely managed to ask if he was feeling alright. He had replied that he was, most certainly, and what possibly could be wrong with him. He had kept sitting long after his coffee was over and was showing no signs of being in a hurry of any kind. They had the usual daily liners. He advised her to take a leave in case she wasn't feeling well. She assured him she was okay and would manage.

For a while she didn't budge from the small round dining table they had kept in the little space outside the pigeonhole of a kitchen. A mere nine hundred square feet flat on the third floor of a government residential complex in the heart of the city; two-bedroomed, attached bath, and a balcony which was common to both the bedrooms. Just a single entry, from the drawing room, which was comparatively bigger than the other rooms, and had the majority of electronic appliances. The 25 inch Philips colour TV set cum DVD player, the Panasonic digital deck among others. The Kelvinator refrigerator and IFB washing machine were somehow crammed in the small dining space, thanks to his excellent space-management skills. The microwave was kept on the top of the 250 litre double-door fridge for the seepage from the kitchen walls would make it hazardous for it to be placed there. The Aquaguard water filter couldn't be helped however.

The splendours of an urban life, she thought. Digitized, calculated, automated. Preprogrammed. Where the members stay together like subatomic particles huddled inside a tortured nucleus. Lack of physical distance would imply lack of mental distance. But that wasn't quite the case, was it?

Who could tell they were living in India? Living in a metropolitan city was almost the same in about any place in the world. Humankind was trapped in a big hall of mirrors, reflecting each other from different angles and multiplying the images. Most cities looked the same. But of course there were subtle differences. The area codes in the telephone numbers, calling cards, the arrangement of particular digits that silently gave out your position in the cosmic coordinates. Then there were the speed factors, efficiency factors, consumer rights awareness factors, standard of living factors, and other scores of minutiae that acted as the sentinels of difference every moment.

Her broadband connection never exceeded 48 kilobytes per second; his sat happily at about 100 megabytes per sec, when he was still there. She would have frequent downtimes, whereas he had a downtime lasting for 17 hours just once in 11 months and they had it flashed in the local newspaper causing three thousand users to change to another network company overnight. "The difference is way too obvious isn't it?" he would regretfully comment, and she had no other choice but to agree. Yet she fought back, "That is not the only index of progress. We need an open approach towards issues, things. Alright, you gain scores as far as materialism is concerned, but isn't it ironical that I read articles on affluenza, the disease called affluence, which cloys your appetite and distorts the taste?" she wasn't sure, however, if she was making much sense, or if that article she had read in a major fortnightly magazine would mean much to the Nissan Sentra driving microbiologist of JHU, who knew that having two cars was any day better than having just one.

The Speaking Tree, the speaking cloud, the Talking Serpent. The rage of the mutes. Spiritual healing as an alternative to the burgeoning physicality of extravaganza. The two sides of code-culture: digits and sutras.

It was 10 when she finally walked into the bath, shampooed, came out and wrapped around a black-bordered dark red synthetic saree with the all-purpose black sleeveless blouse. Applied the sunblock copiously, despite the darkened sky. Her regular doses of kohl and a long black bindi resembling a bisected section of a cone-cum-hemisphere (she liked the 3-D effect of the description) brightened up her face a bit. She took the umbrella out for it had started pouring down by now. The last minute file checks were done in a haste, the lecture attendance register for the two afternoon classes she had with the second and third year students, the textbooks which were the complimentary copies she had received from the publishers for being a part of the MHC faculty, albeit she was still a temporary there. Everything was slid into her pretty Calvin Klein black handbag, one of the first gifts from him, when he had just come back, suitably Americanized.

She was running late already, had the first of her classes scheduled exactly at 11:45 and the next one following immediately after at 12:40. The second was a double lecture but she intended to wind it up within a period and half. That would mean she would get free by around 2:20, quite early for her. During the fag end of the session, at times, she would be required to take extra classes lasting till almost 5 in the evening. Also, she would have to begin early, reach campus by ten approx, though she generally preferred spreading the pressure evenly out, all through the year, so that along with Nalli and Samiran, her erstwhile teachers and now colleagues, she could devote some time to the creative writing society and the film club. She didn't have a very powerful voice to suit the stage. She had never tried at dramatics. Although that was a genre she found immensely inspiring. Like many others. She wasn't choosy. A tendency reflected in almost every sphere of her life: food, clothes, places, interests, favourite actors, movies, cars, gadgets. Just anything decent and workable would do for her. She was open to trying out almost every thing as long as it didn't involve much physical exertion, consequently not too attached to anything either. Another strictly urban trait. Any kind of sweating out would involve elaborate aesthetics in the metropolis. The sports clubs, gymnasiums, stadiums, wide polo grounds, cool swimming pools with crystal clear disinfected water. No, she wasn't the sporty kind either.

The downpour was gearing towards the heavier side. As she climbed down the stairs, she gazed up at the dark grey sky and remembered a line from Keri Hulme's *The Bone People*: "And the rain was fairly pissing down." She improvised it a bit: The hissing rain was pissing down in a fury. She opened her big blackie of an umbrella to shield her from the heaven's untimely blessings. Only if it had started once she had reached the campus. Then gently chided herself: selfish woman!

She stopped an autorickshaw and bargained for a minute. Seventy bucks. On other days it wouldn't exceed twenty, ten for the bus fare and ten for the intracampus rickshaw ride, from the bus stop to MHC gate. Shumonto chided her for being so miserly about her travelling expenses. In fact, it was she who needed the car more than he did, he would argue. A staple Maruti Esteem, dark maroon. He never liked small cars. Said they were unmanly. She chuckled girlishly, and asked, what about a lorry, sire? Nah, soon he would buy a Tata Safari, a steelblue Tata Safari; it had the right curves. Ahem, she would give out a light forced cough.

"But what's the use," he would resume on second thoughts, "if we have to go back then there's absolutely no point buying a new car at the moment."

"Go back, where?"

"States of course, where else?"

"Oh."

"Perhaps Boston. Maa and Dada really want me to come back to them. It'd be nice if we're all packed in the same city. I want my family back, in one place, together."

"Yeah."

"With regular visits to each other's places."

"Yeah."

"And if not Boston, then somewhere nearby, or up north."

"How 'bout NYC?"

"You can't really stay in the heart of the city there; you live in the suburbs and travel to work by car. That's if you're emigrating this late."

"Okay."

"So somewhere up north."

"Yeah."

"Not down south."

"No, not down south of course."

She loved that advice Tridib would give his nephew in Ghosh's *The Shadow Lines*: Imagine with precision. As Ophelia, she developed an immense fascination with maps, atlases, geographies. Especially when she found a screen reflecting a kind of all-space: the online world map. Slowly she would diversify into the outer space, read a bit about the galaxies. She read once that somewhere they had found a diamond star. Or was it a planet? Had she ever bothered looking up the compendious atlases kept in the school or college libraries? Never. There was something about the screen that had maddened her. May be she wanted to locate every trifle of a word uttered by Ash, when he would visit Detroit, Philadelphia, Pittsburgh, Virginia, Ann Arbor among other places. But this required only looking up the political map of USA. Her mind would rebel against her soul and she would click on the links leading up to Artic icecaps, interiors of Africa, or the land of Lula and Pele, her father's much admired political scion and football icon. Then she would wonder, was she really imagining anything? Where was it? Wasn't everything already there, cut up in tiny images, bits of information, figures and statistics, in the names of the capitals and ministers, in the pictures of food and handicrafts, already there, already present, already available and removed at once? Was an act of clicking on a link equivalent to having imagined it altogether? Wasn't imagination something far more original, recreating time and space with little tools of words? Here she was, nicked Ophelia, the almost aphasic woman behind the universal man screaming Words, Words, Words. Why had she nicked herself so? A belated redemption? A salvation of a kind? Wasn't it time that Ophelia too should now quibble with words, no matter how emptied they'd become of substance?

The autorickshaw was rushing down Ring Road, creating a splash every now and then when it sped over the puddles on the asphalt street. She had folded her blackie and kept it aside waiting for the rain to subside so that once she got down it wouldn't be a herculean mission to reach the Arts Block. Not that it was a longish walk from the gate to the staff room, but MHC under the able leadership of Dr. Kanchi Shekhar was fast getting restructured and renovated with quite a few state-of-the-art buildings erected to suit newer needs, so that the little distance was all ornamented with semi-solid cement heaps, dug up soil, mud and brick piles. Covering that quarter kilometer was as good as winning a hurdle race.

Thoughts of Irene Scott came back to her. What came back dammit, she had never quite put her off anyway. The late Irene Scott she should say. One of them. The dead souls. Here she was, a modern Chichikov trying to buy some worth of time by trading in the thoughts of the dead. Could she imagine Irene? How did she look like? The name sounded British to her, a descendent of the great Sir Walter Scott, she mused. Heck, the Scott family would kill her had they had an inkling of her speculations. And anyway, once you fall into that big saucepan called America, you become one of them. America is not a place. It's a state of mind. It's a metaphor. America is a condition every human being should aspire for. America is the spirit of Eros, of creation, carnival, elegant slangs, angelic whores, male female 46 chromosomes, whorish angels gays lesbians transvestites chromosomes don't vary or may be they do depends, black, white, grey, yellow, brown, red, pink and even green. America is a prism refracting all colours, all senses, all souls. It's a cauldron into which people want to fall and get fried to a golden yellow from their present pallor. Or vice-versa.

So what the hell she was? An Anglo-American? African-American with mixed parentage? Indo-American? Latin-American? Anglo-Australian or true blue European living there on a student visa? Well she could be just anything. As one of Ivy's friends had once commented (he had quoted Lyotard perhaps, she didn't remember who exactly, and mentally rephrased it), if you're a lesbian Anglo-Irish oceanographer or a bisexual Indo-Anglian archaeologist living somewhere in Cuba or Pretoria or Lima or Laos, you generate a good little stream of cultural capital.

Should she find out more about the late Irene Scott? But how? She couldn't possibly open other mail accounts! Opening one was preposterous enough, and disastrous too. Hopefully it wouldn't be much, probably he would behave normally in a few days; he had a penchant for digesting blows. He was over the top this morning, and was making no effort to check himself. The bubble would burst in sometime for sure; she had to be prepared for that. A week of remorse would follow. Then another week of expiating the sins. Then he would come out suitably cleansed and sparkling with newfound domestic religiosity. And would get doubly workaholic.

At an instinct she thought of calling up Shoili or Kamya. She desperately needed to talk to someone. If she had genuinely depended on anybody other than him, it would be these two people: her elder sister Shoili Sengupta and best friend Kamya Shankar. And of course, there was Nalli at college. Right now, she needed her sister the most. She tried her number. Switched off. She tried Kamya then. Fortunately, she picked up.

"Heyyy babes! Pleasant surprise gurlosss! Whoooh! What's up with youuuu????"

There speaketh the hyperexcited Kamya Shankar; she laughed a bit.

"Nothing much. Just on my way to campus. How're you?"

"Yeah am fine. My shirtless wonder just left for office. We got up late and you can imagine why."

"Heh, good good! Keep the cradle endlessly rocking!"

She didn't get the literary link of course but lapped up the gist. Forget Walt Whitman, Ivy told herself, versified dreams of salad says, cold nights warmed by robust lines from the American soul. Walt Whitman who lives on. Walt Whitman who is lost somewhere in the stars and stripes. Whose self-weaved dream has in fact preyed on him. America the dream, the vision has preyed on many.

Kamya brought her back from there. Back to where she could be a bit more at ease.

"Oh sure, hun. *Tu bol. Tera kya chal raha hai*?

"Nothing really. Umm, I was just wondering, can we meet today in the evening? … Possible?"

"Today? Alright; but what's the matter?"

"I need to talk. I'll ask Shoili to come too."

"Hang on, what's the fucking matter babes?"

"Nothing much really. But I need to t…talk. Is it possible today, say at 5 at Dilli Haat?"

"You've a deal there."

"Thanks. I'll see you around then. Catchya laterz. Bye."

"Yeah okay. Bye and take care. Love you."

"Love you too. Bye."

Click. Snap. A wired world. A webbed world. The warp and the weft. She felt like touching him a bit at that point. The day was wet and she was showing the symptoms too. Engulfing wetness. Last night was dry. A hot Sahara. She dialled for her oasis.

"Yeah temme."

"You alright?"

"Of course I am. Why do you keep harping on the same line? Say something new."

"I was a bit worried, that's all."

"What about?"

"About last night's episode. Look I need to explain. I'm really sorry. I shouldn't have..."

"Hey look here, no one need be sorry alright? No feeling sorry shit. I'm not saying sorry to you. Am not explaining anything, am I? Then why don't you too feel a li'l less sorry for yourself and me, and give your hyperactive imagination some relief, eh?"

"Well, yeah I guess. I was just thinking..."

"No need. Don't think too much. I've always told you to mend that messy habit of yours. Anyway am busy right now. I'll talk to you later. Okay?"

"Yeah. Just one thing. I'll be meeting Shoili and Kamya in the evening at Dilli Haat. So would you pick me up from there on your way back?"

"Predictable. Sure. So what time?"

"It closes at 9:30-10 approx. Anytime, before that. Gimme a call."

"OK. Bye."

"Yup."

Snappier. As always. She kept holding the phone in her hands and then checked the last call duration. 2 minutes, 21 seconds. She wrote an SMS for Shoili: <Meet me @ Dilli Haat @ 5 sharp. Urgent>. Then she put it on the silent mode to avoid being disturbed during the classes.

At the Inter State Bus Terminus there was a red light at the crossing and the situation seemed mildly worrisome for the stoppage time flashed on the signal in digital red indicated two minutes in the beginning but somehow it wasn't changing. She gathered from the auto driver that the screen had gone defunct and noticed a traffic policeman holding a manual indicator and directing the sea of vehicles. The underground train network was under construction and the Delhi Metro board had the entire city dug up with heaps of soil bordering the wide roads and narrowing them down. Almost after every five minutes one came across the Caution: Work in Progress or the Keep to the Left/Right placards, in English and Hindi.

She was exactly on time for the class with the third year English Honours students with whom she was doing Conrad's *Heart of Darkness*. She scurried through the long Arts Block corridor of MHC and signed the teachers' attendance register once again intruding into Bishakha's space as the 'y' of her first name plunged deep into the tab below hers. Bishakha's elegant black got dabbed by her blotchy blue but she had no time to de-mess.

The attendance was thin today. Rains? Nope, that's not the case. Friday, she thought. A big band of belles and boys were enrolled for the CAT prep courses: Common Aptitude Test for the future administrators of business. Good for them. It'd been barely a month since the beginning of the session but CAT was slated in early November and the task was arduous. She had adroitly skirted that territory when she was graduating. Uninterested, was she? Or simply not formulaic enough? Err, that would be self-exculpatory. Not tactful rather, not organized enough to carry out warfare in two distinct tracts. Anyway, she had given up believing in equations ages back.

"Good morning folks," she began, shifting a tiger-print umbrella a little left towards the walls, seating herself on the teacher's table and dangling her saree-clad legs loosely in the air, "So back to good old Conrad, yeah?"

There was a general affirmative murmur with dispersed 'Good morning Ma'am's for about a minute. In the meantime, the textbooks were drawn out of the blackish, grayish bags, cell phones switched off, notebooks flipped and gel pens de-capped. Not a bad beginning.

"To begin with, I would like someone to read out a portion from the text, in order to witness how things indeed fell apart in the *Heart of Darkness*. Let's turn to page 59 and hear what Conrad has to say. Who's volunteering?"

The familiar hands shot up in an instant. Hmm, she mused awhile.

"Tara, go ahead."

The tall, thin, dusky girl, the Dram Soc vice-president, charged up the room with her resonating voice.

We were wanderers on a prehistoric earth, on an earth that wore the aspect of an unknown planet. We could have fancied ourselves the first of men taking possession of an accursed inheritance, to be subdued at the cost of profound anguish and of excessive toil.... The prehistoric man was cursing us, praying to us, welcoming us—who could tell? We were cut off from the comprehension of our surroundings; we glided past like phantoms, wondering and secretly appalled, as sane men would be before an enthusiastic outbreak in a madhouse, on the edge of the black and incomprehensible frenzy.

"That would do. Thanks Tara." She cleared her throat and recommenced, "What comes through from the lines, as you can see, is the mist of incomprehensibility, a brooding tension at the crossroads of cultural interaction, and a simultaneous fetishization of the Other. Who is this Other? Where is this Other? Is it the White Man in a continent, which happens to be not Europe, not the West, not the 'comprehensible', knowable World as it is merely present as 'a blank space in the map,' the very spot of Conrad's and perhaps every Europeans' boyish boast?' Or is it the indigenous African himself, in his native land, the 'other' in the eyes of the perceiver or the anthropologic European in this case (her self being the quintessential 'other': Europe or Africa, it doesn't really matter, or to be politically correct, didn't matter!)"

She waited for a few responses, some interjections. Yeah, one hand had gone up.

"Yes Akash, ask away."

The confident, baritone voice spoke up, "How do we come to terms with the decidedly racist overtones and the very obvious anti-imperialist critique in these lines? I'd quote this line specifically: *We could have fancied ourselves the first of men taking possession of an accursed inheritance, to be subdued at the cost of profound anguish and of excessive toil.* What's this accursed inheritance referring to, the 'accursed' Africa or the 'accursed colonial enterprise' of the King of Belgium?"

"Good observation. Thanks for bringing the point to our attention Akash. You see, Conrad was serializing his *Heart of Darkness* in 1899, in midst of a sea of ambiguity, haze and as he himself emphasizes, utter incomprehension. Sad indeed for him! But how was poor Conrad to know that these very banalities, to quote the modernist himself, "that ever disfigured history of human conscience and geographical exploration," the harsh metamorphosis of the 'idealized realities of a boy's daydreams!' mind you, a white boy please, were to prove such a boon to the man and writer, to get permanently canonized in English

Literature! For Conrad was a divided man. The fact of his being a European explorer-cum-emissary, on the virtue of his being a White male, provided him with the immense prestige and responsibility of being a loyal servant to the British monarch. But is it such a pretty picture after all? Konrad Korzeniowski was a Pole by birth, who later took up British citizenship, thereby escaping his stigmatic past burdened by oppressions inflicted by imperialist Russia. Hence his imperilled schizophrenic subjectivity couldn't identify with all that on-going sham in the name of 'civilizing mission', he even puns on the word 'progress' and evidently in the very title of his novella itself. No doubt he irreverently mocks at the Belgian imperialism and King Leopold II making an amusement park out of 'Free State Congo', that reaps huge returns, in terms of money and tax free human capital; also throwing a biting satire on the self-proclaimed hubris of civilization, the high-point of imperialist expansion post pan-European Enlightenment! No doubt Conrad's liberal humanist stand was applauded worldwide, that is, all over Europe. He definitely was at the threshold of something far more unsettling, unbecoming for the Eurocentric worldview, that very redundant baggage of an over-glorified nationalism or rather continentalism, if we can say that, that hung around his neck as an albatross."

She generally preferred the extempore, free-wheeling discussions. Her classes were not bland every time, and the present third years were a rather good bunch. It was interactive. They had made it so. She particularly liked the chap Akash, an intelligent face and never overboard with pompous displays of what they called 'attitude'. The neologisms interested her particularly.

Another hand went up.

"Yes, Nirmal?"

"But Ma'am, according to Achebe, Conrad was a bloody racist."

A bit cheeky there, not exactly in the I-want-to-know-both-sides-of-the-deal sense, but prompted surely by the thrill of uttering the word 'bloody' before an audience of 20 odd students.

"Let's look at it this way, Nirmal. There can be multiple viewpoints on the same issue you'd agree, wouldn't you? So let's contextualize things a bit. If you read Edward Said's essay included in the selection, you'd find that Achebe's is a rather hardcore approach towards the subtle texture of Conrad's work. You see a typical modernist trait was to not to succumb to a single cohesive meaning but to open up the text, the lines, the words for indefinite interpretations. As I said, Conrad was at the threshold of it, but not quite at it. Of course there're the trappings of time. He was grappling with it, and was trying to find a way out as best as he could. Ugh, of course the very tools he was working with, the very system of so called Enlightenment was later found wanting and adequately punctured, but let us grant the author who's grappling with the existent tensions of his time the credit for enabling and participating in an on-going cultural debate, no matter how flawed it finally turned out to be. Achebe's view is not politically incorrect, but perhaps it's a slightly one-dimensional way of looking at it."

The trappings of time. She echoed her own words in her mind. Her own words? Not quite. Borrowed epithets.

She didn't bother taking the roll call, rather asked them to put in their names and roll numbers in a loose sheet and hand it over to her in the staff room. Tara agreed to the responsibility.

With the second years she was doing Emile Zola's *Therese Requin*. The class was almost spilling over for she had informed them of the double-lecture almost three days back. This was a batch of voracious scribblers. Not too many would raise any objection to what she would go on rambling about. A monologue, she thought. In reverse. To suit them she had prepared the lecture and made elaborate notes. She almost did a reading-out from her register, lasting for about 80 minutes. By the time she came out she was exhausted with an extremely parched throat. She should carry a bottle of water with her, she re-advised herself.

And the rain was still fairly pissing down.

In the staff-room, Nalli and Samiran were blabbering on some course-restructuring, so she presumed. Nalli spurted out the moment she glided in, "You just have to be on the panel. There's simply no way out. Or the competition is going down the drain."

She was almost pleading. Ivy was bemused.

"Okay, okay. But what happened to our dearest Dr Bakshi? Wasn't she presiding over the whole judgment business?"

"Yeah. But she's busy with the Harmony thing. That's equally important and you know the principal wants nothing to go wrong with our Annual Cultural Integration function after all."

"Capital idea!" Ivy laughed a bit. "So what is it this time, poetry or prose?"

"Aah, I've NOT specified that. They were given the perfect freedom to mess around with genres!"

"I adore you! Am sure they were happy!"

"Yeah am sure too. By the way, hitting D-School in say 10 minutes?"

"Not today, Nalli." She was apologetic, they had planned it yesterday. "It's an emergency I have to meet up my sister today. Family matters."

"Oh family matters will have to be attended to. I'm glad you've become less of a wonky, but in a way since you're hardly penning down anything these days, I guess you were better off as a madhead."

"Heh. Yeah just drop me at ITO. Would take an auto from there."

"Sure."

Her confidantes would be waiting.

FOUR
Lost

In Lab 3 of the Department of Microbiology, AIIMS, Dr. Shumonto Roy was examining a set of virulent strains of group A Streptococci, a heterogeneous group of Gram-positive bacteria, nonmotile, and nonsporulating, broadly responsible for diseases like scarlet fever, rheumatic heart disease, glomerulonephritis, and pneumococcal pneumonia. *S pneumoniae*, a primary cause of serious focal and systemic infections, the first most common cause of community acquired pneumonia in the United States and of fatal bacterial pneumonia in developing countries, was the centre of attraction for an upcoming seminar on medically important Streptococci. Hemorrhagic shock in association with *S pneumoniae* sepsis in previously healthy children had been reported recently in the Asian and African countries. Of major biologic importance was a renewed interest in safe and effective streptococcal vaccines and Dr. Shumonto Roy was determined to do his bit in the march towards a disinfected world.

He looked at his Omega Classic gold and steel watch, 1:25 p.m. Measuring pathogenic potentials of the minute inhabitants of the world was rather tedious and he was already hungry. He took off his sterilized pair of gloves, his lab-apron, and after washing his hands with Dettol liquid soap, made a move towards the hospital canteen to get his regular fill of mutton-dosa and apple juice. When he came back he was full, his gastric case was calmed, but he felt a visceral unrest spreading its ugly wings within him.

He was trying hard to ward off the thoughts of Irene Scott but his blood vessels recorded an increased flow towards the cardiac sac and his right hand fingers inadvertently moved the black cordless mouse of his steelgrey computer making him type out a certain address in the blank space on Internet Explorer 6. He was immediately directed towards a relatively unused alumni mail account, <rshumonto_jhu@jhumatrix.com>, something he hadn't opened for months. He breezed past the list of the senders of the unread mails, then proceeded to reread Irene Scott's old posts. He went through the dates; the last one was sent sometime in March 2001 from Albuquerque. Irene had mentioned some tour campaign she was doing as an extension of her field work in the states of Texas, Oklahoma and New Mexico. This mail was basically an apologia for her inability to make it with him; a defense of her career choice and choosing to stay single as an alternative to settling down after tying the knot.

He opened a picture of a pink-skinned, heavy-bosomed girl in red striped top and dark blue denim midi skirt. Her pony-tailed hair was flaxen and she had a broad face, rather chubby to look at. Irene Scott in October 2000 in front of the Café Nazareth, Baltimore. A night-shot. And the flash light had made her appear whiter than she actually was. What fascinated Shumonto, however, was the 38-C cup-sized chest of Irene. It looked full and milky and conferred a misleading appearance of pregnancy on the twenty-six year old. Men have a strange attraction towards menstruating, gestating and lactating women, he had read that in one of the carnival issues of *Sex it Up the Healthy Way* magazine.

That woman was born to be cherished, Shumonto thought. It was difficult for him to comprehend her decision to stay single. Not that sex was a big deal but she had a peculiarly matronly face that could have posed for a Madonna. That was the face the dead European painters would die for. That woman's undulating body was a thing of pride, a stark painterly pride in demonstrating female physiognomic abundance. A painter with an interest in female musculature, or better, just the conspicuous body, could bring out the precise beauty of a shimmering epidermis with the wealth of evenly distributed adipose beneath, and inside the beatific layer of fat the worthy female components: the warmblooded heart, the consuming stomach, the producing womb, the defecating colons and water-firing bladder. Such a woman could give science its due of Beauty. Such a woman's corpse too would be worth many a glance, a splendor for post-mortem, an exercise in obtaining knowledge. She would give even after she was dead. That woman was born to lend her womb, dead or alive, to the service of mankind, to help it proliferate with beautiful white buds. Buds of men. As a loyal comrade of the global brotherhood, he never thought of singling her out for his private consumption. She must be shared; she was too good to be hoarded and not allowed to bestow her benevolence on the rest of the world. And this woman had decided to undergo hysterectomy, chucking out her capacious uterus and catalytic ovaries to avoid getting pregnant while conducting her excursions to encourage the rights of sex-workers in the predominantly Catholic communities of Texas, New Mexico and parts of Oklahoma.

Irene Scott would say weird things. Nuns and priests ought to marry, or have safe sex irrespective of marriage. That monogamy should not be an issue among free-thinking individuals. That true religion should help oneself open out towards understanding the higher realities of the universe that didn't discriminate between female or male or human and the beast. She would read up fat books of psychotheology, something only she could explain, and go on chattering before an indifferent Shumonto when he would be mad as a bull to fuck a cow in heat. His only gateway to the white feminine was a rather weird specimen; he'd muse after a heady screw.

He clicked on a mail dated 13th January 2001 which had two snaps attached therewith.

From: Irene Scott <ishq_75@hotmail.com>

To: Roy Shumonto <rshumonto_jhu@jhumatrix.com>

Redirected from <blacksabbath75@yahoo.com>

Subject: None

Date: 13 January 2001

Dear Shumi,

I'm in Austin and am mailing you from a cyber café at the UTA campus. We're here for a three-day program in which they'd show us Iranian, French and Mexican documentary films on hygiene abuse in parts of these countries including HIV infections, syphilis, gonorrhoea and other STDs.

I'm reading a paper on ecclesiastical sex and hygiene day after tomorrow, that is on the second day. Wish me luck.

I had written to you earlier but you didn't reply. Are you still upset with me? Look I have made my decision and I hope you'll understand. We can stand by each other in times of need, can't we?

Love as always,

Ishq

P.S. The pics at Houston. I'll write to you from Fort Worth next. I got my folks over there in Dallas so I might make a week's stay.

Standing on the grey pavement of the spectacular Houston Museum of Natural Science was Irene Scott, PhD research scholar, specializing in Social Psychology and Religious Reforms, John Hopkins University.

He clearly remembered the first encounter between them. A busily slide-preparing Shumonto was interrupted by a tall, plump, peach-complexioned girl asking for a few projections she would need to screen for a paper-reading session on the spread of gonadial infections in the neglected convents of South Carolina. Apparently, she had said, god-serving lesbians didn't think it necessary to use protection. Her paper dealt with lack of awareness of both the human rights of hygiene and provision of patent treatment following a lapse of health.

That cold rainy November day had made a significant impact on Shumonto's one-track life and provided a baggy solution to his sexual frustration. He had accompanied Irene to the thinly populated seminar hall in the Arts Building and had sat silently in the first row among the audience while Irene blabbered on harassed nuns, their unaccounted pathologies, their psychic deterioration under habitual duress and the spread of vaginitis, uterine infections and other problems. When summoned he had put up the transparencies, explained a few slides and charted the development of some of the gonadial contagions. He had received the thankful acknowledgement from her with the perfect poise of a newbie nascent in the business of transpigmentorial experimentation. At lunch they talked about Indian and British cuisines and she had to go on listening to a rather excited and patriotic gastro-enthusiast. During the second half of the seminar, they had sat in the last row and napped intermittently nodding their nubile heads. At coffee, they had slipped out of the building and escaped to a nearby cafeteria, Nazareth.

Over cappuccino and banana chips they had exchanged pedigrees. Shumonto could trace the line of her descent to a particularly adrenalin-pumping nano-inch of a cleavage visible to his high resolution 700X eyes; she must have been unaware of it since she was wearing a V-necked three-quarter sleeved brown top with black semi-fit skirt, black tights with black sandals. Nevertheless his auditory faculties had registered her laryngeal outpourings: she hailed from Wicklow, south of Dublin and was in love with the Irish Sea of which she had a collection of 576 postcards. She was a student of MA Social Work and it was her first year in America. Shumonto duly let her know that he was doing his Masters cum Doctoral in Molecular Microbiology and Immunology and that he had never really lived close to the sea.

The sex didn't follow immediately, much to his disappointment. But it helped evaporate a notion he had harboured for years watching the Hollywood flicks: American gals were nymphomaniacs. But Irene wasn't typically American either, so a part of that cherished idea never got exterminated. Nevertheless, they roamed about the university lawns, campus bookshops, discovered newer and cheaper food joints, easy beer outlets, and most importantly music shops. He was a rock fanatic and she tuned in to country lore, jazz, Latino beats and even had a taste for Indian classical in the instrumental versions. They would record CDs, listen in to mp3s, and scream along gulping down canned beer. So their occasional purchases would be something like a Best of Sepultura, Bruce Springsteen in California, Selections: Led Zeppelin on the one hand, while on the other, Sanctus Real, Mediterraneo by Marc Antonie, Aretha Franklin, Sounds of Asia: Sitar and Arabian Strings.

Their first kiss was a kind of a lucky accident. She had gone to his place, a small two-roomed flat he shared with three other guys, to call him for a little party they had fixed for Christmas Eve. In the afternoon, she had been trying his number but his cell phone was on the silent mode for he wanted to sleep. After he woke up he was suddenly struck by an irrepressible need to sort his CDs and folders out, which were piled up in uncouth heaps under the desk, on the side of the bed and even on the window base. In his fervor, he had completely forgotten about his poor cell phone, and Irene, fed up of trying his cell had decided to personally go and drag him out instead to do the last minute needful together. She had found him just in his unironed shorts with a Joe Satriani clenched between his teeth and almost shaken out of his wits at seeing her at his doorstep, seeing him in the state he was in. Nonetheless, she had confidently entered the place which was more of a dishevelled clutter of scattered denims, sneakers, half-stinking T-shirts, and a computer shouting at next to the maximum level. He had hurriedly put on a crumpled tee and explained he was having a hard time finding misplaced CDs. She had offered to help provided he wrapped everything up within half an hour and escorted her to the baker's shop to get the food and booze for the New Year bash. He had reluctantly agreed, wanting very much to be left alone with Satriani and Jimi Hendrix on the strings. However, after rescuing two pairs of discs from mismatched covers she demanded an explanation, and he answered that there was nothing to worry about for the original contents of the discs had been erased to suit his current tastes. She had stared at him in confused disbelief and he had tenderly made her sit on one of the two unkempt single beds asking her not to bother her pretty little head. At this she had feigned offence and exacted an apology, for she was a good 5'8", just two and half inches lesser than him, and under no circumstance could she be attributed the adjective 'little'. A mock fight had ensued which inevitably took to its logical consequences. They faced each other's face at the nearest possible distance for the first time and mouthed the opportunity. Yet the flatmate woke up and barged in unannounced, terminating their primordial hobnob for the time being. At the party, they couldn't eat much and Irene had let her perpetually pony-tailed hair fall lightly down her shoulders protected by a heavy black overcoat. They had finally escaped to Irene's flat and made love and made each other unbelievably happy.

Making love proved to be interdisciplinary educational tours for both of them. He would sketch and explain how the Diplococci looked like a pair of aroused breasts and how the Staphylococcus resembled a stunted penis. He avoided using the word 'castrated' for a morbid fear of something similar befalling him. She in turn told him that sex wasn't a taboo in a communist utopia which was a free sex society. Ideally there would be no need of atrocious institutions like marriage or paternity for the body and soul would belong to the community and no single person could lay an undisputed claim on anybody's body and life. Also, multiple partners would be perfectly feasible a choice to honor the I-don't-know-why-the-hell debased physiological needs and avoid spatio-temporal disconnections.

Their respective flat-mates had been co-operative and in times of the duo's hormonal needs they had routinely vacated the flats for boring arty films at the University Arts Centre. They had been grateful to them forever for those big acts of self-sacrifice. And after he bought a second hand Nissan Sentra (from the collar-flaunting, tattoo-flaunting—tattoos of equations and theories of course—mathematics undergrad student whose cousin was a dealer and had a shop in the retail park area outside the university), he had driven her to the neighboring states of Pennsylvania, New Jersey, Virginia, and New York. She reciprocated by taking him to a few reformist meetings throughout which he got thoroughly bored. They were an obscure bunch of students of theology, sociology, oriental and Hebraic languages, social-evolutionary sciences and other vague sounding fields. To him, who believed only in the efficacy of science and especially the human genome project to unleash the big genetic potential and create engineered gods out of mere mortals, those outlandish disciplines were as good as moronic chants but he was sane enough to keep his opinion to himself. Never did he let Irene know that the kaleidoscope of color patterns, morphological peculiarities, religious affiliations, or linguistic orientations only succeeded in confusing him for he was looking forward to a universalized world eliminated of all prejudicial categories. If that world would permit diversity he didn't know; he wasn't sure whatever theories applied to the world of bacteria, fungi, eukaryotes and other smaller tenants of earth would be equally applicable to the human masters. For example, bacteria could be cultured in controlled set ups with additions and deletions from the culture matrix unlike the latter species. Anyhow, he stopped accompanying her after a few sessions of spiritual drilling.

One fine day, they heard of the insurgency in Afghanistan and the prompted killings of Hindus and Muslims in regions of north-western India. He wanted to evade those prickly issues but she wanted to talk. "What exactly does this frenzy in the name of religion mean?" she had asked. He was amazed, "If educated people like you can go on mindlessly yapping about priests, nuns, alternative lives blah blah blah, why not those illiterate ones who have nothing but their religion to hold on to?" She was aghast, "We are a Catholic reformist group; so we try to better the trapped lives of the members in the lower rungs of the Church ladder. We don't kill, we preach against killing." He had yelled out, "Just fuck off, okay. It's you fuckers who created the mess in the Asian and African economies; how can you forget the centuries of plunders?" Like a big white duck she had trembled inside her God Is Peace T-shirt and sat there immobile until he told her he had work to do and needed to be excused. The next day she got a couple of Jew and Muslim freshmen and screeched at his flat doorstep, "So the Germans killed them five decades ago. Those Germans were Christians. So, ideally, this boy should also become an avenger and kill me off. Right?" He was stunned and sent those boys away, then cooled her off after an hour-long fornication, despite having the flatmates in the next room. Yet now his brown and her white skins seemed to have a discreet presence outside their control.

She had asked him in a concerned manner, "Have you ever faced racial discrimination over here?" He had kept quiet for a while and then narrated a casual incident. He was about to get his US driving license and was taking lessons in a driving school, although back in India he had a working license. There were three instructors, two whites and a black. His lot fell in the batch supervised by the white woman, who was hefty, had an 'immoderate' look about her and fussed around with minutest things. On the last day of his training, he was supposed to undergo a test of driving and she was sitting to his right. She made him jump a red light for she had been insisting to hurry things up and he missed an empty signal by some seconds in order to be co-operative. She failed him precisely for doing that. The next time, it was a wrong way of putting on the seat belt. He had watched other white kids getting through the test as easily as he would imagine and there he was stuck with the bitch. The next Sunday he called up the school and got another instructor to supervise. This time he cleared the test in one go and got his license.

He once told her to go and work in the African or Latin American countries where it would really matter. He was careful not to mention Asia. She had simply answered she would like to work closer home. He had laughed and computed the distance between Wicklow and Baltimore and then compared it with the distances between Wicklow and west coast of Africa: "Which one's shorter?" She had chosen not to comment further. Then, after a while, had murmured in his ears, "I don't want to die of a tsetse fly bite." "No my duckbilled platypus," he had said affectionately, "You'll die a senile, old cranky greatgrandmom here in the heart of Maryland."

His mother had long before asked him to offer puja at a temple of a certain saint Srinath. He had a week off so he had decided to make her happy. Irene wanted to tag along too; he was wary, for deep within he was a trifle embarrassed to confess that he too was god-fearing. He told her that it was primarily to satisfy his mother that he was embarking on such a worthless enterprise. Irene wasn't put off; she informed him that different people visit the house of gods to satisfy another set of people. It was a pretty web of godliness. He had on a whim asked, "Do you really believe in God?" "Crap," she had guffawed, "I believe in the godsmiths." They had great fun travelling to a little nondescript town in New Jersey, ate a lot of pineapple ice-cream, grilled chicken sandwiches, banana chips, fruit cakes and drank cans of chilled beer. She had worn a red North Indian printed long skirt, a loose T-shirt and had lined her grey-blue eyes black. She looked like a hippie, he had told her. His Sentra was rocketing that day; the five hours had gone past in a whiff listening to hair metal and screaming along. The highway was a downy hotline to heaven; they were gliding away unstopped, unstoppably fast.

The temple was a state-of-the-art posh looking building albeit a bit small in size. They were provided with a double-room at the guest house wherein they had a helluva good afternoon of sex in a double-bed. A rare pleasure that was. Irene loved the stuff they passed off as authentic Bengali cookery, served on banana leaves but along with fork and spoons to cater to wider audience. Apparently, a disciple of Baba Srinath was conducting a selective goodwill tour to promote peace and happiness in the world. They were handed over a neat looking brochure printed in both English and Bengali script on opposite sides of the leaflet. It informed them of an upcoming evening meditation session.

The disciple, Sri Priyonath, was addressing a medium gathering in the large hall with a huge wall-painting of Sri Srinath, speaking on 'Enhancing the Inner Beauty of the Soul'. The audience comprised both Indian and American crowd, and there was an interpreter to translate the disciple's Bengali wisdom into English. He talked of pragmatic spirituality and Shumonto watched Irene's eyes light up with a flame of acknowledgement. She felt a deep connection with the guru's lexis of truth and her upgraded religiosity went through spells of meditative moods. The next day the guru was reflecting on the effect of meditation on the unconscious and the link between the universal and individual soul. He answered queries from the soul-searchers captivated by his divine rhetoric. Also, it was on the second day that the session was televised for future broadcast on the Spirit and Soul Channel.

Irene, seized by a compulsive whim of interrogation, made a request to ask the guru some questions in private. She was granted permission and Shumonto kept grudging about her having spoilt the whole evening. She came out delightfully beaming. He could smell faint traces of male cologne emanating from her flesh. He didn't mention it to her.

Soon after she forcibly took him to another of her congregations. She hadn't told him what it was about so he remained crabby during the drive. They got down before something that looked like an old farmhouse to him. He wanted to know what she was up to. In return, she gave him a pamphlet proclaiming a statement by a certain Jason Agamemnon, a sex-abuse victim brutalized by a church bishop. The names of the ecclesiasts were kept secret for the sake of confidentiality but Shumonto knew what the evening was going to be like. He was developing a sharp distaste for Irene's incessant correction mania. She was adamant; she begged him to stay with her for the evening and that it was going to be his last time in the clutches of reformist zealots. He went inside following her, appearing shorter than her for she was wearing three-inch high heels. She looked like a grizzly bear, he thought, a white female bear out of its hibernation.

Irene, in fact, was gathering compliments that evening from her male comrades who were unanimous in conferring a queer gaze on him. He felt humiliated within. Sat huddled in an inconspicuous corner while she kept lolling around chatting up people in casuals and fetching him the champagne and snacks from time to time. An old man came up to him and asked, "Are you a Catholic?" When he said no, the man was surprised. "A Protestant then?" He replied he wasn't Christian. He was Hindu. The man seemed baffled, "Then what are you doing here?" He had no answers. The man introduced himself, Edward Simpson, retired bank officer, devout Catholic. Then he asked, "So your Hindu priests too must equally abuse innocent people. What do you do about them?" He had sheepishly said, "Not everywhere. We don't have it everywhere." Simpson had persisted, "But what about the places where this happens? Sexual abuse in the name of religion?" He had said aloud, "I'm not really sure but I guess there are laws to take care of such things." Under his breath he had muttered, "Fuck off asshole."

Irene started staying off for longer periods touring to talk about rights and spread awareness among various kinds of victims. When she met him next she declared she was going to chuck out the twin ovaries and uterus from her system. He was shocked. "But why?" he had asked. "To avoid getting pregnant in case of casual rapes or casual sex at times when protection isn't handy," she had answered coolly. "Occupational hazards." She mentioned. "But don't you wanna have kids ever?" He was exponentially perplexed. "I would adopt one I guess." He had never asked her anything about her body again.

She would mail him from different places, often after months. He soon got involved with an Iranian girl and Irene's absence started seeming the normal thing. Meanwhile, he got homesick again, started spending time online, chatting up fellow Indians and Bengalis. He met Ophelia after quite a few abortive cases of virtual romance and decided that Ivy was practical enough not to get entangled with him. Slowly Irene Scott became confined to an occasional offliner or sporadic smileys without a text.

Dr. Shumonto Roy spent the rest of the afternoon reading up the posts of Irene Scott. He wondered if it was worth telling everything to his wife. He decided against it. Yet he kept reading the last six mails of Irene. How could she get AIDS after that operation, he was bemused. Had she taken to drugs? But she never had such inclinations, he rectified himself. A soul of a nun in the body of a plump cat. Or was it the other way round? Soul of a cat in heat in the body of an archpriestess?

He tried remembering the last time they were in bed together. A faint memory. Suddenly, he felt uneasy and started sweating in the air-conditioned lab. Then went out and registered for a voluntary ELISA test. It took him five minutes to know whether he was slated for another rendezvous with Irene Scott sometime soon in the future. The results were congratulatory.

FIVE
League

At 5 o' clock that evening, Ivy Roy was scampering through the busy streets of New Delhi among the honking cars, the mountains of buses with their exhaust pipes pumping out the sweaty soot from the city's nostrils. It was always the same circular ride, the Inner Circle, Ring Road that ran all through the city like a girdling snake. The traffic jam at Defence Colony flyover had eaten up 20 minutes and she was lagging behind. Nothing uncanny about running behind though; she had got used to a reverse timeclock that moved slower by a minute with every passing day.

Both Kamya and Shoili had their own cars; Kamya drove a white Hyundai Santro while Shoili had a second hand dark blue Maruti Zen, for which she was paying a monthly installment of Rs 3,500. Travelling was less of a problem for these two rather mobile women, going anywhere within and outside the city at the shortest notice. Unlike Ivy, her elder sister and best friend were both widely travelled, although still within the country. Shoili had of course her MA in Human Rights from the University of Kent but she had come back to work in India. Her frequent visits had been to Bombay, from where they were coordinating a network of women's self-employment programmes in the regions of interior Maharashtra and Madhya Pradesh. Shoili worked as a legal consultant for an NGO called Jaagaran which looked into the legal prejudices against poor women and sex workers who were often thrown out of their jobs and were in desperate need of rehabilitation. She had her own practice too but that was basically meant as an excuse to own visiting cards.

Kamya on the other hand worked as a PRO in a small software company based in Noida but having a branch in South Extension. She was a verbose lady with a penchant for putting the blandest ideas in the choicest phrases, impressing most of her clients rather smoothly. However, she was a staunch South Indian brahmin with a strict distaste towards anything remotely non-vegetarian. Even the smell of eggs would make her swoon and in case she happened to come near fried fish she would lose her wits as easily as she would misplace Ivy's audio cassettes. They were old buddies and initially stayed in the same colony, not far from Ivy's present location. After her marriage with Raghav Ravindran three years back, she had moved southwestwards, where they still had affordable and slightly spacious flats for the Indian middleclass. The typical double-income-no-kids syndrome was fast catching on in Delhi, following Bombay in the lead.

The auto stopped at the Dilli Haat gate at about 5:36 and Ivy scuttled through the inclined terrace to reach the counter. Shoili and Kamya were already there with the entry tickets, waiting for their damsel in distress. Ivy donned the role rather too often: she was perpetually running into serious problems that made a difference of life and death to her. Shoili, who had literally seen a lot more of the world, advised her younger sister to get tougher and take life head on. For Shoili, Ivy was a puny little bourgeoisie caught in the stagnant pool of lesser glitz, mistaking the tiny ripples in her crazy pond for gigantic tides. A butterfly of a sister, she would reflect, garbed in fresh plumes of anguish, and searching in verses what one called a solution. She wanted Ivy to drop in at their rehab camps for once; she should know what misery could be like.

They made a quick circuit of the place before settling for a shade less stone table with slabs on raised platforms for benches. It was particularly balmy and breezy with the sky still showing signs of potential shower and the stone tiles wet and dark having been drenched in water all day. The tiny streams still ran in haphazard directions in the minute gulfs between the ridges on the tiles; the carvings collected the pouring fluids of the city, the jug of a sky bucketed the condensed vapour, erstwhile the tears, saliva, urine, sweat.

They sat on one half of the square stone table, adjacent to each other. The weekend college crowd in denims and kurtas thronged the place, to grab their share of the afterbath perfumed air. The ground had that intoxicating scent, that which emanates from a scorched earth impregnated by the first droplet of rain. The Off-Season Indian Monsoon. The enticement of that no-season could only be experienced, never described. And Kamya's long *ghaghra* skirt, most probably bought from one of these ethnic stalls showcasing and selling indigenous Indian handlooms, refracted the dance of water and light breaking them into a bacchic order of colours. It was a shimmery peacock blue, with a glazy overtone that gradually blended into a rainbow at the border. An inverted flowing river balanced on a spectral arc of a boat. A miniature for the lid of a sky on the tumbler of the world.

They were sitting at a place lined by regional food joints, at a little distance from the clothes and artefact stalls that greet the visitors on entering the atypical mart. It was the aroma of the food that particularly enthralled people; fusion food like fusion music filled up everyone with a potential that seemed to say I too can mix and match. A village in the heart of the city; an amnesiac idyll in the concrete jungle that was meant to sensitize people towards their rural brethren; yet that also made them wince with relief: Oh how beautiful the jute bag looks! It's such a *lovely* idea to spend some time in the villages. Though the Haat had its charms: a pretty offering at the altar of the city; a boogie-woogie of cuisine, craft and culture; a cinematic little India staged on a six-acre space with grub festivals, puppet-shows, exhibitions, small time street-theatre.

They placed an order of fried pork momos, thukpa, vegetable chowmein and mixed fruit-beers. The Tibetan plaza was by far one of the best though earlier they used to roam about and try out little things at as many stalls as possible. No state was left out; they would begin alphabetically to avoid leaving out. Often Shoili would take promotional coupons from them and win a free snack.

The young Nepalese boy who took their order was rather slow to deliver. Ivy meanwhile opened the lid of the ketchup jar and slipped a spoonful into her mouth. Shoili was offended, "Just lay your hands off the ketchup woman! When will you ever change your ways?"

Kamya was milder, "She's disturbed. Let her be."

Glancing sideways and observing a busy Rajasthani potter, Shoili deigned to comment, "Yeah so what's the source of her disturbance this time? What has our dear brother-in-law done? Or is it someone brand new?"

Ivy didn't mind her sister's prickly snubs; she knew that her Shoiiii had a wild tongue that would shoot to sustain itself. She also knew that some of the soundest advices that had made her life a little more organized were Shoiii's gifts to her Aye. And one of them was *not* to marry Dr. Shumonto Roy. She announced in a low voice,

"Yesterday I discovered that he had a girlfriend back in the States whom he had stopped meeting for quite sometime and who is now dead."

"Oh, really?" Kamya was quick to respond, with the required sympathy.

"Yes." Ivy exhaled.

"And how exactly did you make the discovery?" Shoili as usual was terse and official.

"I was just going through the YM message archives. I saw this unread message from him asking me to try open one of his mail accounts and I found mails from the girl there," Ivy replied meekly.

"The dead girl, you mean?" Shoili clarified.

Yes, Ivy nodded.

"Well now that she's dead I don't see a problem. Forget about it and don't tell me just 'cause he had a gf back there you're going to throw tantrums at your place." Objective Shoili.

"No, all that is fine. But the problem lies somewhere else. You should have read those mails. The girl's all hell bent on meeting him up, that is when she was mailing him, and since he couldn't reply 'coz he never got them, his account was temporarily blocked, the girl went nuts. But the real problem is that the girl died of AIDS and she was depressed and wanted him to be there. And now there's a friend of this female who mails and blames him for her death. And this guy has almost internalized the horseshit and isn't behaving normally since last night."

"Quite a twist," said Kamya. "So what do you plan to do now? Take him to a shrink?"

"For godsake, he's not turned mad yet."

"Yeah, heh, I was just kidding. Okay on a serious note, what next?"

"Stop the cheap spy-book shit alright?" Shoili jutted out. "Shumonto-da has got a sort of a shock and needs time to recover. That's all. Don't blow it out of proportion. Just give him time and he'll be okay."

The thukpa was a definite tongue-teaser and the sisters immersed themselves in the culinary delight for the time being. Kamya sat there with a grumpy face nibbling at her veg chow. Shoili asked after a while, mouthing in a full momo,

"So what was she called?"

"Irene Scott."

"Sounds British to me."

"You never know."

"Yeah and where exactly did they meet? Any idea?"

"None whatsoever."

"Must have been a colleague at his university. Or a junior." Kamya offered her reflections.

"Could be. You know his brother is settled in Boston for quite a while. Could be a mutual friend too. Though in the mail she had asked him to come to Dallas and meet her. So she was writing from Dallas."

"Hmm. He has somebody in Dallas you know of?"

"Not really. Might have a friend or something but am not sure."

"Well. See it's nothing basically. I don't see anything particularly nerve-racking over here. He's just a little ruffled mentally. Will get back to normal in a few days' time. Just don't poke him unnecessarily. Leave him alone and he would sort it out."

The evening was a glittering one. The newly bathed leaves rustled past each other, shining in the orange incandescence of the neon lights. The stalls were lit up, the craftsmen looked happy after a day's sell off. The turbaned Rajasthani potter had sold off the swan-necked clay wine-holder, with a painting of a hunting blue eagle on its outer surface. The world looked satiated for a while; the oppressive weight of the day had partly shed itself.

They got momos and chicken biryani packed for Shumonto and shoved off from the Tibetan plaza. Moved around for sometime stopping at the handloom shops and tinkering with bangles, danglers, embroidered *cholis*. At a little well-lit corner, a Mizo dance performance was going on; they watched the girls wrapped in red, blue and green matching their steps to the beats of the outlandish drum. They had coffee and sweet curd at the Bengali stall and came out of the Haat. It was nearing 9. Kamya drove off; she had her hubby waiting and had already received three frantic calls about a few misplaced objects: an unironed trouser, a wet towel drying in the balcony and the CD, Signatures—Evergreen Love Songs.

Shoili took out a packet from her handbag and gave it to her. It contained a book and a pack of two CDs. Ashish Nandy's *Return from Exile* and *Ghazals* of Mirza Ghalib, in the voice of Jagjit and Chitra Singh.

"Hey I'd been looking for the book. It was out of stock I was told," Ivy feigned gasping with excitement.

"Yeah it wasn't available but I got it from our Daryaganj dealer on a request. He's been getting me some rare stuff of late. I'll show you some time. Come over on Sunday."

"I don't know. Depends on his mood. He gets irritated looking at my sullen face throughout the day but that's all he would do. At the most he'd hit that 777 and get smashed. It's such a terror to have him on the driver's seat then. Twice have I taken an auto to get back home and arranged for the car to be sent back. It's ridiculous. Plus you know he's basically friendless over here. Everyone is scattered over in States, his batchmates, his family and now even his mom. He's desperate to go back. These 10 months have been difficult for him."

"But do you really want to settle there?"

"I don't know. I've the PhD thing though. Was thinking of taking the GRE and TOEFL early next year. But settling down is a different ballgame altogether. You know I am sure mixing up would never pose a problem for me. I mean look at him for instance, he's imbibed most of the traits you know, but does he really have friends from non-Indian origin? Hardly. He had his colleagues of course; I'm not counting them. But, otherwise? Every time on a vacation he would go and meet up one of his college time chums. Or go to his bro's place, stay there in Boston for a week or two and come back to make love to those Micrococci or whatever they're called. Once he even went to this weird bong temple to offer a puja. And even while chatting, all he would do was to mix with the junkies of Kolkata Online and abuse copiously. All and sundry. Before I met him I used to frequent so many other rooms. I know my experience is virtual, but in my own way I tried knowing the world. I didn't shut it out. I used to have those Australian buds remember? That Jenna and Alec. Then there were a few from South Africa too. I've lost touch yes but at least I talked to people. He's strange in a way. You know of it and I don't know why I keep rehearsing my blues before you!"

"That's alright. Don't worry about it. But you still do love him, eh?"

"Bullcrap. I mean I do. I ought to anyway. I mean even if I hadn't married him, I would've still felt a funny thing for this guy. This entire husbandry is silly, but nice in a way. Feels good to stay warm at nights. Plus there's this consolation that at least I'm there to take care of him. He's awfully self-sufficient you know, almost irksomely proper and correct. But you have to create a need somewhere. I think he's stuck with me. I'm the wrongest thing that could've happened to him. But if it hadn't been me he would have been still more miserable with another. Perhaps that's the case with me too. Born miserables."

"Hmm."

"Just imagine. Can I ever ask him to come and watch a Pirandello or a Miller with me? Would I ever recite an Eliot or Lawrence to him? And do I have any interest in his bacillus and *E. coli*—that's all I know of his field—and do I ever bother? Just too horribly different worlds we inhabit. At times I feel like an ET with him."

"Knotty issues. Staying out of it is good you see!"

"It would have been a case of sheer escapism for me. You know if I had to love a chap chanting Marx or Derrida, I ought to have been with Tushar Prasad or Mitakshar Thakur. But you know how things fizzled out between us and I have never even missed them. They don't need partners, they need a blank cassette which they would fill up with their chitterlings. But here I am, caught up with someone who barely lets a wrong emotion out. Barely feels vulnerable, barely gets heady and intoxicated. At times, I feel it's better to let him get drunk; he would yap a while then and talk nonsense. That would be soft rock to my ears."

"But what about this Scott? She's definitely not Indian, and according to you his ex-girlfriend too! I don't see why you should call him xenophobic after knowing that."

"Yeah Miss Scott! True she's like an unravelled gene sequence, to put it in his phraseology. It's weird she died of AIDS. Wonder how she got it. Sleeping around? Perhaps, a way to de-stress. Or could be a reckless injection. I don't know. Am I supposed to feel sorry for her? For him? How am I supposed to react? And if he keeps me out of all this then what am I supposed to say to him, how am I supposed to behave I am not sure. And what, pray, is the meaning of getting married and sharing a bed if we close out the secrets from each other?"

"Don't gimme that crap. Everyone has secrets to hide and they're better hidden. But I don't think it's that important. You meet so many people. In fact people have more bfs and gfs than proper friends these days. Dating in dating out. No big deal. I shouldn't be telling this to you now. You're 26 for godsake!"

"You know I really don't want to know about this Irene Scott. I mean somewhere I have a hunch that things didn't go alright between them and there are more skeletons in the cupboard. I just don't want him to face all that all over again."

"Hmm. Let's hope he doesn't have to."

Shumonto came from the parking lot looking tired. His eyes were sunken and he was reeking of rum. He wasn't staggering though. Fucking nerves, Ivy cringed within.

"Are you guys through?" he asked in a casual way.

"We never are. Let's have a coffee together." Shoili tried her hands at buffering.

"Alright." No resistance. No penalties for that invisible offensive distress.

They had a Georgia at the Coke counter; it was milky and sugary and he flinched and made faces while sipping. By 9:45 he was caught in a red light at the AIIMS junction. Ivy was silent. A juvenile voice streamed out from Radio City, "Good Evening Delhi. Welcome to Maruti Suzuki Traffic Beat...The stoppage time at Def Col flyover is about two minutes. No accidents reported so far. Time for a cruise with your sweetheart, what say?" In another instant John Denver was dished out, You Fill Up My Senses, Like A Night In The Forest, Like The Mountains In Springtime, Like A Walk In The Rain…

SIX

Saturdays had always been a disappointment for Ivy. She never went to a school that had Saturdays off. At college it was a half day, though the afternoon film-screening was a redeemer. Only once she had started teaching could she finally lie back and relax during the weekend.

But then there were other things to do. Visiting the British Council and American Center for re-issuing or returning books, video cassettes, CDs, journals. Occasional catching up with a friend over a matinee show. A play at the Habitat or BC Pal Audi. Or Kamani, in case she had managed a pass. Rarely a musical function; she preferred tuning in at home, with the lights turned off and herself sprawled over on the unmade bed, with a Graham Greene or Gunter Grass carelessly thrown aside for a post-10-minute-siesta reading. Everything followed its own course; she found something lyrical about her systemic anarchy.

She had hardly ever stayed alone, or ventured out alone, unlike Shoili. The untravelled one; she would spend her Sundays doing the prescribed readings for the Monday classes. During long breaks when there would be no difference between weekdays and the weekend, she too would register no weekly change in her moods that fluctuated vehemently during working sessions. There would be a phantasmagoric hum all around, as her mother's thuds echoed from the muffling walls catering to the general lull. Shoili wasn't there; she was at Kent. Baba believed in snoozing the Sundays away. Maa would screech along with the pressure cooker, or doze off during unbecoming summer afternoons. Her invisible entrapment would loiter around and complain like an unsung bollywood heroine. Ivy knew she would someday cast that second lead as a primadonna in her directorial debut.

Home is where the hearth is. The *chullah*, the stove. Ivy, forever cut out from entering the kitchen by a self-imposed vanity, never grasped that little truth. Food was always served to her, to her father, to her sister; she was as good as a son languishing in inactivity. She would secretly congratulate herself on that, to have mastered that important art of not getting affected by another's physical rigours. As a penance, however, she would attract cerebral unsoundness periodically, fall into bouts of depression, feel rootless, fuckless, and pre-identified by a pre-existent three-letter name.

So, life was the same old circus for her. Watching the kittens growing into fine cats filling up the cat-sty. Parents busy in an intra marital affair, Ma tending the plants, Baba editing typescripts of economics articles, Ma ordering spicy fruit-chats from the hawkers who yell out their discreet aromatic presence to the world, and everyone generally happy with the way the chicken capsicum turned out finally after inputs from three repeats of the Sunday Gourmet on Zee. By 11, the piglet would pretend to fall asleep in her pigeonhole of a room and the let the sow and pig take over the travelling show, moving from the drawing room to the adjacent big bedroom. She would at times imagine sounds of 'oink oink' coming from it. Aah, she would tell herself, after the *iillish* with mustard, they are now having the dessert, a nightlong languid copulatory ceremony.

At times when life would start showing signs of getting as boring as a never-ending prelude to an unembarked on excursion, she would take adequate measures. Solve crosswords, text-twists or word-racer on the Yahoo Games site with an unexampled ferocity, or wait for her ex-boyfriends' surprise calls.

Then she found a solution. She took the tour of a virtual life and started blogging.

******

The Story of O.

I've nothing to do with the letter O. Yet a persistent fantasy of mine is Ophelia walking out from her grave and cruising this discotheque of a world under a flurry of fluorescent lights. I'm obsessed with the letter O.

I'm Ivy. Silly and puny Ivy. Would you do me a favour? Call me Ophelia.

******

I know her for some time unspecified.

Do I want to know her at all?

What for? In order to desire her?

Where's my desire leading me to?

She's merely a line of words, one after the other.

She doesn't exist for me in any other form, nor I for her.

Both are phrases, words, letters, signs.

My name is my shame. Their capricious glances betray their guilt, the three letters in my name.

They will conjure up a thousand reasons for me to love it. But need I pay any heed to that? Need I caress that protrusion in want of another's touch? Let me desiccate the roundness and drain it of those acid juices flowing in there. They'll call me a witch. Let them. Who have they spared anyway? Assigned a virgin to become the eternal mother! What if I reverse the equation a bit? I'll get kicks out of that, apart from the ones I'm already getting from within.

And treading those strange lines, from my spheres and distension, to those invisible constellations, those unseen galaxies flooded with alien symbols and shibboleths, wherein my flesh dissolves away to find new horizons, hasn't that announced the trumpets of a quiet storm? How silent all that is! Like the calm Pacific, gentle, warm, huge, soft. I became the protean being and assumed myself once again. And wasn't that a discovery by itself? After all I hadn't had a chance in my atonal life to sway to the tunes of my inner music. So what had I found, a mirror perhaps?

Perhaps not a mirror though. But something that breaks off the reflection into a million unwarranted images, each with a voice of its own, eyes to seek and look around, each like a flittering little birdie anxious to stretch its own wings. And fly away. I saw myself reproduced from every corner of that labyrinthine maze, whose surfaces were varnished with imperceptible metals, purer than gold.

Walking the streets of a virgin city, with strange nameplates to lure. Come across a thousand twists and turns, yet take any route whatsoever. It doesn't need a guide, there's no one to show you around, for everyone, like you, is an explorer on the unconquered moon. With its dark spots, its craters, its abysses. Then its peaks, mountains, valleys. You find a million yourselves calling out from every corner. "Hey you! Can you hear me?"

And amid a million signs that go uncaught, you chance upon something after all. Suddenly, it becomes the oasis you were looking for, you realize that it was all a desert with palm mirages all around. And luckily you've found a whole pool whence you were searching for mere droplets.

They say you get to name your child. The very first act of naming: giving a being a proper noun that has to be carried on the back for a lifetime. Who named me? My mother or father? Or someone like an old relation asserting his or her last claim on the bloodline? Yet, all that is immaterial. I just know that I didn't have any contribution in the words that were entered in the register against my birth number. We have a naming ceremony as well! We get named. And all my life I felt a strange pang while uttering that always-alien word—my name. It would haunt me everywhere. I became it, for rather than it being synonymous with me, it was there everywhere before me. School registers, attendance sheets, bank drafts, on credit cards, on letters. Where was I?

It was a mocking stranger. Forever it taunted me with its apparent grandeur and sneered at my plainness. "You don't deserve me!" I would hear its jibes at unwanted times. Then I rebelled. Finally, I put that enemy of mine in the cage of visa gold and let it sulk. For in the unreal city you get to name yourself as many times as you want. You are whatever you desire to be. You are all that you want at once. And you name yourself like your fellow comrades in the holy crusade. Instant nirvana.

I am saddled with my bulge. So is Ophelia. Together we are not.

******

Logging Ophelia/ alias Poison Ivy/alias Olive/alias Oleander/alias (_____) into the network

Welcome Ophelia to the Lattice, the quagmire of dreams, desires, underground souls and ids. It's here that you'll find out who you really are. Lead on. Your instincts will be your only torch.

Poison Ivy, here you won't find faces, only masks. Isn't that a relief, the foreknowledge?

But you can take flights Olive, go higher and higher, farther and still farther, much beyond your wildest fancy.

Caution: It's always to the moon and BACK.

Oleander, remember that paradise is only a pretty projection of hell.

******

BLACK SABBATH: Oye Ophelia!! Long Time No See!!

BEELZEBOOB: Oops hey! LTNS indeed! How have you been man?

GLADIATOR: Ophelia, pretty woman (??) //Smiles

GORY WARWILLED AMBUSH: Ophaaaaaa *amar Ophaaaa*// kissie//kissie

HYDRAULIC POPPY: Oph//Smiles. How are you? Long time eh?

-- Thanks every buddy! //Smiles. This is overwhelming. Though I guess it hasn't been a week even.

BEELZEBOOB: You're a weakness. Kolkata Online had missed you Oph.

HYDRAULIC POPPY: True. We missed our Red Sonja the Bloodthirsty! //winking

-- LOL. Call from the battlefront. Guys, I'm the student admission councillor again, though it's two months from now. I need a better job than that. //Sigh. The Campus isn't going to let me be in peace I guess.

GORY WARWILLED AMBUSH: Bah, Oph, what do you need a job for? Bloody hell you live in an 1,100 square feet South Delhi flat all to yourself (who's counting ur momma-dadda?) and am sure your dadda won't let you die starving. Do something more fruitful other than squeak before a bunch of nincompoops in the Injunland. But yeah, don't write a book for Chrissake! We've dozens flowing in here; everyday we receive about 10 or more. Imagine my plight; I actually have to flip through some of them! And what do they talk about? Still harping on slaughtered holy cows, unclad dirty *sadhus* or dowry-struck slaughtered women! In fact, cows and women come in a combo pack. Gawd, I go up in flames sitting here in CA dammit!

-- Bushy, I got no such plans munchkins. Stay happy with your Californication classes.

GORY WARWILLED AMBUSH: Don't! Don't ya call me munchkins. Heck you'll drive away the smattering of female following that I have here.

BEELZEBOOB: Laughing My Ass Off! Bushy, she can't help it. You call yourself a cherub and you expect others not to notice! Rather the cherub presiding over all the other cherubs ruling from the White Palace. //winking

GORY WARWILLED AMBUSH: By Lucifer and by Ginsberg, Belze, I'll belch ya hard for sounding like a 400 year old musty epic. You cronies of Injunland will never learn. Opha to come back to you, squeaking or squealing over rusty stuff won't do. Of course, I can have a private session with you in my private escalator to heaven and drill it in ya: How to public it with bad liners.

-- Hmm Bushy, Grand ol' Sire, I'm sure thy omnipotent benevolence will lead me from darkness to light.

GORY WARWILLED AMBUSH: Hold it! Don't ya thee thy me, like Mellors did to Connie once. Though you can Johnny me and I can Jane you.

-- Agreed Grand Sire. But I can't be mothering your steeds. I won't let the loyal crone of Injunland be couched on luxury and damned incest.

HYDRAULIC POPPY: LMAO, you had it from the horse's mouth, Bushy!

GORY WARWILLED AMBUSH: Mare, Poppy. Or the Women's Lib will put you up for drying till death.

BEELZEBOOB: You've a new job Bushy, that of a soothsayer! Get suitably apparelled love! Come to my boutique and I'll give you a few spare alkhallas to don and thus profitably con. //Heart

GORY WARWILLED AMBUSH: Your squalid Dhakuria *dorjikhana* Belze? That dingy tailors' shop? Who the heck has given you the license to call it a Boutique, eh?

BEELZEBOOB: Grrrrr Gory. Heinous. Horrendous.

GORY WARWILLED AMBUSH: There! You've learnt the art of soothsaying at last. My sessions weren't a waste altogether. If ya find yourself in dearth of adjectives just hop on to amro-dick-shunnery.com.

-- Bushy, you're sinking. Need a recharge.

GORY WARWILLED AMBUSH: Yeah yeah, come to me my Sonja. We'll fence and recharge all night long.

-- You're confusing the timezones Bushy. Anyway, I'll be right back. //Coffee break

******

The floor needs a cleaning. It's been an hour since mom's yodelling.

Yeah. Heck. Me's a Mophelia for a while.

Cups and mops. A 24 year old should be used to them.

Not always.

Especially if there're no knotty issues. No vermillion excess or shankha-pala to flaunt. Not yet.

Cool kurtis and Jaipuri skirts. Kurtis and jeans. At times sarees. Casually yours.

******

Put your finger in the hole and stop the world from pouring in. Shut out the world there.

Chat screen minimized. Time for some milky sugary coffee.

A passport is a fiction of an individual. We all live in passports, as numbers and secret codes. Your chat-ids are fictions too; you multiply yourself every time you hide behind a new name, mirroring guises.

Back to Dali's ascending nuclear Christ. Nucleus or blastocoel? Protons or germ cells? Christ diving into the atom. Mrs. Dali in red alert, waiting to devour the God. A good manly pair of feet there. Soles rather. Souls. Duo.

A case of theogeometry. A perfect desktop theme.

Imagine yourself living alone in an 1100 square feet South Delhi flat! Sucks. Aah, but still that's heaven. Really?

Yeah, I always loved prancing around like a ghost on the prowl.

Living alone would be chic, eh?

Well yeah, no answering to anyone, no accountability. It's living like a princess.

But you have to make your own coffee every time.

No maid business dammit. I don't like a snooping eye around me.

Old melody on Radio Ga Ga. AIR SUPPLY, *All by myself, don't wanna be.*

They have no sense of timing. Especially the Soft Rock station.

******

Blue worlds. Traffic signals at crossroads. Ever ramifying, dissenting, breaking out. Gossamer's web? See the thin red line bisecting her blue form. Shades of blue, in ripples, vanishing circles of her eyes. She comes in fast forward or slow motion, hers is a flux of images, stills in flow, moving frames, concave and convex reflections; superimposed or overexposed. She perceives in packets, in bits, in digits, 0 or 1.

This patchy blue woman staring at me is you; this bleached fool dipped in Robin blue, getting her odd blotches all over, divided in the middle with that flaming red-spring of a line—crooked to the end. *The webcam's perpetually hazy.*

Your battles have always been petty.

The world hasn't changed. Mom had seen war pictures in black and white; I see them in colour. The moment I thought I tripped on the meaning, it vanished.

It's good that the world to me is nothing but a gallery of distinct paintings, disconnected pieces lying wantonly here and there, without a purpose. The theoreticians impose the purpose on them and make a veritable labyrinth out of it, a labyrinth too big and mazy for anyone to make a way through. The theoreticians pretend they have the route, or else they prance about in funky herds so that even the sojourn through the blind tubes becomes bearable. Or if they chance upon the door out, as the likes of Galileo did, or the saints perhaps, it was the same—madness. Why you madmen, why do you want to destroy my little cocoon and put me in an asylum that you've erected to serve your ends, only to find yourselves as entrapped as me?

The universe is breeding copiously. It's a multiverse now; it procreates with a marathon speed. Everyone is allotted a personal universe to tinker around with. Some still feel entrapped, and claustrophobic, like I do. I scream in vain; even if people hear me they are too afraid to scream along. They are afraid of noise, they love music.

I cannot distinguish faces anymore; it's just a formless mass, a callous of deindividuated points, a blur with shifting focus. You can adjust the lens at times but that doesn't make much of a difference.

They say behind every face lurks an undisclosed story, the unsung histories that are destined to go down the drain. But come to think of it, one word says it all: decay. Nothing quite dies; it lives on in the insidious alleys of time, like fantastic gnomes. What fills me with cold horror is to think of myself being just another of these shadow-boxers, just another point in the indistinct blur.

Holy mediocrity!

Smug, *comfortably numb*.

[Bridget Jones had it at last; Marc Darcy was hot of course, even in the New York snow. But as far as I'm concerned, it's a never-ending oscillation between Jones and the other Bridget (Alworthy, Tom Jones' semi-incestuous mommy) and the gulf between the two is quite unbridgeable. Literary Bridgets leave compendious sons, heavyweight and kind of formidable. I mean I could never fantasize about Tom in my loo (well smarty Jones never went as far as procreation) and therefore I'm left a Joan of Ache.]

> Where the mind is without fear
> And the head is held high
> Where knowledge is free
> Where the world has not been broken up into fragments by narrow domestic words
> Where the words come out from depth of truth
> Where tireless striving stretches its arms towards perfection
> Where the clear stream of reason has not lost its way into the dreary desert sands of dead habits
> Where the mind is led forward by thee
> Into ever-widening thought and action
> Into that heaven of freedom my father,
> Lead my cunt-try away

I thought you'd gimme some TLC. That's Tender Love and Care.

******

It's almost 3 a.m. Brilliant moonshine outside. Let's versify the moment.

> [I've become less of me, yet more of me
> I'm amalgamated now, for you flow within my secret channels
> As an infested circulation

C'mon dude, at exactly 3:02 a.m. you can knock me down
Dazzle my screen, monitor my beats
I keep my windows ajar
At all odd hours

I'm chairing a congregation of rustic moods
Guested by xexox sheets, piles untouched, tabled thoughts, bracelets of hair
Itinerary of my perpetual paranoia

And this ghost-white lamp that's trying to outdo the slyest moonshine
Is threatening a pseudo-seduction
To the autoseduced
Aggravated by the last contact

Had I been on marijuana
I would have hurled swimming heavens at you from point blank range
And made you screech

Your frozen axons are heating mine up in this strained nocturnal nexus
My blood will coagulate
And become a lump of self-abuse
Time you show up

Or cease being the muse
For godsake lemme try my hands at lesser aches, pretenses, just yet again
Before I miss the last wake up call]

Who was that for? *Who says that fictions only and false hair become a verse*?

******

Bono said the other day that I should set the voice mail active. He wanted to leave messages. He wanted to *communicate.*

-- Turn on the voice mode, Ivy.

Turn me on Bono.

-- Half the time you keep your cell phone off. Or else you have run out of validity. Or else you're entertaining cheap calls from your so-called online friends.

Okay so you think we still retain our validity eh? And cheap calls?? Some of them are ISDs!!

-- C'mon Ivy, get a grip. Do stuff. Get back to your regular schedule and grab a bittuva sense.

And Bono aka Mitakshar Thakur is two years my junior. Just above twenty-two. Not yet finished his MA. Archdebater with lotsa CUM, Clarity of Un-violated Mind.

Communication.

Ivy has a computer, 24-hour broadband internet connection, five email accounts, three instant messengers installed, a webcam, a cell phone, a landline, a letterbox, a Panasonic stereo-system with all kinds of Radio channels and a colour TV with cable connection with 89 channels.

In addition, Ivy has a pair of ears, a pair of eyes with diminishing returns, therefore three pairs of soft lenses to compensate, a pair of spectacles for nocturnal use, and last but not the least, a mouth that can speak, squeak, squeal, scream, screech, score and scare.

Finally, she has her skin.

Yet they are still in search of communication.

Insertions. They're simply putting in more insertions. And hyper-links. Constant improvisation is the way of life. No first draft available of their life stories. Your mistakes get erased. A peculiar quality of the digitized world. No scope for errors. All or none policy.

Is there a subjective space? My little space that's just mine, no matter how unclean, howmuchsoever error-ridden? And a personal time? Is she perceiving the world as disconnected images and finding unforeseen correlations amongst them, bombarded with images/snaps/ feelings?

This art of well-timing seems to never be within reach. The world has goofed up its time-infrastructure.

How much has the world moved ahead in the gap between her thought and the next jiffy?

Is she nothing but a photographic imitator of time?

******

In the heart of this unreal city there are as many closed secrets as there are open secrets. And in the dusty roads find shelter the dissipated but warm home-truths and the cold but bosom-borne hard-facts never seem to leave one. The skyscrapers act as mental-ladders to youthful aspirations, while the blazing firmament of summer generously pours in condescension. People look as high up as they look down upon.

-- If you take a look at our company growth-rate graph, it takes a dip at this point which is attributed to the faulty manufacturing strategy…

-- Ashoka the Great was a preacher of non-violence, that is after taking refuge in Buddhism…' 'Teacher I lost my pencil.'.." ..Slap!

-- What the hell Miravai! You're late again for the *bartan*! There's no water in the tap.

-- Hey Pooja! Guess what? Aman gave me this I Love You card. He's such an asshole! But I'm so excited about that hunky-dory friend of his, Meghnad!

-- Mamma who rules a condom? Oh you don't know! A Con. Just like a King ruling his Kingdom! Chunky told me but Woooonyaanh Woooonyaanh why are you hitting me?

-- Fuckin' bastard! Why the fuck do you keep a fuckin' mobile if you gotta keep that fuckin' thing switched off all the fuckin' time!!

-- Arre Barfiji! What are you doing in that lightless corner of the country? If you want the political limelight, learn to have the mango and have the *goothli* too! Come over to the capital *man*… No, no, I didn't wish to be anti-feminist! I very much meant you were a power-packed woman. Err, it was just a slip of the tongue.

******

The Capital hardly sleeps; it buzzes with activity. The political upheavals, the economic downstream, the Hindutva rightwing, the leftover post-Marxists' Leftism, the decentralized intellectual milieu and the scattered everyday life being the centre of everything. Big shopping malls have been erected, air conditioned and you find everything under the sun there; cross the road and there's Roadcross, the supermarket, no heat, no sweat, only consumer's pleasure! No problem zone, the beggar girls are shooed away, who knows they could be prostitutes! Unnecessary trouble-makers. Now who's going to stand for an hour in the queue, remember the Uphaar tragedy! We can have the tickets in black. To walk the ramp you only need the height, rest can be worked out, and a whole industry is functioning thereby. There's the Chavi Dalmia Fashion Week at the Intercontinental, but these slum-dwellers in the adjacent *maidan* may create a scene. The eminent politician spoke against consumerising nudity, a capital story! The blind saint Padmalochan attended the Astronomy Seminar and lectured on 'looking' into the future and forecasting destiny by seeing what's on the stars. The government has ordered the transport vehicles to switch over to compressed natural gas as a fuel from diesel or petrol; the situation is getting inflammable, they have called for a bus-strike tomorrow, burnt down six buses by spilling gasoline and setting them afire. Luckily, just three received minor burns. Here's a talk on Kripa Nahta's Liar, it's about lesbians and society hypocrites. Wow! The teachers are asking for a pay-hike again and now the MPs too! Kewl, there's no college tomorrow. Pollution is quadrupled; the demand for cars is not going anywhere. We need to have a greener city; other states should go green with envy. Get exotic plants, we have to project our indigenous flora. The Wonder bra can make the teenagers look like women; it gives them a boost. Phil Gates has opened the floodgates of the IT industry; every home has a window! The real-estate thing has had a crash of late. This is the age of Post-structuralism and Deconstruction. The Sad Adam will be torn into pieces for having a functional crimson circulation, by a pair of bushy white rats who can't get enough of the biting-into-other's-cake syndrome. The omnipresent, stupefying, ineffable, bewildering phantasms! Phenomenal!

******

Let's disturb the film of appearances, shall we, the dull routine of pseudo-objectivity!

After all, it's a comedy of broken solitudes, prevailing separateness, formless private worlds dissolving into a broth of bubbling insignificances in a cauldron of time, fried in the oil of events.

******

Serenading Ophelia. That's the name of a silly photo album. Why silly? No idea. Perhaps because none were clicked by her. But something she had searched and stored in her personal space. Marionette Monologues. Yes with two capital M's. Alliterated.

She has some mad scribbles too. On herself. And a few letters. For herself. By herself and a few others. So she thinks. She thinks she's CC, Central Character of whatever That Will Follow. Alliteration once again, heck! A personal museum dedicated to a namesake, but memorializing the not yet dead self. Crazy to say the least, yet not uncommon. Quite tomb-like, though mobile, portable 'cause wireless. The namesake's perhaps an excuse for tomb-making albeit a virtual one, a gimmick for self-aggrandizement, an apology for self-love, a case for holding an identity card that sanctions melancholy, a well-chosen glum to be worn like rouge while marching on intangible ramps, wearing e-cerebral high-heels, which often flounder, break, stumble on wayward microchips that like disobedient uncouth kids laugh at her unseemliness, then discard them to walk barefoot on the vague gravestone, with indecipherable greetings, complaints, desires and dates, then lap up the illegibility (to give it her own changing colours) for self-promotion, pretending a mingling, faking a compoundness, then ending up, not quite unwittingly, lodging the dislodged, or the never-quite-lodged, yet-unlaunched, waiting for a flight. Yet always fearing a crash, at times dying and living with it, often drowning in the sky.

But we aren't concerned with what she scribbles. For the moment. Anyway she doesn't have a sound grammar. And she does a lot of those stupid spelling errors. I mean *commits* them. Not *does,* that would sound trivial. Faulty sentence-construction, too wordy at times, too adjectival. Anyway that's not exactly what we're going to deal with. Let's focus on Serenading Ophelia now. It's a photo album, alright. For that's what it stores and parades once you click the link. It would lead you to this violet background white-lettered photo space, in which you'd see images and a small adjunct text with each. There's some music as well to delight you, of course how else would O be crooned to, sung to, thus persuaded to pose and parade before her? The images are photographs of Ophelia on canvas, painted since 1775 to 1926. The dates are not exactly incidental. They were present on the first link on the first page of a Google search called 'Ophelia paintings'. She clicked on each of those links, each a painting since 18th century, spanning the 19th and first three decades of the 20th. She didn't download all of them to her computer. She didn't like all of them. Some didn't fit the bill. For example, some were too orthodox, or too male in perception. Perhaps she was looking for Ophelias she could identify with, or Ophelia that could shock her

she isn't a painting of Ophelia. She's a picture of herself, without a smell or sound, or perhaps carrying a sense of smell and sound with her, perceptible only to her, and to the photographer who took her snap, at a little distance from the same grey pavement on which she was posing happily with her small kid-umbrella.

At the 11th second, the monitor would get partially blanked, _040607540_alyson_citrine would give way to 280_barricade. A black and white snap of a long street, banked on both sides by deserted brick buildings, which are actually clusters of flats. Bombed out flats. It's London Blitz in all its devastated glory, with sooted walls and roofs, an ashened sky, the serenity of smog drooping like an old salivating man on the brink of death bent on a terrified city, the victim of collective rape, amongst many other victims lined in a casual cemetery. Had it been Venice and the street a canal, the debris inside those crumbling houses would have flown into the stream, it would have been a shade of mild red at places. Now perhaps they have the Metro running beneath that street which is no longer itself but a plasticsurgeried model with a sparkling sootfree face. The operations had been extremely successful to erase the last traces of a past scar.

Third came Benjamin West's Ophelia, originally an engraving from Boydell's Shakespeare Prints. "XLV. ACT IV, SCENE V. Elsineur. King, Queen, Laertes, Ophelia, &c. Painted by B. West, President of the Royal Academy. Engraved by F. Legat." The actual site said quite a few other things, that the original painting by West was bought by a Mr. Felton and shipped to America and exhibited in a museum in Philadelphia, that a reviewer for *Examiner* (1808) described Ophelia in the original canvas as "robed in white; her flaxen locks hang in loose disorder over her forehead and down to her waist; with her left hand extended she carelessly strews around the rue and thyme; her eyes exhibit a wandering mind and delicious indecisiveness, yet she is gentle; rage makes no part of her character." In her slideshow, however, somewhere in between the 20th second and the 30th tick of her screen timer, she felt West giving her something quite indescribable, something more than the fate of a tragic virgin. But before she could tell what, the slide had the next offering.

She smiled. And paused the show. This image was familiar, almost personal. It was called (she had called it) *eee*. Thrice written, uttered at once in one go, kind of a compound utterance, the fifth letter of the English alphabet. It produced a sound effect she liked. This was a gift from a person she knew, a loved one. An image of his loved one. A snap in black and white yet again, but a weird one. A tulip twig and a straightened out string of barbed wire in a broken glass bottle and a barebacked woman in the background scratching a grey wall. It was hazy. She loved the haze. The prominent veined hands were clutching a nothing, scrounging for a nothing.

She had her fill, then clicked on the tiny black horizontal isolateral triangle indicating 'play': now the title read Ernest Hebert, Ophelia, c.1910. Meanwhile, Billy Joel's Leningrad faded out to the emergent soundbytes of Simple Minds' Don't You Forget About Me on the Launchcast Radio of Yahoo Messenger. Change of mood. And the thorn-diademed, kohl-rimmed woman winked at her from her archaic face. She liked this one, the mocking-at-angst look of it, and scores of outlandish flowers strewn in her dishevelled hair that stood out like pockets of puddles in a dug up road. She selected this one to feature on the display board of both the Yahoo and MSN Messengers, so that she would beam as a black and white beacon when her blinker showed she was online. Job done, she smirked at herself, pouted and threw a kiss at the photosphere while tossing the idea of putting one of her own webcammed snap [that she would take right then, right there, of the pout] in the series. But on second thoughts, decided against it.

She fleeted past the next three rapidly, all three were coloured. The titles read Francis Danby, Disappointed Love, 1821; George Frederic Watts, Ophelia, c.1864; John W. Waterhouse, Ophelia, c.1894. Ophelia hiding her face, a musing Ophelia, Ophelia admiring/bemoaning herself in the lap of green. The image strip popped up whenever she brought the cursor to hover on the picture and she clicked randomly on the 12th and 13th. Madeleine Lemaire, Ophelia, 1880s, PREAULT Antoine-Augustin, Ophelia. A tit-flaunting or perhaps oblivious to her half bare self witchlike seductress, a sculpted-in-black venal Venus now arrested after a digital transmigration.

She looked at John Bell's 1775 mischievous flower-girl with a magic wand in her hand. A joke of a kind, she mused? Was Bell sure to whom he was handing over the stick?

To step out of herself and merge into those discoloured spaces, those grey leaves, skies, wilted flowers (known through the shades and lines), those maniac eyes and swinging breasts that challenge you: Enter at your peril. Now Cerci, Sycorax, Medusa, who was once a Penelope, Miranda, Andromeda. I love Cerci, I rejoice Medusa and the way they enthrall. I don't want role-models, I want friends, lovers. They all are lovers. Sita couldn't love but one man, what a miser! Couldn't give more than one man, couldn't disseminate herself but fissioning into two replicates of the one. What a shame to waste a whole lotta love on one body, on its fixed monotone, on its non-pliantness. Though there were them who loved. They who loved them. They who loved them back. At times, almost loving. But why them, why falling back on them yet again? Because they drowned, all of them? Drowning in the earth or fire, it's still letting yourself go. Turning to cinders or decomposed into the elements, post-burial decay into one's origins. They aren't one, they are all themselves, denied selves for token selves, mere faces and multiple wombs. Shut up, for godsake, stop senseless straying into nothing. Stop harping on clichés. Stop vomiting old names. No more proper nouns. No more names. None of them.

That wasn't her, was it, staring back at her from the glaring screen? She would have wished it had been her, a bit like her, a bit of her, had it been something but O. Yet wishing might bring to life unasked for things. She didn't know if she was wishing to be like her, to be her, for she had a fate to fear, silences and muteness to fear, neurosis and loneliness to fear, death and desires to fear. (How silly, she thought, to say desire's going from zero to one, whereas actually it's going from one hundred to one hundred and one! But was she jumbling up needs and desires? Then for desire to be really so, mustn't it go from zero to minus one, ever-fleeting?) No, it was messy, she knew, despite repeated attempts to unclutter the mess, it was still quite the same. She knew. Plus all she was looking at were mere set of dead images; frozen, figs of fancy, mere works of art, merely to be looked at, and relegated to blissful amnesia once she was satiated. The logic of pure satiation, a hedonistic desire to look, analyse, distance and analyse, interpret and connote, connote to further connote, until it became an endless cycle of interpretation and connotation, a self-germinating intelligent design, a self-perpetuating body of reflecting surfaces admiring each other in a game of deadly reproduction. Leave me alone, she cried, not aloud of course. But who was seeking?

SEVEN

Hearth

Shumonto was watching the reality show *Wrong Miracles* on Tele Today. He had just finished with a pilfering Jerry and chasing Tom on Cartoon Network. After *Wrong Miracles* he would switch over to *The Gadget World* on Discovery, followed by *Business India* on NDTV, then *Khana Khazana* by Sanjeev Kapur on Zee.

His wife was making stray jaunts from the kitchen to the drawing room. It was understood; he wouldn't cook for the day. He wouldn't offer any iota of help, wouldn't take a bath, would take hours to sip the tea, would be roughing it up with his chat-room junkies and littering heaps of verbal debris. In other words, he wouldn't move his butt.

At about 12:30 in the afternoon, Ivy gave up.

"Are you going to have some breakfast?" she asked, annoyed.

"What have you made?" A nonchalant counter question.

"Nothing yet."

"Then?"

"But I will."

"And what you will?"

"Bread omelette."

"And what have you had since morning?"

"Nothing. Just tea."

"And why's that?"

"I overstuffed myself yesterday."

"Are you dieting?"

"No."

Ivy felt well-stocked. He was speaking up finally. After hours of audio-silence.

She made the toasts and a double-egg omelette. She liked it well-fried, with lots of chopped onion and green chillies. He would separate the chillies first, keep them at a corner of the plate, inspect the toasts for awhile, make a few observations, compare it with a McBurger, think about having stocks of mayonnaise handy, then patiently wait for her to get the ketchup from the fridge. That was how it usually turned out with him during his downtimes.

A quickie for a breakfast. Quickies interspersed between the races for a disinfected world and a verbalized world. Quickies inserted between double takes and gyrations.

He came to keep the dirty plate in the sink. The kitchen was in a clutter. He could see sons of cockroaches swimming in the grubby pan; there were oil smudges on the sideboard, the wiper was lying on the floor. She hadn't put the lid back over the drain-mouth. That was why the brown battalion had an unblocked ingress. *Periplaneta americana* vs. *Blatta orientalis*, he mused. The roaches there and the roaches here. Which were the ones that were more repulsive? Could repulsion be mapped? Formatted into types, classified into discreet grids, given a color, a basis, an antidote?

Hygiene. Wouldn't she make things a bit more hygienic, he bewildered. Without hygiene the world would be colonized by the little masters. That would be a particularly unwanted scenario.

Foul women. Like she chanted, fair is foul and foul is fair.

He was half tempted to leave the mess as it was. On second thoughts he remained. Ran water from the bucket over the dishes in the sink, sprayed some Baygon roachkill and put the lid back. Picked up the cleaning rag and hung it on the rod. Took a bit of soap-water, soaked a rough cloth-scrap and wiped clean the smudges. Nothing was sparkling still. But no outrageous look anymore.

She was cuddled up in the bed with her glasses on and a small book on her side. He had seen it earlier; *The Politics of Postmodernism*, by a Linda Hutcheon. It was lying on her study table for quite a few days, she hadn't bothered opening. Perhaps she really didn't have anything else to do, he concluded. She would doze off in a while, she was showing the signs.

Should he talk to her, he was wondering. But he needed an excuse.

"Do we have a nail-cutter?" he let out finally.

She glanced up, took off her glasses, straightened out her legs under the sheet, and rubbed her neck. "A nail-cutter?" he said again.

"Yeah, we do. It's in the left drawer of the dressing table."

"Okay, thanks."

"Are your nails long enough yet?"

"Put on your glasses," he advised.

"Well you can tell me yourself. I think you hardly need a nail trimming. They are just fine."

"Leave that to me."

"Do you mean your toe-nails?"

"Both."

He didn't feel like bragging about cleaning up the kitchen. Not the right time, he thought. Anyway she didn't need telling. She would notice it herself and feel good. But she should remember that he hated clutter. Now. Things had changed for him. He's no more a reckless bachelor.

He settled on the nearby couch and began working on his rather clean and short nails. Made them cleaner, shorter and shapelier. He could sense her gaze on him.

"You want some help?" she asked, good-naturedly.

"Yeah, with the toes," he answered frankly.

She got up and let the rim of her nightie fall and cover her legs. Came up to him, sat on her knees and started evening the toe-nails out. Took turns to file them as she had read in the Ladies' Home Journal, an e-zine delivered to her Inbox on a monthly basis. He watched her, bemused at her absolute focus on the little irrelevant extensions of his bodily appendages. She looked up at him and smiled. He made a similar gesture; good work it said.

"Are you sure you won't eat something?" he offered, genuinely.

"Might try your head if you lemme." She spurted out, without looking up.

"Erm, that's not on the menu," he was coolly curt.

"Well then I guess nothing it is." She remarked.

"I can get you something light from the market. Make some noodles if nothing else."

"I'm not hungry."

"You never are."

"Says who?"

"I do."

"You're wrong."

"I'm not."

record straight. This is also investment. Making the right contacts. Expanding your horizons. The globe's at your feet then.

I alternate between staring at her and staring at the grey floor. With a twisting of my lips to suggest a deep impact.

-- One more thing, Bishakha resumes, I'm editing a critical edition on the earliest women writers from India. We'll be covering from Mirabai to Toru Dutt. You can see it'll be on regional literature basically, barring Dutt. So, if you like, you might as well think about contributing something. What do you say?

That'll be great, I reply instantly.

She's always been a real help. If Nalli's a soul-guard, she's the depravity-terminator, path-paver and a scholar-maker.

-- Good. Look in for something substantial. You want to stick to the originals in Bengali or dip into translations?

Actually, I would like to work on something other than Bengali. It's already overrepresented.

-- Oh, alright then. Yeah, you're quite right there. I already have five bookings for Bengali and we've to limit ourselves to twelve. The Global Lens and Co. series editors won't accept more than that.

I nod my head, sympathetically.

-- Fine then. I might be going to Sahitya one of these days. Would you like to come with me? You've a membership I hope?

Oh yes, of course I do. I spurt out, genuinely pleased and grateful. After yesterday's fiasco today seems a very heaven. Actually, it's a glimpse of heaven after a rather longish drag of five months.

The staff room is buzzing with human voices of every kind and decibel. It's 11:30 and it's crammed with people. Lecturers, readers, senior readers, a few assistant professors. Then the regular faces. Bhanuji, our head staffroom manager, Dineshji, the peon, Lataji, staff-helper. They're constantly moving in and out, running desperate errands. Transferring calls from staffroom to the administrative section back and forth. Sticking up fresh posters and notices on the boards. Answering a few student queries if a staff member is present or not. The usual scene. The scene I've cherished for seven years now.

The autumn break is over. It's already two days of regular schedule. MHC doesn't waste a single working day killing time. The curriculum clock has been ticking accurately with only minor lapses ever since.

The torch of being one of the best is a heavy onus to carry forward. MHC accomplishes it with a robotic finesse.

Breeze (Samiran Dutt is a balmy and affectionately bizarre dude) and Malti Bakshi glide in together. Breeze (with a coupla CDs in his hands as expected) always had an irrepressible itch to go on yapping and performing literary calisthenics before an awed bunch way after the bell had rung, but Malti Bakhshi too? What's wrong? She looks positively spaced out and thumps her weight on the next couch beside Bishakha.

The English faculty is slowly assimilating. It's recess so the rest should also be joining in anytime. Bipin Ghosh, the HOD, then C.L.R. Jayavardana (who's significantly named and gets addressed as James), Kaya Singh who is the co-coordinator of Gestus, the dramatic society, along with Breeze, then Ambreen Mirza the pass out from JNU and a recent recruitment. She's about my age and she is a temporary. I'm an ad hoc.

Six months back the faculty would have included me. [I'm desperate to come back here.]

Six years ago, it would have included Mahendra Raina and Rahul Raj Verma. The two giants of Delhi academic and theatre circle. They retired together like good old crones and are doubly active now with their theatre group, Mimic. That was when I was in the second year of my graduation.

A process of good-humoured self-elimination. To avoid contamination.

Nalli (Dr. Nalini Subhramanium, PhD in Early American Fiction from Delhi University) shoots the jittery concern.

-- Is everything all right, Malti?

-- Like hell it is Nalli, Bakshi commences her plaintiff mono act which seems to have all the signs of becoming a prolonged gall-breathing at the Top Gun. Perhaps she's coming from the principal's office.

She resumes, after taking a breath.

-- How can they do it? Take away my course without even informing me? Without calling me up for once?

Nalli tries to defend the accused.

-- Bipin tried contacting you yesterday Malti. Your cell was switched off.

No change still. Bakshi continues unhindered.

-- What tried contacting me Nalli? Alright, so I wasn't reachable, but at least they could have stalled the decision till today. What was all the big hurry about? And hadn't I informed the office and Bishakha that I wouldn't be coming on the 16th? Goddammit, I too can have some family business to attend. My sons had their school Parents-Teachers-Meeting and it was absolutely necessary for me to be there because they haven't been doing very well lately. I had enough reasons to be stressed out; and to pile on everything, what I get to hear first thing in the morning today? That my syllabus has been scissored without me having an inkling of it! I ask you Nalli, you're a senior reader too. Do I deserve this after years of service?

Pregnant pause.

Guess everyone is staring at the floor right now, except for Breeze who's fiddling with his CDs, apparently trying to find a suitable pocket in his black Adidas handbag to slide them in. I wish I could just vanish right now, without delaying for a moment, feeling like a perfect intruder, an eavesdropper who gets to hear stuff that's too pungent to bear. I should have gotten used to intradepartmental bickerings by now but unfortunately I'm psychologically clumsy enough to take it uneasy.

Bishakha the smoothie arbitrates between the boiling Bakshi and the absent Bipin.

-- Malti, I understand. Please take it easy. We'll re-schedule it in case you've a problem with the staff decision. We were getting late and had to wrap it up yesterday itself. There's a hell lot to cover remember, and we thought you were already overburdened so we scrapped a few.

Bakshi rewinds herself.

-- But do I deserve this Bishakha? Not even being told about the changes! It's humiliating you know. I shouldn't be saying it before a girl who's been my student here but I need to forewarn her against the kind of politics that's running beneath. In her own college. My case should be a lesson to you Ivy.

Damn. Damn. Why me? Why me always?

Smoothie's turn.

-- Calm down Malti. We'll sort it out. And it's not politics for heaven's sake dear. We were just trying to be a little more efficient, that's all. I'm sure you would've done exactly the same thing had you been in charge. And c'mon, the syllabus has had such a major cleansing operation. There are so many new things to teach. Wouldn't it be better to cooperate as much as possible? It's only a minor issue dear, don't take it to heart.

And Smoothie is younger than Bakshi, much younger. Public relations!

-- Alright Bishakha. But I want to talk it out with Bipin first. I'm not agreeing to your so-called decisions until then.

Peace! Signs of truce! Many rounds of silent applaud for Smoothie.

Breeze acts the little devil now.

-- But Bipin has gone to receive Steve Rhys folks.

Calm little devil.

-- Oh, fantastic! So now what Bishakha?

Smoothie glares at Breeze without throwing even a glance at him.

-- We'll talk it out today itself Malti. It's my responsibility now, since I was equally involved.

That's what Smoothie loves doing: being responsible and being in charge. The secret commander of MHC Eng Fac. She resumes in a conclusive air.

-- The Steve Rhys thing has been arranged in haste Malti. He was only going to talk at the Arts Faculty but Bipin and I coaxed him to try it out here as well. Two seminars back to back isn't a joke I guess. He's been unbelievably kind to me, that too after years of audio silence from Bipin's side. Anyway, we'll talk on our way back. The thing begins sharp at one and I must go and check with the Seminar Hall. Come with me, they all listen to you. I'll be such a mess all by myself.

Bakshi has cooled. She had to.

-- Yeah alright. I'm feeling claustrophobic inside. I desperately need some fresh air.

Breeze bursts out hysterically once they leave. Nalli claws at him.

-- Heck you had almost sent her up in flames Samiran.

-- I couldn't help it Nalli! I think it's my birth right to laugh at clowns.

-- C'mon, Samiran. She could've been your teacher for all you know.

-- Yeah I know that. Anyway, what's Ivy Sengupta up to finally? Didn't see you yesterday.

I had to pay my very first visit to SLC, I duly inform him.

-- Good, so what's the situation like? Koel Pathan made you sulk alone in the Staff Colosseum for the whole day, eh?

Good heavens! How do you know? Practising occult science as a side business, are you? Samiran the Thelemite?

-- Hehe, madam, I was once at her doors too. Long story!

No kidding!!

-- Really. Ask Nalli. It was Mahendra Raina who plucked me out of the muck and set me up here, for good.

Sounds like a fairy tale. Oberon fixed the despondent Puck and ever since the magic wand never went to another's hand. Wow! No wonder he wanted you here. Gestus wouldn't have been what it is, without you.

-- You speaketh the truth my lady.

Sagnik Borghein, from the Sociology department rushes in. He and Breeze are inseparable duo. I've heard people saying they recreate the magic of Raina and Verma.

-- Hola Dawtto!!

Vintage Sagnik. Deliberately irks Dutt with that Assamese inflection of his.

-- Yeah Bog.

-- Steve Rhys is here today, eh?

-- So I gather.

-- Bishakha, I tell you, is a mastermind! In all the positive sense of it I mean (that's apprehending Nalli's 'quizzically yours' look). Dawtto, tell her to fix Amartya Sen for the department fest, eh? What say you? We'll tag along with Economics dept and can have a gala time gorging on Sen! That's of course if he's in India then.

-- Forget about it. Keep me out of this lobbying shit.

-- What lobbying Dawtto? Sen won't mind, and Bishakha is always ready to utilize her 'contacts', eh? Ha ha ha!!!

-- Do it yourself Bog if you're even one per cent serious about it. Though, honestly, it'll be a wonderful opportunity to listen to the veteran. I missed him at IHC last time; he was there with Romila Thapar if I'm not wrong.

-- So you've been co-opted to my bogey eh Dawtto? It'll be a perfect image-booster I tell you. What say you Nalini Subhramanium?

Nalli casts a tired glance at him and prefers to stay silent after a shrug.

-- And what about thee Poison Ivy?

That'll be Sen-sible of us and Sen-sational for the rest, I contribute to the tabloidish atmosphere.

-- Ahh Ha ha ha!! Rumour in the making! Ivy wilt thou join me in circulating it? Spreading its ripples all over the campus? Time we make October Fools out of people. April is a dead month anyway.

Nalli grabs the last words. Those old and familiar ones.

-- *April is the cruellest month.*

******

The Seminar Hall is jam-packed as expected. Suddenly everyone's on time, courtesy Professor Emeritus Steve Rhys, University of California. I forget the exact place. A chum of Spivak perhaps. She should have a talk lined up too, here in Delhi, but that's for the next year I guess.

People are coming in huge tides despite the short notice. Oh, now I know, they all have been redirected from the previous talk at the main Faculty. What is Rhys speaking on, by the way? Nalli's not sure. Neither is Breeze.

There are six long rectangular tables arranged in a row at one side of the second-floor corridor, covering the entire length of the Hall. So that while Rhys talks, one can peer out to appreciate the latest publications, both his, and of his compatriots in the world fraternity.

The Hall is a huge room covered with red carpet, red cushioned chairs and posh looking brown curtains that begin from the roof almost, hiding the air conditioners and speakers behind them. The entire faculty is pouring in; there's a general hum that rises appreciably high as it approaches one. At the very front, the panel table with digital microphones, bottled water, and other paraphernalia. On the wallboard facing the huge crowd is written a note in gargantuan fonts:

MH College welcomes His
Hon'ble Professor Emeritus Steve Rhys
The self-proclaimed Man of Translation
Who doesn't belong to any institution or nation!

It's a big sport and the cheerleaders are post-30 on an average. The big hero arrives with an uproar and a huge round of applaud. A gigantic man of over six feet, dressed in a metallic blue casual shirt and off white trousers. Slightly balding with silvery tufts and perhaps too starkly pink for an Indian ambience. Followed by the principal and Bipin Ghosh, dwarfing both.

The usual bouquet presentation, followed by the princi's all too predictable welcome address. Bipin takes over and without wasting a single jiffy in quibbling hands, it's all over to the intended, expected and anticipated man. Steve Rhys begins thus.

-- I'm overwhelmed, brothers and sisters of India!

An ear-splitting round of clapping that seems to last for eternity. And there's that familiar pang in my lower abdomen. Sheeit. I should have known.

Steve Rhys, a disembodied mouth. An O. A pink O with pink insides and a shifting floor. The seminar's in full swing within minutes, but I'm falling into a pit of blankness. For the rest, the pink O has a tag, for me it's no more no less than the SLC peon who offered me tea. The audience becomes a community of disembodied ears and hands that go up periodically. The claimers to a wholeness have dozed off and my irritation attains an erotic appeal with the throbbing ache climaxing exactly at the moment Rhys offers a temporary conclusion and drinks from the Bisleri bottle. Rhys' fiery spirit apparently cuts an interjection short. I'm beginning to decipher the codes of mimicry, beholding the swimming world with almost closing eyes, regarding the skin peeling off from the palm, as it often does, as the cellophane comes off a paperback when it's time to collect dust, get dog-ears, flappy encumbrances, like digressions for an impatient reader fed on pot-boilers.

Nalli excuses me out, creating a minor disturbance through the hall, as we traverse almost half the length of the hall for the nearest exit. We rush to the ladies' loo where I wash and clean myself. Then block out the hole.

At the staffroom, Nalli offers me Pyricontin and the tranquilizer relaxes me after a while.

We come back after almost 50 minutes. There's no point going in at the very fag end. Instead we stay outside, inspecting the books on display. I graze through the titles randomly, at times bothering to open the cover page and look inside. *Discovering Diaspora, The Violence of Memory, Translated Shame, Polysystems of Communication after Technological Revolution, Literature in the Net-Age: An E-valuation.* Almost all the major publishing houses have their editions, a parade of enchanters from everywhere, the world in a nutshell waiting to be cracked.

The technologies of terminologies. The terminologies of technologies. Mutually enabling. Symbiotic. Enabling us brown Shylocks to hoard and weigh chunks of cerebral flesh in different beam balances. Outside the seminar halls, the world moves on. Or does it, without infesting the red carpeted, comfy-cushioned-chaired, well-lighted, audio-video-powered, discussion auditoriums? The world is furiously scribbling its transient changes; it's 'work in progress'. It has past embarrassments that it wishes to hide desperately, push them under the very red carpets that cover the seminar rooms in various corners of the world. It's a trifle strange, how the rubrics change. How they resurrect old nomenclatures to erase a recent blunder. How they pull out a hyphen and send it centre-stage, or dig out a lost third bracket to celebrate a 'third world', something they don't quite know what to do with. Like the unfound nuclear weapons, the word 'new' chases them in their crazy nightmares. Oh just where to put it, just where exactly to put it so that it just stops vexing the canon-makers for a while. But no, that cannot be. The canon-makers have a lot of wallets to take care of, or may be bank lockers of publishing houses and media barons and politicos and columnists and reviewers and critics and counter-critics and theorists and antitheorists and writers and unwriters. The unacknowledged war of the old and new. The red and white. The black and white. The brown and white. The yellow and white. The VIBGYOR and white. Obsolete? The colour-scheme is obsolete? Is it past the post? Is it gone for good? What about the embarrassment of that remembrance or are you too ashamed to recall? That *nostalgia*? Where have you shoved it off? Buried under the weight of terminologies? Heh, you could bury the very womb that generated the army of terms after all? But you couldn't possibly, eh? You must enshrine the nostalgia well, inter it periodically and reinstall it to keep the show going. The show must go on. We need the grants. We need the research and development. We need a level playing field. We need the standardized foundational myths to erect a museum showcasing liberty, equality and fraternity and how wonderfully we are striving, slouching towards that *one* goal. It's the goal of a glocalized world to make it into a pretty cosmo-village [where you cannot mention the pillage but singsong eu-logic chorus to the Techno-Terminus]. But, of course I don't mean it. I mean nothing actually. I'm not responsible. No, don't say I am. I wasn't in the panel. I don't know Steve Rhys. I'm not sure what 'polysystems' may signify. I couldn't care less. But I ought to. I got lectures to deliver. No matter how puny I seem to be, I still got *lectures* to deliver. I too have to generate a battery of critics. They are little larvae now, small and feverishly eating on the slop. They need to grow fat, then prune that fat to fit themselves in a standard panel-chair. With differing colour-schemes. Any of the VIBGYOR. Or a shade. It's called differential gradation. And it's at the offering end of the *gradient*. The receiving end is at the other extreme end. It includes, in the order of diminishing powers: the non-panellists, the non-interjectors, the non-jargondecipherers, the non-comprehenders, the non-facultymembers, the non-starcollegians, the non-topscorers, the non-desiringtobetopscorers, the non-identitycardholders, the non-Englishemulators, the non-fluentEnglishspeakers. Oh beauty! What an absolutely violent *hypertrophy of difference*! Oh beauty, you have actually managed to store, remember and utilize *that* phrase! Oh hell, what does it mean though? Oh hell, *recall* immediately, the meaning, damn it's the passport to the cultural supermarket you aspire to shop from and be displayed as well. Oh damn your genealogical anxieties, oh rather don't damn them yet, *use* them, *beat them out to suit your needs, howl* and *scream* as fits you fine. Join the chorus. You can never be the lead singer anyway. So just join the chorus.

People have started coming out of the hall. So it has ended, I ask a familiar face. Yes, it has, what a pity you missed it—the crisp reply.

What did he basically talk about? I ask half-apologetically.

-- I'll give you what he gave us as the 'topic'. "Active Imagination as the force bridging the Gap between the Original and the Translation, irrespective of the Centre-Margin Alignment."

Aaaah, great!

They're making a beeline towards the buffet section. Bishakha comes out and duly enlightens our starving selves, with a What-the-hell-happened-to-you-in-the-middle-of-it-all look. I throw back a try-and-understand. She returns an oh-I-see.

Rhys comes out at last, accompanied by Bipin and the University mascots. Bishakha drags me and Nalli along. The buffet is suitably ethnic north-Indian, typically Delhiite. Vegetable salad, veg fried rice, dahi bara, naan, dal makhani, shahi panir, aalu gobi, gajar ka halua, rasgullas, vanilla ice cream, tea and coffee.

Columns of pretty porcelain plates disappear slowly as the serpentine line moves forward. I observe from a distance as Nalli prepares a plate for me comprising dahi bara, dal makhani and salads only. Not in a state for much consumption today.

The line has broken up into small circles of individuals playing the chummy-chummy game. Bishakha and Bipin act the coordinators once again, becoming the revolving moons introducing the stars across constellations. The circles form, dissolve away, then reform in a newer combination. I try computing the mathematical equivalent of possible permutations and fail miserably.

Fragments of sentences reach me from everywhere.

-- Steve, do meet Dr. Eshwar Prasad, from Orissa. He's come all the way from Bhubaneshwar to listen to you.

-- Professor Rhys, what do you think of our collaborative effort - "The Bengali Renaissance: A Predated Cosmopolitanism?"

Rhys: Am afraid I haven't gone through it yet, but sounds challenging. Here's the thumbs up from me.

-- Aah Stevie dear, you must do something about my upcoming edition. Gimme something to ensure a tornado and meteoring sales (Foxee Lady from SLR)

Rhys: I'll surely mail you, sweets.

-- Steve, taste the aalu gobi, authentic Indian stuff I tell you! Your plate is empty man, what the hell? *Bhaiya, daliye inke plate mein thoru aur*!

Rhys: Am afraid I can't. I find it a bit spicy and considering my age…

-- Oh puuhhleeeez, keep your dietchart at bay for once and dig into the mistress of spice. She's warm and caressing, eh?

I move towards where they're serving coffee from the vending machine. The smell of vanilla makes me puky almost, for some irrational reason I can't fathom. Once again the world starts blurring out, till I barely feel a strong hand supporting me by the slightest touch.

-- You alright young lady?

Rhys! The towering Rhys!

I regain a bit of my lost strength.

Am f..f..fine, thanks a lot.

-- I saw you escorted out at the beginning of the talk. May I know the reason? I won't be surprised if you tell me that Steve, you peeve, the moment you announced the godforsaken topic I fell sick.

I smile a little. Sir, I'm so awfully sorry I missed it. Unfortunately, I had a severe attack of abdominal cramps and I had to retire.

-- Cramps and I have a long association you know. (Dancing eyes, with a tinge of tenderness.)

-- And don't you Sir me now. Call me Steve, Stevie the peevie.

Yeah, Steve.

--That's a good girl. So what do I call you?

Oh am so sorry. I'm Ivy. Ivy Sengupta.

-- Err, which of the two? So-sorry or Ivy Sengupta?

[Hehmm. Scratch my head. Bad manners?]

-- Shall we walk to that window Ivy, to get little fresh air. I'm allergic to staying in AC for too long at a stretch.

Oh sure. Please. (Why on earth is he talking to me??????? Heck what if I black out in another microjiffy? Nalllllliii where are you?)

He resumes once we've reached our destination.

-- It's not rare actually that I'm conversing with someone who hasn't given an earshot to even a scrap of my talk. Hehe.

[Great so Steve Rhys is a sadist hell-bent on humiliating me. He's picked his scapegoat with care. A hapless, clipped-winged duckling.]

-- It's positively refreshing!

-- With a touch of intrigue about it.

-- I'm an avid reader of murder mysteries.

-- Don't you talk?

Yyyeahh, I mean, eehh, well, ahem…

-- Well?

I have a question for you Steve. (I've no idea where on earth it sprang from but at least he isn't going to call me a nascent dumbfuck back to his Californian crones.)

-- Shoot.

Well, I'm not sure if you're aware of it but have you, ever, visited an online chat-room? I mean, the way they talk, of course via typing, and am not talking of those Internet voice-conferences, especially you know, if you consider an Indian or African chat room or Russian for that matter where the script is English but reads different, makes those alien sounds, what would you call that? A sort of translation?

-- Hmm, interesting. Can you elaborate a bit further?

Yeah. I mean I've been thinking about it. And you know, since this component of imagination, as you said, becomes a kind of a bridge between two languages, cultures blah blah blah and umm err you know the whole idea of talking via a computer screen to invisible people who could be just anybodies, anywhere and practically one just doesn't know, do you see a kind of bridging over happening here? Like what I mean is that, umm... you know basically two things happen on chats. You speak in English or you speak in your own tongue with the English script. When you speak in your tongue, I mean the look of it, those words, phrases, and of course those icons and images that take the place of gestures and moods and stuff like that, do you see it as a new kind of development in language or a translation? Is there a difference and if so, what exactly is happening here?

-- Well, I don't really get the time for chatting but yeah, I've been reading about it. Umm I would call it a sociocultural phenomenon, you know, like centuries back you had those first Bible public-reading sessions. Different, but kind of similar. An assemblage but not quite an assembly hmm? Too many voices, too many names, random names, utterances, familiar script but alien words. Or like injecting words into the script. Attempting impregnation. Perhaps to find a fruit somewhere, form seeds of something new. With a lot of play of imagination oh yes. A little icon that smiles at you and its clone smiles back at the addressee. Yet you two smile in your own unique way, your muscles flex, your lips curve, there could be or not be dimples...

-- Steveee...Hell, we've been looking for you! What on earth are you doing out here? Get inside.

A troop of imposters there. I wish I had an IDS, Intrusion Detection System, was reading about it in some damned little technomag. Rhys looks a bit embarrassed perhaps.

-- I was just chatting with this interesting young lady here.

-- C'mon, there're so many waiting for you and the cab will be here any moment now.

-- Yeah alright. Gimme a sec. Aah, Ivy! Why don't you mail me hmm? Take it from Bishakha and do it. I would be expecting to hear from you. And one more thing, you might as well try writing a research paper on the thing we just discussed. I would help you in every way I can, that's a deal!

I smile back. Yeah. (A slow half-teasing, half-sighing one.)

-- Ciao then. Keep ticking.

Goodbye Steve.

So two tentative assignations, hmm? Good news for Nalli. //Smiles

NINE

Ghost

"The Moon, she hangs like a cruel portrait
soft winds whisper the bidding of trees
as this tragedy starts with a shattered glass heart
and the Midnightmare trampling of dreams
But no, no tears please
Fear and pain may accompany Death
But it is desire that shepherds its certainty
as We shall see..."

She was divinity's creature
That kissed in cold mirrors
A Queen of Snows
Far beyond compare
Lips attuned to symmetry
Sought Her everywhere
Dark liquored eyes
An Arabian nightmare...

She shone on watercolors
Of my pondlife as pearl
Until those who couldn't have Her
Cut Her free of this World

And I embraced
Where lovers rot...
Her ghost in the fog
Her ghost in the fog

It was difficult to understand what he was up to. She watched him for a fortnight: come back home the usual time, open a stashed away bottle of chilled beer or rum (he had given up whisky on the doctors' insistence earlier), get stoned on either or both, watch a worthless film on HBO, never switch over to Zee MGM even if they were showing *Casablanca* or *When Harry Met Sally* or *Chicago*; then at about 12 sharp turn on the computer, put on the stored mp3 'Her Ghost in

The Fog' by the British black metal band Cradle of Filth, listen to the same song over and over again until it would strike one; then whisper to her that he could feel her between them in the bed, she was there looking at the duo, that British bands had contributed the most to quality rock, that black metal reminded him of her, of his salad days, that she was a Cleopatra, then on knowing that the queen was tawny he would edit it to pink Cleopatra, the prowess-goddess, worthy of male respect, who was born to devour and be devoured at the end, but who led a heroic life, a Joan of Arc, a Florence Nightingale with a hyperactive sex life, but well-deserved, the only woman he didn't want to cage up, the only woman he liked to see roving around even if the champagne she would get him from the shelves would taste bitter, the only self-sufficient woman he had come across, the only selfless woman he had ever known, the woman to give him the best sex of his life, the woman to offer herself generously at the altar of his masculinity, the woman who crossed barriers of colour and religion to make love to a *Blatta orientalis* like him, the woman whose sexual ambition and performance excelled his and he wasn't ashamed to admit that for once, the woman who always stayed a nun-nymphomaniac and never surrendered to the mediocrity of a whore-ice maiden, she who had kissed him first, she the bold one, she who had soothed an initially awed him, she who had let him suck her beautiful breasts, simply because they were white and big and milky, although she wasn't ever pregnant, they looked as if she was perpetually lactating, she who would let him fuck her on days when she would be chumming bearing the pain of her contracting uterus and his onward thrusts, she who was always wet for him, nursing his wilting narcissi of drooping conscience, confidence, she who was in a nutshell Irene Scott.

In the morning of course, his selectively amnesiac memory would have deleted the entire tape of his nocturnal oratory, making him rather apologetic about not remembering a segment of his precious nightlife, giving him a rather puzzled face that could pass off as one deserved by innocent microbiologists who only knew the sexology and endocrinology of bacilli and cocci.

He could have written a Brown Skin, White Masks during those nights. He had to merely substitute the word nigger with the genus *Blatta* and there they would have had an intergeneric discourse on sex. Miscegenation with a twist. A Gregor meets an Othello and undergoes a digital reconfiguration: *Suppose all that you have always valued in your life was shown to be an illusion. What if your precious beliefs, maxims, platitudes, and traditions were inverted and distorted beyond recognition? You suddenly realize that what is good is bad; what is beauty is foul; what is virtue, vice. What if all your points of reference were to shift: North becomes South; black becomes white; deviant becomes saint; saint becomes deviant. Suppose that this transformation—a metamorphosis of perception—were to come to you and you alone. Suddenly you awake, and in utter solitude you discover that your values have reversed along with you: you are a roach*! And thence scream to your dead alabaster of a Desdemona, "Put out that light, and then, put out that light!" For the roach of course was the *Blatta*.

He was attempting something unthinkable during those nights. He was rejecting precision and considering suppositions. He was going against his grain, against himself. Of course under the intoxicating effect of alcohol in his blood stream. The typical case of involuntary deviation, a matter of straying. Just for the time being. Just while the white moon up there behind their bedroom curtains made a pass at him, just while it made sure it was a lifeless dead ghost, just while it convinced him that it would never speak up on its own behalf, it wouldn't commit the sin of self-defence, that he was free to call her a nun, a whore, a nun-whore, a saint, a priestess, a slut, a diseased cunt, an ethereal soul, a queen of snow, an Irish nightmare, a pinkplumpkin.

She would love him for his authorial endeavours. There, he was creating something at last. He was breaking free of his electronic calipers, his amplifying lenses, and entering the dim, dark and obscure. No matter for however miniscule a time. He was fabricating too. He too was taking refuge in metaphors. He was becoming a poet unawares.

So he wasn't unimpressionable. So there was a flesh and soul that had permanently etched its presence on his mind. So he was human, not yet a *Homo robot*. So he could offer penile salvation to a hungry hole. So he too could admit being a flaccid rod in search of blind tubes. So he too had his wet sense of humour. So he could brand and re-brand, shuffle and re-shuffle, and get out of mental bottlenecks about fixity of anything beyond one micron in diameter. And he too could rejoice in absurdity.

Yet everything was to end up in denial. That self-effacing brat of the moon would wind up her moonshine as the dawn broke. In the morning he would wake up trebly sobered, erased off any traces of imaginative reconstruction of Irene Scott, whose only identity would be confined to being his late, Catholic, white ex-girlfriend, now dead and probably buried.

So he would leave her high and dry. She realized that hunger was for Irene, for that ex-member of their sisterhood who had attained the status of the supremo in his eyes. Irene was the quintessential actress, the perfect performer. And here she was to observe her reflections on a broken mirror of his memory, coloured by the light of his inventions. She was only a scribbler, Irene was the one scribbled about. But no, Irene too must have had things to speak. Her speech was a mystery to him. He couldn't penetrate her there. Perhaps he could never ever make an entry into the reservoir of her soul. He was a reluctant poet. He hated ardour. He preferred proportion. He liked cadence. He liked rhythm. He liked soft lyrics. Matter of fact dreams. Comprehensible fantasies. Comfortable numbness. Understandable dumbness. He liked the language of simple gestures that had simple meanings. And measurable exactness of complexities that he could put in a formula and solve at his own pace, which tended to be swift. Speed.

******

The bed was housing her grave. She was right there, between him and her. She made Ivy feel like the other woman. She made Ivy cringe in pain, of dejection, of rejection, of sexual inadequacy, of a lost competition, with a ghost. She exploded into Ivy's world as a series of six tiny bombs followed by the holocausts by nights. Now she reigned her bordello, ubiquitously. She was carving her dead cells viciously in a lethal mission. Ivy felt sure that she was alive and had become a bad destiny. The she's were confusing her now. The she's were getting mixed up. Both screamed 'I' first, both said I reign, I win.

Mirror image. She felt like an optical isomer. Just the directions were opposite. Irene—the realization of Ivy's wildest fantasies, Frankenstein's female monster with the horrendous end. Irene played out the script, Ivy secretly nurtured within. A theatrical queen till the end.

******

She penned down a long hate poem the night he didn't drink and muttered the name Ishq while making out.

Ghost's Fingerprints

Tracking him down she leaves her marks
For him to gorge on
As she devours her mortal lover
Ravishing her corpse in her grave
Where flesh and blood failed
The bodiless took over
Pushing him to the brink of a kiss
She lays down her thorn bed
For him to toss and turn
She puts out the torch in the man's cave heart
Asking him to walk in blindness
Collecting her bones for souvenirs of love
Whose flame flashed once more for a penultimate breath
He's now a man possessed, seemingly so
Yet is it not that last straw he feeds himself
To flirt with his deceived self
His Narcissus now sucks milken honeydew
From tunnels of wilted flowers
His pride in loving the dead, in self-assault
His newfound bliss in hedonistic martyrdom
She infected him with germs of sick hermits
Medusa you stoned this Pursues, this self-reflector
And shackled this hapless Andromeda
To the eternal chains of secondary dispensability

******

I, woman, write my Eve
Eve, woman, before Adam's consort
But ribbed nevertheless
I have turned my bones to flesh
Bent the rods of iron fortresses
Wherein my hormones were rendered poison
My juicy viva locked up in capsules of laws
That they called reason
I, woman, tempest of the blood

Will now turn the narcissi and devour
The fragrance of wilderness
I will spread my black panoply
To wrap the cosmos with love

******

My man, your libidinal Eve's territory is dark
It's lightless and slimy
Her body a venus flytrap
And she bathes every moment to scrape off the mucus
At times the self-guarding knives that you have given her
Dig in deep and make her bleed
She bathes in blood
To douse you in her milken honeydew
She's happy with her stickyfingers
And grappling with the impossible subject
She's altered her thesauruses now
Where can she keep the mutation?
She's only a bit of that everywoman
And her tendrils will fasten you fine
Her truth is her debauchery
Her true woman versus her true love
If only it was selflove

******

The night's a bellowing bitch in heat
And her ghost barks from its underside
She's all around me, her claws leaving
Trails of hot red on my sore flesh
She poses as if I'm a porn pulsar
A Mary Magdalene before her Holy Maryness
She's the blackest hole in the centre of my cosmos
Her lethal absent presence between the firefly and shallow sea
What do I do when the other woman is a burnt corpse?
Am I to let a vampire feast on my blood till it dawns?
Lady Lucifer's postmortem lechery revealed an unqualified appetite
She's sucking her biographer's portals
Double-annihilation and a half-blind spectator
Twin gladiators fencing on icicles of inorganic love
Two claimants of a moron.

******

Medicated drama queen in her last stupor

Slashes her wrist to open the channels of self
Her crimson life, her red splendor
The prodigal Eve, squanders its quintessence
Most selfish in her ultimate breath
She murmurs praises to her delight
Victoria curves her foaming mouth
To sound her trumpets of glory
Dying Medusa laughs at all the fools
Who shed tears at her farewell
Who don't know how she has reclaimed her confiscated self
Once again, as she hears her own birth cry
Hanging on to the umbilical chain
Ghost's adieu, the never quite gone

******

Ivy Roy had turned herself into a petty woman-hater. She had joined the ranks of her hubby in making the women responsible for her woes. She had started believing in the Original Sin. Her battalion of theories had failed her. No amount of reasoning could make her feel redeemed. In the process she'd taken a toll on herself. She'd started feeling a revulsion towards the idea of female flesh, the idea of copulation.

She dreamt of herself locked in the bathroom with the water level rising, the drain clogged letting out armies of roaches, and Irene Scott orchestrating the whole opera from the shut panes of the window.

******

She never let him know of her dream. He never asked her how she was feeling about the presence of the late ex-girlfriend in between them. He simply skirted those questions. If he read them in her eyes he didn't mention. If he thought she was getting colder towards him he felt all the more better. He started coming home late from work. He would drive around the city for whole evenings. He would turn on his oldest and choicest CDs and play them in the car. He wouldn't give the female colleagues a lift unless it was unavoidable. He avoided male company like rats. He started getting DVDs home and watched old timers. He was drinking like a fish again. He was binging on whiskies too. He missed hitting down a motorcycle by seconds. He paid fines for overspeeding and jumping empty redlights twice.

******

Meetings with Kamya and Shoili were not helping. Dilli Haat looked like a fake stage put up for Irene to gorge on. She could be that puppeteer. She could be the woman doing the dance on the brass plate. The chameleon.

******

He listened to Celine Dion's "It's All Coming Back To Me" the whole evening while driving around. Returned home at two. Was relieved to find her really drowsy. Slipped into the spare room and slept soundly. Dreamlessly.

******

They were staging *Goodbye Desdemona* at Kamani that Friday evening. She didn't leave the keys with a neighbour for they weren't really familiar. She didn't bother returning right after the show. Chatted with Barry John and his troop. Agreed to do a write-up on contemporary urban theatre. The Delhi scene. Met Mahendra Raina and refreshed memories. Had the Georgia a good four times. Kept her cell phone switched off through out. He never bothered calling up anyway. Shoili dropped her home at 1:30. There was no sign of him. He was back next morning, smelling heavily of Nina Ricci, fragrance for women, by women. There weren't any lip impressions though.

******

She spent the weekend at Shoili's. Inhaled a lot of Malboro lights. Shoili was smoking heavily. And was missing Kanu a lot. Kanupriya Sehgal. Shoili's present partner. A year back it was Kushal Moitro. Shoili was obsessed with the letter K.

She went online and found him logged on, systematically self-depreciating. The other chatters greeted her, whoever recognized Ophelia. He didn't bother of course. He didn't even bother logging off. They were discussing his escalating online notoriety in the mainroom. They were saying that Ash was messaging every chat-nick with the remotest resemblance to a female kind and auctioning his tool. They were laughing at him. On other days, he would have silenced everyone in a matter of minutes with his lightening sharpness of mind. Today, he wasn't bothered.

None of them went offline for quite a while. He got tired of random roughing up after sometime and settled down reading the indiatimes news. In about 10-minutes Kolkata Online timed him out from the server. He was there on the Yahoo though. He was listening to Cradle of Filth again. Then a bit of Nirvana, some Pearl Jam, some Greenday, Coldplay, Matchbox 20.

She finally posted him a message, "You alright?"

"Yeah."

She was thinking of the things he still didn't know about her or her people. Shoili's bisexuality, for example. He had met Kushal on their marriage. But of Kanu he had no clue. Kanu was the network coordinator in the Maharashtra region, in charge of organizing adult workshops in about 40 shortlisted villages. Shoili and she toured the areas together, video-shot, prepared a 10-minute documentary for grant purposes and further awareness, got a lot of village women involved in the process. Shoili was her second girlfriend. She was Shoili's first.

She thought of Bono and Tushar, her college time boyfriends. He had merely asked once on chat if she had been engaged with anyone before. She had said a simple yes. He had never troubled her anymore on that front. Never bothered asking how many and how often. She reciprocated by not interrogating him on those sensitive issues either. Only, while kidding would he confess half-jokingly at times that Irish coffee and women were the only source of heat in that isolated stashed up northern coast. She would merely laugh at his cracks.

She opened BBC NEWS Online and read on Iraq and the search for Saddam. The next Presidential election in the States was due for 2004. She only wished that it was America that had the much-hyped regime change. It was difficult to dream of the Big Apple during those moments. She read the comments posted by eager watchers of the action flick unfolding on the world-stage. Most of them expressed rage, many exhaled helpless sighs. It hurt her to think that he had been there in that country which was busy defaming itself before a global audience. She was sick of the scramble for power. Like everyone else. But then on second thoughts she felt perhaps that was indeed the place for him. He still called it the land of the free. Free for those who could discriminate and not have a veil of delusion over their eyes. Some of the fiercest intellectuals were there. Chomsky and the gang. She wondered how would living in Paris or London differ from living in New York or Los Angeles or Boston. She, who had hardly trodden beyond her city, tethered to her desktop. She, who hadn't yet been to Puri or Benares, was hypothetically tabulating the plus and minus of Paris or Boston.

******

He opened his mailbox again. Read the last six posts from her. Then opened Richa Arora's mail and sent a reply.

Hi Richa,

This is Shumonto Roy.

I had no clue of Irene's passing away until a few days back when I was clearing my jammed mail archives. The account to which you had posted me the news of her demise was out of use for a pretty long time. So I hadn't the faintest idea of what all happened to her and the odd circumstances of her death. I'll be grateful if you let me know every detail of her untimely end. This is important for me because I think I've got myself implicated, however unwittingly, in this pathetic situation and I'm shocked beyond limits because of it.

May be I'll come over to Dallas if need arises. I would like to meet the folks she had worked with. And I would unearth the reasons for her contracting the deadly virus. I hope you would cooperate with me in every way possible.

Post me ASAP.

Shumonto Roy

******

On an impulse she typed Irene Scott JHU Social Psychology on the Google search bar. There were about 23,129 different results displayed in 0.38 seconds. After a few misses, she came upon a blog site on page 3: www.jhualumnibloggers.org/cathref.scotti/quixotica.

That day she discovered that Scott was a compulsive blogger and landed on the moon of her soul. And it wasn't barren.

TEN
Bysche

"So what are we going to call it?"

The room was a small, ill-lit, ill-used one on the second floor of the Arts Bloc of MHC. End of November afternoon, sublime in its own way. The outside had the sheen of perfection, tinge of silken gold strewn in the clear light of day, carrying the lingering fragrance of innumerable poppies, marigolds, roses and tulips. MHC lawns looked better from the top. The long corridor had been a witness to a 102 summers and winters; the Arts Bloc was the first to be erected during those times when the lecturers were mostly English. The garden was a majestic grid of crisscrossing rows of flowerbeds, in yellows, reds, violets, oranges, at times blues. It was inviting; they wanted to hold the inaugural session of the poetry club beneath the shades of eucalypti. But that was not to be. It was just watered and the soil was too wet. The sneakers would sink in, the gardener had expressed his irritation. He had taken care to plant those potted palms lining the main lane running parallel to the lawns and the Arts Bloc; he hated it if the students ever trampled on even a blade of grass. But they wouldn't listen; they would come walking in, running in and loll around in the softness of the lawn, often be sprawled on each others' laps, boys and girls in cozy groups lazing in the meager winter warmth, huddled too close, too heedless for a *mali* of 54. The not-so-old sturdy man in off white pajamas and checked kurtas would give them angry stares at times, but after a while would be found crosslegged under the huge peepal tree, sitting on the round cement platform and listening to the ceaseless chatters of the young mouths. So young, he would think. So nubile, so agile, so feckless. He would deduce scraps from their Hinglish banters, guffaws and blush during a particularly earwrenching anecdote. The adrenalizing little stories, called SMS jokes, often in crude Hindi. And as Ivy imagined Lekhan *mali* interpreting those alien fragments of digital prattle, she smiled a bit. He was there, snoozing under the same peepal tree, with his archaic black Solidaire tape recorder on his lap, the remnant of the *beedi* he was smoking still held in his middle and index fingers of the right hand carelessly balanced on the slightly lifted right knee. A solitary man, oblivious of being under another woman's gaze.

"So what are we going to call it?" she thought, after taking her eyes off the sleeping Lekhan and focusing them back on the desks she could see in the Room 84 of Arts Bloc. She wasn't inside yet. The students were still coming in, in scattered groups of one or two, and some she hadn't even seen before. They all looked quite lost, and seeing her standing beside the brick-railing of the corridor opposite the door to the room 84, they felt doubly so. Some wondered if she too was a student; she was wearing a red Jaipuri long skirt embroidered in black, tight black slax underneath to protect from the chill. Her black Kashmiri pure wool shawl was one of her favourites. She just had to wear a full sleeved white cotton short kurta under it to stay warm within. They were trendily dressed; in colorful sweatshirts, denim jeans and sneakers. She meandered to the times when she was in Sampad Lal College as an ad hoc the last academic session, that was just a year and a half back, until March 2002.

-- Your basic task, Ms Sengupta, is to create a thriving ECA for us.

Pathan had said. Koel Pathan, in her posh triple-AC room had looked like a perfect business executive who knew her job too well. She's, however, Dr Koel Pathan, MA LLB, University of West Virginia, and apparently after getting disillusioned with her unremarkable law practice in the United States, had gone on to do a doctoral in Canadian literature, specializing in Margaret Atwood's theme of survival as the basic issue in Canada, and presently she was the Principal, Sampad Lal College, a good 10-buck rickshaw ride from MHC. Dr Pathan, as her colleagues addressed her, was a rather tall, hefty woman who could have, with a little patience, climbed the top echelons of the law circles for she handled the legal quibbles rather excellently and within three years, SLC, from a nondescript, below-average college had grown into becoming one of the biggest (in terms of land area and size of the buildings) campus centers. How exactly she had managed to get such huge amounts of grants for the expansion of her college issued was something nobody thought worth pondering on. Looking at Ivy through her gold-rimmed glasses, with a smiling face bearing a serious intent, she had resumed--

-- As you know we have a good Science faculty, a fine Sports complex and we have quite a few records in that field. We have some of the national level certificate holders and we actively promote a good sports environment. But of course we can't neglect the other areas of equal importance, and that's precisely the reason why I want you to establish an Extra-Curricular Activity committee. You have the right background, Ms Sengupta, and the best thing is that you're young. It will be easier for the students to identify with you.

Ivy had been staring at the back of her black state-of-the-art PC, going extremely well with the rest of the set-up. The ice-blue wall-papered smug office of Dr Pathan hadn't stopped impressing her for the last half an hour. She had continued,

-- However, Ms Sengupta, since you're on an ad hoc post, the college cannot let you handle the money matters. At least not officially. So there'll be a convener, and you'll have three more people on the board. They'll be representing the Hindi department and the Science and Commerce faculties. So the four of you will have to cooperate and make it work.

Ivy had nodded her head in an insignificant way and remembered Nalli's dictum: Stick around. Pathan had looked at her quizzically,

-- Any problem, Ms Sengupta?

Ivy had shaken her head furiously to denote an affirmation. Then in a stagy-jitter had added,

"But I was thinking, Dr Pathan, ehh, that, in case, I, I mean, in case there arise differences amongst our approaches, you know, conflicting viewpoints and messy things like that, I was just wondering if I would be the right person to take up such an important responsibility and represent the English department, considering that I've barely begun teaching here, the students or teachers hardly know me, and..."

Pathan had cut her short.

-- You don't have to worry about that. I'll handle it. All you have to do is arrange meetings and start off a few working societies. Begin with the basic ones like a film club, debating society or creative writing society etc. It just needs to be launched and can grow gradually.

"Right … I think I'll begin with the creative writing thing, since that's what interests me the most. And films can be screened on a weekly basis, but we need a place for that, and a slightly big television set, and a DVD player. And it'll be good if we have a video membership in one of the good libraries."

Pathan had looked mildly pleased.

-- Fine! You begin with creative writing then. Meanwhile, collect your time-table, and your share of the syllabus from the office. They'll also give you the attendance register.

She was the boss. Coming out from her ice-blue office, Ivy had taken some time to look around. It was bustling with young faces of every hue and size. Girls and boys dressed trendily in denim jeans and colourful tops, fake branded tees, shoes, with ranges of body art. Ivy divided the girls in two arbitrary categories: with or without heavy doses of make-up; it was hard to distinguish otherwise. Guys were tall and brawny and almost half of them in sleeveless tights flaunting the diligently sculpted arms. Everyone well-armed with cell phones, smart-looking college-bags, the cool-age hairdos with multiple streaks of purple, brown or gold in their meticulously maintained crops. Rich kids mostly. With enough money to secure college admission despite the percentage. Interestingly, SLC didn't bring out a high cut-off list during the admission time. It had a nominal fee of course, but accepted fair amounts of donations from the students' willing parents. Apparently, it didn't refuse admission to someone who would only pay the official fee. More than happy to secure the Rs 3,850 from anyone who's willing to pay, provided s/he had a first-division in the higher secondary examination.

In striking contrast to the spectral human figures loitering in the corridors and lawns, once again the walls had attracted her attention by being sinisterly bare. The beautiful shade of lemon green seemed to harbour a sense of lonesomeness without any attempt at filling in the blanks. At intervals there were large life-sized paintings by artists she couldn't mentally locate but apparently contemporary in style and theme. The paintings were put up in a rather random fashion, perhaps according to size and colour, and not in order to mean anything more than what they were intended to do—cover up the stark emptiness all around.

And she had thought of Bysche or Ozymandias as the name for the creative writing club she would organize there. It had never taken flight. The money had gone into the music and choreography societies. They reaped good returns. The girls and boys were much at ease to flex their limbs than toss around the pens and tinker with sheets. She wasn't ready to accept there was a difference however. It couldn't have been. MHC too had its relaxed moments. The tiff over the English Annual Festival sponsorship was just one such instance. The students had demanded Cosmopolitan to be the main banner to be put up inside the Arts Bloc walls. But there were wrangles. The faculty had unanimously opposed, even Bishakha and Nalli. Samiran was quiet as usual. He would never take sides. It was Nalli who had informed her about the whole fiasco; how the festival was called off and the students had a week-long mass-bunk as a gesture of anti-authoritarianism. Nalli had winked and asked, "So you think they did right?" She had smiled and said, "I too would have had a great time bunking! Would have caught up on the entire IHC Cinemania had I been that lucky!"

Now she watched the fellows in their casual but measured way-lessness. They knew it to be somewhat official, so had bothered to communicate through polite whispers. The assemblage had just a mere 9-10 still. It was 2:40 already. Nalli would've barely got over with her last class for the day. Samiran and Bishakha wouldn't be coming; they were busy elsewhere. Things more important like the Debating Society that Bishakha channelled, or Projekt, the MHC cine club run by Samiran were happening at other places within the MHC walls. Those had packed attendance of course. Soon Malti Bakshi would be holding the half-yearly Meditation workshop in the ECA room, making it completely inaccessible for almost two to three days. Samiran would lose his wits despite knowing that it was inevitable. One of his screening schedules would have to be postponed. It was always a jumble, always a scramble for the keys to the AV room, the DVDs, the mics, the speakers. The Indian and Western Music societies too would have no place to practise during those two days. They had their competitions coming up with the onset of the festival season in the university. MHC always had too little room for all these myriad events happening in its campus. Space management was a big issue, always in jeopardy, always causing ceaseless hassles to the staff and students. MHC was building two new sections to accommodate the extra load. There would also be book stalls by different publishers specializing in academic works. But all that would still take sometime. It was a run for the office signatures now, the stamps and the endless circles round the administrative counters. Yet, everything throbbed in a weird way. Ivy felt things coming alive, each moment staging a little theatre with a cached story to tell. There was always a pretty little history peering from the moment's shoulders. There were always pasts, comparisons with what had happened hitherto.

There was a green-backed ladybug crawling on the railing at a little distance from the point she had rested her elbows on. It was hopping around, making sudden unannounced flights to nowhere and coming back to where it belonged. Terra firma. Terra mortara, she corrected herself.

Their cell phones were buzzing at odd tones. She remembered the entry that had won the first prize in the Fakespeare contest, an extempore writing competition on the theme: Yells the Cell. It was some Zoology Honours guy that had walked away with the booty, and the lions of literature were left snarling at his goatee. She had seen him barely for a minute or so with Nalli at the staffroom; she was absent on the day they had declared the results. She took out the printed A4 sheets and started reading again.

Sense, Matrix and Sexaphorisms

Err you mean SMS? That's precisely what my chilled-out global brothers and sisters are going to yell out at me!! So there, my frozen fellows, that's indeed what I hope to engage you with, the SMS in a not-so-new light, also drawing your kind attention to the Sexagenarian's Mobiphobia Syndrome!!

Can it be written about? Will the very visible hands of the stern and wrathful censor board (we do have it, alas!), descending straight from the likes of Jehovah, ever let such improper things be 'Voiced' aloud, in a presumably prestigious mag like this? I seriously don't know! Am I being a lunatic in attempting to enter the seemingly impenetrable, the inscrutable and break the TABOO!!? And have the audacity to make my prosaic subaltern whims be heard?? Preposterous perhaps! Nevertheless, ignorance has the historical testimony of being absolute bliss, and I'm not going to think about this 'article' once I hand it over to dear Mr. Editor! Then dump it, or gulp it!

Now to confront the blistering accusation that's looming large in every reader's popped out eyeballs (from the editorial board to the electrifying babes)! How could I get away with a title as juicy and alluring, therefore abominable and to be kept away at any cost (of course only under public gaze; what's the loo for otherwise)! I humbly admit that the reason is the most obvious one. You all know it, and though I'm not bitten by the deadliest virus on earth, aka Honesty, I still feel compelled to confess that it is simply to attract attention. Perhaps you enlightened beings will halt a bit, and glance a while into its ostensibly trivial content.

Too long an introduction? Of course, for a generation that's symbolized by the BEEP and the BLURB, indicating how time-tied it is, qualified by the single word 'complacency', which in the latest lingo would get translated into "Honey-I-simply-don't-have-a-second-to-spare-for-all-that-shit," it is certainly criminal of me to thus detain their distinguished selves. I humbly beg your pardon.

But I do have a point to prove with all my banter balderdash. The words beginning with a capital letter each in the title are all linked, in my skewed field of vision, to connote just one idea, which is a disastrous reality as well! That being that, we are the only generation which doesn't quite realize how hopelessly drugged we all are. It's gone too deep, from each cell to cell! Every other age, which preceded us, at least knew that it was inebriated. The hash was something that couldn't just deny its concrete existence. We, by God's grace, whatsoever that is, happily don't know and have not the slightest inclination to know either. It's no less than a wonder that it is us only who bask in the glory of being infotained and technosuavy.

Does this ring a tone, I mean a bell somewhere in your minds? (Too much of an assumption?) Our cellular dudes and dudettes certainly can shake their bonbons to the latest tunes coming out of that little God called Mobile Phone, which can metamorphose from a musical Apollo to a shooting Cupid in no-time, but perhaps will 'think' a thousand times before switching it off in a theatre hall during a performance! Oh don't blame them, you last few philosophers alive, for they really don't know what they are doing! The M-factor is working too bad you see! The Matrix is all around us, we are all plugged beings, merely bio-batteries for these electronic divinities! A thought is never our own, it's simply a programmed entity put into our minds, which in turn are nothing but the cool-joints where a signal meets another, a tune kicks a tune, a joke slaps a joke and a message dethrones a lesser peer! Don't bother if you fail to extract an iota of sense from the staggering heap of exchanges. Mind you, although you're being astoundingly moral in your inexplicable discomfort, that I'll term as 'see-sickness', but you have to understand that they are simply resorting to a new means of conversation which has engineered benefits as listed below:

Firstly, there's no need to open your mouth, thus you can contribute to conservation of physical energy. The Matrix has established arterial connections with the heart of every user and non-user so that the cardiologists read the chart as 'beep beep' instead of the old boring 'lub dupp'. This has enthused every individual to live at a higher state of excitability, which albeit is an illusion but manages to bring out a heightened sense of being a witness to the cell culture.

Secondly, you don't have to apply your brains, which implies that you are conserving intellectual energy that's circulating in the Matrix. You have been already fed with the correct (for once) information that the energy supply is very limited and most of the times you'd be stumbling on the 'Access Denied' placard.

Thirdly, the World Wide Warp allows for the interchangeability of any tune/tone/joke/lewd comment called message with just any other. The rate of substitutability is admirably high, therefore none of them can claim to etch an impression in your cerebrum. You in any case do not have any rights over your brains, so what's the point in messing up the patents anyway?

Fourthly, you, in an unwitting collaboration with the deus ex machina (that's God in the Gadget! Bingo!) are furnishing the New Speak, the language that truly dispels all borders, barriers and prejudices for it's continuously evolving, and doesn't quite require any preformed knowledge of the vestigial terminologies. You are perfectly 'free' to enter your version of it without the atrocious burden of being meaningful at once!

Lastly, the Matrix very benevolently once again, tries its best to clear out the mist covering the sexual lenses of Gen-Now, by pamphleteering extensively the dos and don'ts of sex and the solemn features of the eternally-cherished gender battle. If a few disturbed eyebrows are raised at the fact that sexual liberation is cited as the same as sexual liaison and the various strains of feminist humours commonplaced with avoidable-ways-of-male-bashing, they are to be puckered at their own peril!

Cautionary Note: The Matrix does not hold itself responsible for a defiant rebellious cerebrum that occasions to step out of the system. Ever since Descartes has been undone, and the raging notion of 'I blink, therefore I am' thoroughly instituted by the 21st century Pandemonium in the Pocket, it's only for a devastatingly virus-affected unit to go haywire like that. The System duly believes in exterminating the brutes. And when you observe that the digital dove dances to the jazziest beeps in the screen, you go bacchantic over the most picturesque truth ever known! Watch out! The MMS's Gonna Get You!

She cogitated if he was equally interested in versifying. There was something mockingly unserious about his style. A nascent cynic there. The wall magazine had put it up for a month almost. She had seen students deliberating over it often. When it was taken off people had come asking if it could be put on display once again. Apparently they found it funny, especially the MMS bit. There were stray cases of porn in the cellular circulation and the campus had it rocking the debating societies for weeks. A little catchy piece of modern critique. Tabloidish enough, she thought. Who was on the judges' panel, she wondered. Nalli had forgotten to mention that.

She saw them coming from the other end of the corridor. "I had asked Ashish to meet me in the staffroom. I wanted him to come for our first session." Nalli exhaled, flushed after climbing the stairs.

"That's all very good." She recast her eyes on the tall thin boy beside Nalli, well-armoured with ponytail and a long bottle-green kurta. Specially for the meet? she wondered.

"Good afternoon Ma'am, I'm quite keen to join the poetry club," he spurted out to ward off his all too evident uneasiness.

"You write poetry?" she asked, offhandedly.

"Not really. However, I at times write stuff and compose my own tunes. I've shown Nalini Ma'am my writings."

"I see. Lyricist?" *Sarcastic? But why?*

Nalli butted in, "Yeah you read his lyrics and wonder what's the angst all about! Ivy, in fact you must. All weird ideas these kids of today dabble with!"

"Weird, Ma'am?" He looked a bit taken aback.

"Oh everything but Yeats and Shakespeare and Dylan is weird for me."

"Bob Dylan?"

"Dylan Thomas. An English poet of the 30s-40s. Bob too, he was a poet in his own accord."

"Okay, I got a bit mixed up there."

"Getting mixed up is good. Confusion is healthy. Don't you worry about that. Just don't forget to show it to her."

"Yeah."

He resembled a face. All too sinister a semblance. She quickly graphed a hypothetically emaciated Shumonto and the search was complete. Disturbingly so.

About 16 had assembled for the meet. She put the question before that meager gathering.

"So what are we going to call our poetry club?"

"Verses?"

"Verse libre!"

"Nonsequitur?"

"That was good. Anything else?"

"Metaphor?"

"Alriiiight…"

"Cadence?'

"Umm.."

"You too suggest something Ma'am."

"Yeah, well, I sort of had thought of a name. I picked up Bysche, Shelley's middle name. You folks like it?"

"Yeah, sounds cool."

"Okay. Bysche is cool. Alright. But.. I sort of liked Nonsequiter better. So which one?'

"Ma'am, what if the poems don't turn out to be nonsequiturs?"

"Aah, that's a possibility."

"Heh, let's have a vote."

"How 'bout Bysche's Nonsequitur?"

"Hehe. Considering that nonsequitur would be anathema to Bysche!"

"But may be it will be cool. Bysche would have nonsequitured, had he lived long enough."

"You have a point there."

"Yeah, well now?"

"Let's keep it. Bysche's Nonsequitur."

They began reading out their works. Jittery voices, little squeaks and squeals from reticent souls. Still shy, still amazed at their hearts' capacity to absorb aches, still baffled at small wonders, still intoxicated with first feelings. Not yet fatigued, not yet deadened. The neat-looking girl was whispering from the second last row -

What is that a woman wants?/A man? -- Oh yes! That she can never deny!/But then besides what else haunts/Her, as she gazes at the starry sky?/Love is everywhere; love is nowhere--/So what if the moon casts a silver spell?/Why is the heart heavy when everything's /Looking for an angel from the heaven who fell!/On an orange morning or a golden noon/Or a violet night with a shady tone/One can hear her softly croon/Songs of love, or lost love, one of her own

/Women, wine and wealth are a man's choice!/But what if she decides to choose?/Why does she hide it? Why can't she voice?/Who the hell are men to think it loose?/She's soft and gentle, I agree/She leans on a man, I can't deny/The 'Rules of Love', her passive degree

But alone out she gives a solitary sigh./A fragrant love, a cushioning love,/An engulfing love; but a vacuum still/Remains in her heart, confused and mauve/Wanting ever; thinking in what to fill?

She had settled herself in the right-hand corner and had closed her eyes to do justice to the words. Juvenilia, she smiled to herself. She had to put those slashes, dots and sporadic nonsenses to indicate the lines; the child had rushed through it without much of a pause anywhere. She told herself to actually see the poem; its shape and the look of each line. Pop song stuff: Nalli would say. They'd come up with words like bootilicious in no time, she would exclaim, positively horrified. Linguistic evolution, eh?

How old were these kids? 19? 20? Less than a decade younger to her. But it takes a day to change the world, mutate the dreams and souls, infiltrate the words. Shumonto's had changed almost overnight. His visa had been rejected for almost no apparent reason at all. Safety purposes, the university had to look into the faculty's wellbeing. Enough to postpone an assignment indefinitely or make a surreptitious intra-departmental transfer of responsibilities. Enough to fund a gene-atlas and gene-graph a spliced world, with markers like ethnicity, colour, nose-length, semblance to apes.

Nalli's boy was sitting huddled a few benches away from hers. He was nodding his head occasionally. When Nalli asked him to read out from his works, he was puzzled.

"But I haven't got anything today."

"I had asked you to get some." A disappointed Nalli there, with her brows puckered up like a second bracket.

"I thought I would listen to others today. Alright, I can recite one from memory though."

"Please go ahead." Slanting afternoon rays of hope. Beaming Nalli.

"It's a very short one though."

"Let's hear it first."

The baritone got deepened as the words started ejecting themselves out from a strange cavern. Almost every word was emphasized and for a dozen of seconds they were booming within the cobwebby walls of the ill-illuminated Room No. 84 of the Arts Bloc.

History is déjà vu
Again and again
Of badmouthing
Ill-breeding
Acid rains…
Wake up
From wonderland
To nightmare
Of today
Yelling
"Error!"

ELEVEN

Link

He had made himself quite cozy in the spare room. The pillows had a brand new look about them that made them quite tempting to rest his head on. A dark blue with sky blue stripes—the covers, of the pillows and the bed. Of course the mattress too was firmer and inviting, just enough to ward off recollections of a girdled up quiescent Ivy by his side.

She was sleeping in their regular bedroom. Or waking perhaps, he didn't quite care. Firstly, because he could do absolutely nothing to help her for the time being. Did she need help? He didn't know. Had she asked him ever for help of that kind? Nope. Had she relied on gestures? He couldn't fathom. He wondered if he had ever tried reading her face. He wondered if he would succeed if he did try ever. Ashes don't connect, they're the residue once disconnection sets in, when a body is burnt and is made to disintegrate, when it goes back to the elements, to individual atoms of existence, self-contained, self-extinguishing.

She said it was the ghost of Irene Scott that had come in between them, that he was romancing a nothing, a phantom. Truly, that couldn't be the case. Irene was dead. She had died for him even before she contacted that virus. When she left him for those projects of hers she gradually faded away. It was so slow, natural. He didn't even come to know of it until he suddenly found her gone one day and didn't feel a thing. Nothing really stirred him for that matter, nothing ever made a deep impact. He didn't even miss having sex with her; Taebba knew her job very well. Another order of whiteness, another grade of paleness. Iranian soft-complexion vs. Irish milkiness. It was always a comparative analysis for him, always related and relative. But he let them exist simultaneously. Nothing was better than the other. He just assorted them in a convenient system of classification that's all, to mark them better. In fact, he hardly had things to talk about with Taebba for she was an year junior to him in the same course. And neither of them wanted to go back to the fungi or lyceum after a good one. So he would wrap it up as soon as it was over, smoke a cigarette and drive back home. The drives were unusually soothing; he would cruise around for two to three hours at a stretch on those empty night lanes bordered by tall conifers. He wouldn't stargaze though, that wasn't quite him. But yes, his CDs would be playing all along. He would feel pretty happy then, if happiness was not having a burden peering over your shoulders. To be free in the land of the free. To be not faced with that driving-instructor, to be not faced with snooping traffic signals after every minute, to have nothing to distinguish between, no tables to draw, no lenses to see through.

The ghost of Irene Scott. He wondered if the past could really be why he's not with his wife presently. Why the two had camped separately under the same roof. That used to happen a century back when the beds would be separate and would accommodate just one after the act. The idea of a double-bed was a bit romantic, he thought. And really needless. It was forcibly joining two separate sleeps together. Two sleeping bodies, two distinct nightmares, two different streams of consciousness united by law and law only. Under the misnomer called love. He let out a light chuckle. He really didn't want Ivy next to him. Had he ever? He wasn't sure. He wasn't even sure if he had desired Irene to be next to him. Desire was a silly term. It really didn't exist. It was much easier to define an exact need to go get a sedan or a disc or a portable stereo. He could go through the catalogues then. He could pick and choose. He could junk. He could collect, display, shelve, pile up, go back whenever he wanted, or completely forget and yet feel free. Needs and wants were so much better to deal with. It was desire that was messy. That's why gods had allotted the poets to tinker with it. The unwanted souls with the unwanted roles. Happy clubbing.

Why wasn't he with Ivy right now? His wife. His better-half. Perhaps bitter-half would be more accurate. And rightfully so. Ivy the bitter one, the neglected one, the pitiable one, the saddled one with just one man to look forward to. Why didn't she opt for anyone else? What was it? Why him? It was as if neither spoke about it when he returned to his country after a gap of six years with the perfect intention of going back. And had not the war begun and his stay extended, he would've been back there in Baltimore piercing through those familiar sets of microscope lenses. Did they get married in a haste? In a way, since there was nothing else to do. Her M.Phil was over, he had no real project up his sleeves. They liked each other's company as a matter of fact, although he didn't really know too many women in Delhi. Yet he had had his share of trying out. Of picking and choosing. And he knew it to be an endless process for an eager eye. And he was sure that Ivy certainly wasn't a junkyard material. She wasn't display stuff either, he didn't care about anything to put it on show. Except for himself perhaps.

Inadvertently she had been a witness, a confession box for him. She had been a part of his life, however virtual, for almost quarter to three years. If he calculated the days spent with either, Irene would come a close second, although he had met her six years back. But not always was she there, the busybee, often to his great relief. The campus was huge and travelling inside was a bit of a big deal in winters. He hadn't seen so many frozen nights and days before. In the first year of their affair they would really make an effort to be as close to each other as possible. But then the lab works were getting more strenuous every day. During the weekdays he just would be too tired even for a lingering kiss. The weekends were better but making out would be a bit difficult with the flatmates hovering around who couldn't really be sent out in the freezing air. Things were slowing down, and nobody was complaining. She started having her excursions when the weather got summery and began staying away for long, often months. At times he would miss her then, during those long Sunday siestas all by himself, with the gang out for a beach ball or watersport of a kind. Those were the sporadic moments of desire, if getting frustrated about not having a decent fuck could be called desire. He would irritably come online then, and mess around like a jungle king, who had a right to fornicate every living or dead female, who had the right to penetrate fantasies, often to create them, to discard them, to toy around with permutations and combinations of fantasias, to declare them before a faceless set of chat-IDs like Satan's own verses. Ash the archantagonist, a befitting role to play. And after three years of ceaseless shadowboxing, he found a second in Ophelia. A listening ear, a child-woman, an independent but unprejudiced mind. He was spending almost the entire day with her, at work they would talk as he would be recording his readings of the rate of proliferation of the *Staphylococcus* in the culture matrix at different temperatures. Often he would reply after 30 minutes, at times even after a whole day in case his experiment didn't allow him to focus elsewhere. She was quite an owl, she hardly used to sleep. Her summer vacations would be on then, and nightly crusades of the chat rooms her favourite way to kill time. She would tell him about the latest headline flashed on BBC NEWS Online, for he didn't have enough time to look everything up himself. She wouldn't mind if he didn't reply; it was understood that she'd understand. He really was busy. Unlike her. For whom the only business was freedom. To do anything, talk to anyone, read anything and write whatever. Freedom bounce, that's what she called her state. Lucky bum, he'd say. But within, he would wonder if he could handle so much of worklessness. Nothing to do was a deadly state, scary and repulsive. Do something, he'd advise her, take up a small summer job, get involved. But she wouldn't pay heed. Sitting up nights guarding the gates of Pandemonium, she'd say. Watchgirl of the night, she'd say, a night-crooner, a loneranger in a nightbar.

He never bothered understanding her. She was there like the hands are just there, to serve a purpose. It was as if she was destined to give him company when everyone else had logged off and retired to their real lives. She would still remain, like a pond that just refused to dry up. A sink to drain his day-long reflections, irritations, soft joys, mere exchanges, minor notes, lesser resolutions, daily trifles, wrong miracles. There she was, a disembodied ear, a rewritable compact disc. The screen always kept her blinker on. It would say idle. It would say be right back. She was inseparably there. And mysteriously it never bored him. Not seeing her for a whole day often made him wonder where she had disappeared. He could love certain things that promised complete submission to his whims: his computers, his cell phone, his Nissan Sentra. He liked to be served. A real aristocrat. He liked to see his detractors adequately pummeled; he liked the battles and he liked to be the winner. Yet after dusk he needed a bed, a TV, and something female and serviceable: Irene's breasts, recollections of Irene's breasts, Taebba's craft, the screen with innumerable instant messaging windows from ostensibly female-sounding chat-nicks, and finally like an inconspicuous recorder, Ophelia's chat-window buried beneath the layers of virtual rendezvous.

He reached for the laptop right in the bed, turned it on half-cuddling the machine. Was she there? No, she wasn't. He checked the time. 1:46 a.m. Merely the twilight for Ophelia three years back. Not anymore. Now it was post-midnight. A jet black night. Was she invisible? But he had no way to verify. He couldn't possibly send a message to ask her. She who was tucked in the bed next door, next room. She whose soap scent still hung around, who might as well just knock and come in anytime for a book or old issues of Frontline. This was where they kept the archives; she wouldn't sell them off. They were piling up; they were now twin towers themselves. He wondered if there was a helicopter buzzing around to bring the twin paper columns down.

He entered Gazebo, a virtual joint for Indians all over the world. He was a frequenter there as well, though his best netpals were from Kolkata Online. He greeted a few familiar nicks, got welcomes in return. They were chatting about different things, e-bay turnovers in 2002-03, pros and cons of coffee addiction, illegal music download softwares, Sygate firewall, exotic recipes for Indian kitchen, Indianization of pasta, pizza, lasagna (which became lazzania in chat parlance).

He made his debut for the night:

-- Well, McAlooTikki Burgers are quite a rage somewhere out there. The cuisine-pimps are doing good for themselves. Long live biriyanization of the tongue, both the lingo n gastro way.

Her jargons. They didn't seem to leave him. Did any one notice what he said? Yeah, an oldie there.

STOICMALE: hey Ash buddy, yeah dude, my dotter is pretty mad over those mcaloos. She calls em yum-aloos heh .. so hows baltimore doin?

-- That's history stoic .. am in India now .. the war has fucked me up big time n am stuck here for I dunno how long

STOICMALE: really? whn did ya get back?

-- Last July .. was scheduled to go back n join the department but apparently the seats have got filled up now .. bloody pretenders .. as if the war's our doing .. see how they've cut down on the visas dammit .. I tell u these mothafukkers really shove it up ur azz man

RASPBERRY: Ash get grip on ur tongue dude .. we've been trying to de-gutter n clean up the online sewage pipes .. dontya mess it up all now

-- Sod off rasp, don't try to attract my attention .. or u'll gain a second entry into the 'ravished by Ash' list

RASPBERRY: heh Ash, when does the loose then pervy side of u take u over? u wanna wage war dude? eh am ready

STOICMALE: don't invite trouble raspy .. u a sweet gal .. don't nudge him in the wrong place hun

RASPBERRY: okay so Ash got company in clapping .. Stoic Eunuch is flapping his twin calipers to impress the monarch of dunces .. gees!

-- Rasp clam up shrimpet .. or u'll be put in a vacuum pump n be duly sucked outta de system ..

STOICMALE: ignore her Ash .. temme .. hows things back there?

-- Sucks man .. I'm desperately waiting for my visa to be sanctioned so that I can leave ASAP .. I had a helluva project coming up my way when the war thing happened ..

STOICMALE: swear .. these shitty fanatics of the mid-east

-- Hey hang it dude .. it's not the Mid-East that's the cause .. they've been rubbed on the wrong side for years now .. the rage of the oppressed n underprivileged

He was surprised at his own words. Borrowed words rather.

STOICMALE: whatevah, I know that one day they might mistake me for a mullah coz I sport a turban and beat me up in the middle of a crowded road with everyone staring like they r watching circus

--That's the problem dude .. our visas get rejected bcoz we resemble them .. that's y they dump their virtual junk into our kitties to get the shittiest things done .. that's why we've the call centers mushrooming like bacteria an we think there! We've come a long way .. we've made PROGRESS!

STOICMALE: they had a survey recently .. free-bay has registered a growth rate of 25-30% at the end of last month .. now something like 20 billion doesn't get counted coz they think that's petty cash .. they take the employment count often without considering the income from these net malls n project a wrong image .. as if asians have snatched off the good payrolls from the market n r solely responsible for the downturn if any

-- Yeah the present govt talks about a Christendom n the Axis of Evil at this age .. but what else can u expect whn morons run the show man? Making a religion n holy war of every shit around and shitting around with their own .. heard of those escalating AIDS cases in the convents and other places? Bunch of pedophiles n faggots hurl infamies at others .. heck .. what effrontery!

STOICMALE: hey that's more in downtowns .. the kallu areas .. that's the breeding ground of all the STD menace .. but dude apna desh too not far behind eh? giving south africa a run for the top position in the AIDS chart !

--That's a misconception people love to believe Stoic .. and especially we brownies .. man the downtowns r ill-furbished .. if they make u live in a ghetto how long can u keep fussing about hygiene? And the worst cases are where the social-activists n scholars get the virus man .. while trying to wipe it off .. it happened with a friend of mine wud u believe it? She died of AIDS doing campaigns for AIDS awareness! Bullocks to the life man

STOICMALE: hey that's really sad .. was she an indian?

-- No, Irish .. a very close friend .. we hadn't been in touch for a while tho .. I got to know of her death coupla months back .. positively horrifying .. n what was her crime? Trying to drill some sense in the southern parishes to keep the church shit-free, practise safe sex n not keep the priests starving for flesh n salivating at the mention of kids instead

STOICMALE: hmm .. hey but catholics are like that eh?

-- Like what?

STOICMALE: u know, hypocrites?

-- Gimme someone who isn't man .. nonsense .. I had gone to this Bong saint's spiritual confo once .. on mom's insistence of course .. n had this late friend with me then .. fuck u wudnt believe wht I had seen with mine own two eyes man .. saint making out with devotees after the session n getting hard cash donated for institutional funds .. symbiosis man that's the only word that came to my mind .. nexus plexus

STOICMALE: but christlovers esplly dude!

-- No way, it's not religion man, neither is it the fukkin skin .. we Indians are the suckers man .. we suck up to them peach-fleshed gods to ensure the bloody due promotion .. n keep an Afro-American at bay coz we think that they're gonna bilk us real bad n snatch off the payhike .. while at the end of the day we consider our bootlicking selves lucky in case our promotion hasn't been freely slid into another's pocket n u can guess very well who's that another .. but we wudn't budge .. we wud still kiss the bleached ass n wait for his kindness to put us in his good books

STOICMALE: is it better back there, in india?

-- Better? huh .. fukkin iconic void dude, that's what my wifey says abt the whole thing .. man living in New Delhi and after being mauled over by the mall culture u really wonder where u are .. almost every second umrican thing is here .. selling like hotcakes .. from britney's belly-button posters to princess of new york caps .. the latest there is the hippest here .. n imagine what they take out of us? pictures of women getting raped, remote widow-burnings, dirt n filth and splash their next day headlines .. the fukken gen is living on borrowed dreams really

STOICMALE: but dude the money, isn't it coming from there, the mnc's .. thnx to the call centers so many young folks rnt jobless

-- Yeah sure! If speaking the latest fad in a grafted accent is smart-jobbing! If streaking ur hair to make it look flaxen is fashion oh yeah thn why not?

STOICMALE: gawd, these young folks got money dude, n money speaks

-- Easy money man .. fukken easy money .. alright good for them handful of folks who wud have to sulk otherwise sniffing for jobs .. but clearing other people's virtual toilet aint great jobbing, eh? BPO? Alrght so there we've so much work in hand .. u know it's such a crazy state that even beginning to complain is a herculean task .. such a loop man .. such deepened infiltration that to cut all that out wud be to yodel from the cheese bin like the senile n decaying left over of the hard core communists .. who see their red betrayed in every darn decision ..

STOICMALE: well MTV gen it is, what can one do?

-- so the only criterion for landing up juicy jobs is a cowboy accent, yeah? Look at ourselves okay .. wht we write isn't half like the way we speak which fortunately or unfortunately is still a conversational standard English .. but whos going to tell its Indians talking looking at our chat-room posts, eh? And if we speak in vernacular using the English alphabets we're accused of being parochials, toads in bogs unfit for the cosmo world.. n this is a small reality .. wht abt tht 80 % unaccented folks out there, without jobs, without MTV, without getting their existence recorded?

STOICMALE: wht do u wanna say finally dude? u say all that good patriotic jingles n thn u r going mad to come back to the States .. the same u !!

-- Yeah I know .. I dunno if I should hate myself for that .. u know my wifey doesn't wanna go n settle there .. she has loads of friends here .. n says she'd be lost in a brand new place .. I get hysterical .. I say fuk it belle .. India is more umrica than umrica herself .. at least in the 'attitude' if not the amenities

STOICMALE: they put good ads on tv u know .. say its all well back home .. feels good .. even if it's half as good as here …

-- Indeed they do .. fukkin campaigns to get the votes nothing else .. a phantom of expectations from a phantom of progress .. n man it's weird for folks like me .. I feel outta place everywhere .. here n there

STOICMALE: wonder what we're dude? where's our place in the world? I carry my turban n soul everywhere .. they still look at me as if I was the first sikh they ve seen .. over there my folks laugh at my umrican accent .. or if I say I can't have cow s milk unpasteurised

--We live in a middle-space u know .. cyberland tucked between the east n west .. past n present .. space n time don't matter much for us .. although they do but still they don't .. it's both night n day now .. it's the same everywhere .. just relatively above or below the scale man .. that's a cynic's wisdom for u .. anyway am signing off .. it's 2:30 already n I got this mess of a job tomorrow ..

STOICMALE: more slides eh?

-- U betcha! Adios man

He logged off from the chat not because he was sleepy. Or not only because he was sleepy. His outlook express had flashed:

'Message received: from Richa Arora; Subject: None.'

TWELVE

Hyphen

Bono spread-eagled on the bed. My bed.

Still can't fathom why he should lie there, after the deed is over. We do it to each other as a favour, friendly charity.

4:30 p.m. on a Saturday. It's not an off for him though; he has his papers to do. And this is a footnote to his story. A little cross-reference.

He has crept out of his library rather early and before hitting the Habitat thought of hitting on me.

There's an understanding between us. A kind of unstated one. Something like a temporary arrangement which is going on for almost two years now. A crash course in home-making, house-keeping.

-- So you had a good start yesterday, huh?

He says, part-interrogative, part-declamatory.

Yeah, you can say that. Finally reading a paper at the MHC/LSR colloquium. So I can claim to have a sort of a vocation. At least for the time-being. Something to keep me busy, that's all. Anyway, lot of stuff happening there, as usual. It's barely a coupla days, but the campus is spilling over.

-- Well Miss Ivy Sengupta, not everyone likes to hibernate all year round like you.

His white striped shirt is a little creased. He used to be more conscious of his appearance erstwhile.

-- What are you looking at?

Your shirt isn't ironed properly.

-- Never mind. I didn't get time today. I can't handle everything by myself including the laundry.

Of course. Indian men are exempted from doing the laundry.

-- No dammit, the maid didn't turn up. I'll tell mamma of every bit of her callousness. Even the dishes have to be washed and the kitchen cleaned but hello no sign of madam Chhanni. I actually tried doing the dishes last night but you know I just had to give it all up after 10 minutes or so. Just not my cup of tea.

Yeah, I know.

He moves his hands to touch mine, touches me for an instant, the lightest press of camaraderie, then slides them under his head to make a comfortable headgear. The bedsheet is crumpled, almost falling off in a heap at the rear end. I slither out and put it in order once again, whatever order that can be achieved without making him move his somnolent butt.

I'm making some coffee. Okay?

-- Yeah, lemme take a tiny nap until then.

He grins raising his head and almost instantly dives back into the space between the two pillows. Pulls one over his face and shuts out the last traces of dimming light.

His cell phone makes a sharp ringing tone. A blue Nokia 3310. The commonest.

-- I'm not taking it. Hey, just put it on silent please.

Muffled drowsy words. From an ostensibly satiated man who wants nothing but to give in to the dictates of a sleepy bunch of nerve axons. A tired body.

> Man has no Body distinct from his Soul; for that call'd Body is a portion of Soul discern'd by the five Senses, the chief inlets of Soul in this age.
>
> Energy is the only life, and is from the Body; and Reason is the bound or outward circumference of Energy.
>
> Energy is Eternal Delight.

William Blake believed in souls perhaps. Who knows?

******

An eleven hundred square feet South Delhi flat all to yourself. Living alone since yesterday, which happened to be Friday, 20th October 2000. Maa and Baba there in Kolkata for a brief visit. Bono checks in, checks out at his own will. Bono, aka, Mitakshar Thakur, 21, MA Previous, English, Delhi University, who's happily tucked into that six by six cushiony bed of mine, with a yellow printed bedcover that's almost done to death by sheer neglect.

Yet this flat is rather stuffy. Too many of those age-old furniture cramming every corner of it. Not much space to move around, except for the room I have kept the desktop in. Technically, it'll be a study, with my books stacked in unseemly piles, scattered all over, even on the floor. Plus all the old magazines, month-old heap of newspapers, dot pens, pencils, markers, refills, broken earrings, spare mosquito-repellents, just anything can be found just anywhere. I've never tethered anything to a particular spot.

Three years back it was a difficult situation. Ma wanted to live in Delhi, while Baba developed his final and this time incorrigible bout of selective nostalgia for homeland. Kolkata, three centuries old young nubile struggling Kolkata, enticed my father like never before. Ma protested, no one wants to stay there, can't you see people migrating to Delhi everyday? She had her own reasons of course: severe bronchitis. Kolkata: humid, sweaty, sultry, taxing for an asthma-prone middle-aged woman who had fallen in love with *Dilli* some 25 years back. But it was decided of course. The packers would have come and executed the operation in just two days. Ma wouldn't have touched a single thing. Wouldn't have spoken to him during those 17 hours they would be huddled inside Rajdhani Express. Wonder if she's ever gonna cozily settle in that Salt Lake City house, with her plants, cats, and Colex Inhalers.

Of course I am an issue for them. At 20-something, a daughter becomes a vertical snake if not already de-hooded. Maa was noticing signs of decay in me: moral and otherwise. Shoili was beyond repair of course, and had been hatching plans of moving to Bombay since long back, had applied for her postgraduation from TISS, Tata Institute of Social Sciences, but got through Kent instead. Else, she'd have been busy with numerous NGOs and wouldn't have bothered satisfying Maa by tying the knot. Instead, she'd have tied a red bandana around her head and marched for almost every rally shaking the strife-ridden city. Unlike the rest of the young enthusiasts she continues saying Bombay. Mumbai wouldn't come so easy; why no one knows better than me.

Ma seems perpetually heartbroken for I decline those offers from NRI Bongs arranged by our flocks of global relations. She asks if I like someone. I say no one in particular. She calls it venomous and now after several futile tries, concentrates on plants and pets instead. Her daughters are not stable, she thinks. She had some hope in me, for I often wear sarees to college; we have too many of those fancy functions called seminars. She is, meanwhile, reconciling to her fate and gearing up for an eventual eco-friendly life, all set to make a cat-park of her Salt Lake City house.

Once Shoiiii and I talked about it: Should we adopt kids?

-- I have to do a lot of moving around Aye (that's what she calls her little sister). I can't give a kid enough time. Anyway, I got too many to take care of already. We are running three schools for street children and I have to periodically inspect them and do all sorts of stuff you know. You have a sedentary life, why don't you give it a shot?

But it's not just giving it a shot, it's someone's life dammit.

-- Yeah, true. Plus Ma would get furious. May be later you can think about it seriously. Say after 30. But that's if your partner's okay with it. I want no hang ups from either side.

You know what they think? Adopted kids are worse than kids outside wedlock.

-- Yeah, so isn't it great that by another say 100 years people would prefer adopting children instead of wasting time in stray reduplication?

You sound optimistic.

-- The hell I am. We'll have bio-engineered, white-fleshed, Roman-nosed, Amro-brained, moon-bred, standardized kidbanks and we'll get our pick easily. Then who the fuck would, fuckforbid, while away nine-months of preprogrammed life feeling awkward and all ballooned up? Moreover, in case they want some ethnic brands, we can always outsource them, right?

******

I prefer Nescafe to filter coffee that Bono drools on. So I keep a stock of both and make separate mugs with very different combinations. Mine all sugary, milky, frothy. He prefers it strong and generally black. At times we exchange our mugs, at times he adds some milk and sugar and puts on a grouchy face for the next couple of hours.

Coffee is ready. But Bono isn't. He's fast asleep. His limbs are stretched and bent in a form that mildly resembles a distorted *swastika*. Despite the dysfunctional AC, the room is cooler than the rest. Fair-faced Bono sleeps with his mouth slightly open, with that gentle motion of a leaf half-swaying in the lightest breeze. Is that delight? The combined delight of the flesh and soul that flows forth from an involuntary suspension of the self, though immersed in self-love and worldly-love? Then why don't those affections of truth, goodness and satiation run through me? Why do I feel that my blood circulation is a secret channel for the devils' colloquia, chanting satanic verses for the envy of all that's sacred and beatified?

I check Bono's cell phone. Three missed calls. Two new messages. A voice-mail.

I come back to my own pandemonium and switch on the monitor. The comp is always on, and if am not home, it's on standby generally. Game number 2873 of Free Cell still awaiting my next move, the score has sunk to zero, thanks to the time lag.

YM Radio demands: Are you Idle?

On a kinder note: Click here to resume.

I close it altogether. Two friends online. Gramercy, Prozac.

Do I want to talk to either of the two right now? Ummm?

I role the cursor over their blinkers. The yellow smiley winks at me.

There! Prozac's idle for last three seconds. Five. Nine. A minute. One minute 17 seconds. Three minutes 48 seconds.

May be something else. Someone brand new. Dig deeper and often you find tillers of the same cohort. Terra Incognita, here I come.

Turn on some raw music. Unsentimental. Discordant. To suit the haphazard mood. Reckless in the late afternoon sun. Smelling the incipient dusk.

> I need a guilt to nurture, a secret to hide
> my womanscape must copulate now, sow some germs of innovation
> my intimate Sahara has dried up many an oasis of tenderness and am forever thirsty
> am not your Ceres, Juno or Venus, am none of them but am fertile with a dash of metaphoric barrenness to proffer up during defensive moods
> am not a static image but a circling hot nude moon stripped of bikini clouds
> am piranhas trapped in prolix fields, am stingray fighting somnolence, am ichthyosaur renegotiating extinction
> my clan is at war with history but I've gone astray and heading nowhere

> looking for a place to hoard my illicit bliss that they call ineffectual and eunuchlike
> but I say it's still undigitized, it's forever falling apart but coming together too, and that 'eunuchlike' is emotionally incorrect
> yet they're forever building new lexicons and prodding me into buying some
> I'm incapable of a legitimate fury to call my own, or a consummate passion, though I have drives and needs and I think I love as well
> I don't dream of building citadels, I don't dream at all, or may be I do, those puny daysights that chase you while you're shitting, eating, mating
> I sort of like them too, posing as this self-confessed self-satirist living off instincts and animus pools, dissolving odd equations and disproving all axioms.

Turn on Radio GaGa and play the Ambient station. Fusion music. Soothing. Undisturbing, a bit soporific.

Create the mood. For the embrace of the unknown.

******

Now Playing:

Artist: Lili Haydn

Song: The Promised Land (Feat. George Clinton & Pharaoh Sanders)

Album: Light Blue Sky

Welcome to **Gazebo**

Room Users: 24

Olive Beetch enters our Room.

Private Message from Drab: Wanna blotch up your pretty face baby?

Private Message from Male_Dignity: Hi there, I'm 32/male/Bangalore, working as a business consultant in an MNC. Interested in a decent chat?

Private Message from oo-Laa-laa: a/s/l ??

Private Message from 9811235232: Gimme a call, pleaseeeee, I m dying to talk to you.

Private Message from Provoke Me: will ya?

Private Message from Statue of Liberty: Heya, liberal male from the Big Apple. Wanna bite?

Private Message from tRoTteR: hi, from Singapore here, coming to India in dEcEmBeR, any ladies from Bombay/Pune interested in meeting up? Contact me: everready4it@hotmail.com <mailto:everready4it@hotmail.com>

Screens flooded within no time. The screech of the message alert wrenching the pinna off. Deactivate it. Close the windows. Ignore the buggers.

Wait and watch.

Update the profile meanwhile. How 'bout 20/f/xxx, hm? Cool. Suitably placeless. Love being the womanchild.

Finally.

Slash: is your bark as bad as yr bite ;-)

Olive Beetch: i dont goddamn bite

Infuriated? Dramatics of the virtual. The right Gesture begeteth the right Effect.

Slash: hmm .. glad to hear that.. in fact nor do i

Olive Beetch: i dont bark either

Slash: god, i really asked for it, no? sorry and cheers .. i am sure you are a darling sweetheart, soft spoken and full of light and joy

Calmer. Calmer.

Olive Beetch: never mind .. though the latter stuff was also exaggerated .. i'm neither that sweet or joyous

Slash: aw, what else? trying to keep you interested in this window.. your time and attention must be in great demand and i am sitting here twiddling my thumbs

Olive Beetch: very true .. i'm kinda havin' a hard time .. fingers achin', sometimes wrong messages too .. damn

Slash: i can imagine.. tell me, how many chats going on?

Not a single one honey, if you deliver me to the Promised Land that is.

Olive Beetch: never strain ur brain sire .. make it useful otherwise

Slash: one can try, but try one must .. and this is brain dead biz anyway .. hardly u wud call it intellectually challenging, eh? so what do you study, young lady?

Olive Beetch: oh challenges! .. as far as they r concerned i'm everready

Slash: hmm

Olive Beetch: young lady .. hmm quite presumptuous

Slash: well 20 isnt too old is it .. so just taking a liberty

Olive Beetch: huh .. u did go n peep into tht profile phooh

Slash: of course .. isnt that what it is for? but sorry anyway .. didnt mean to intrude

Olive Beetch: no .. thts meant 4 intrudin .. kinda self-advertisin .. lol

Yeah, heck! What else did I make it for? That's the Venus flytrap and you're lured!

Slash: burglar alrms going off here!! but no foto i notice .. care to send one?

Photo? Aaahha! Demanding drone here! Sulk for a second sweets.

Slash: doing some intruding of your own? or busy?

Olive Beetch: oh ya there u come again! such a relief!

Slash: huh??

Olive Beetch: hehe

Slash: wrong window, eh?

Olive Beetch: nope nope .. now i'm gettin selective .. activating the sieve of mind .. anyway whts like ur age or u an ageless chauvinistic male too .. typically male tht is?

Slash: provocative young lady .. i must add .. good show! and the last man standing, gets the virtual rose, eh? that wud surely do my chauvinistic though battered ego a load of good

Olive Beetch: hey ol' man [if i go with ur word] a rose is packed with a thorn .. kinda divine justice, say what?

Slash: u're spilling drops of blood milady

Olive Beetch: i kinda like bloodshed .. so rose is more thn welcome

Slash: gory goree .. heh heh

Olive Beetch: hmm yeah grotesque .. but whtsoever... yeah so sir ...wht keeps u occupied

Slash: thoughts, milady, mere thoughts .. do you stay on that side of the net, or also step into the real world?

Olive Beetch: i m firmly rooted to terra firma

Indeed?

Slash: good, then the show must go on!!!

Olive Beetch: what a gay idea!

Slash: oh i want to be gay

Slash: but not in that sort of a way
Slash: no homoerotics and narcotics
Slash: lol
Olive Beetch: hmm
Olive Beetch: okay..
Olive Beetch: but wont it be a good change
Olive Beetch: for a while
Olive Beetch: they say its always welcome
Olive Beetch: a change tht is..
Slash: lol no milady i dont think so
Slash: i dont think that i can ever get my mind off women to spare even a second thot to men
Olive Beetch: hmmm .. good occupation
Olive Beetch: sir!
Olive Beetch: but thn u wudnt spare a single woman
Olive Beetch: if u cud .. correct?
Slash: well even the best of us arent that lucky lol
Olive Beetch: we all live in a state of semi-fantasy
Olive Beetch: do we not?
Slash: now thats a crazy proposition
Slash: if i could well what wouldn't i do
Slash: i live in a total one@state of fantasy
Olive Beetch: wow .. join the gang
Slash: reminds me of a crazy hoarding to advertise a las vegas casino
Olive Beetch: in fact the cyber world is much more real in some ways
Olive Beetch: oh wats tht?
Slash: it said god save me from what i want
Olive Beetch: haha
Olive Beetch: right!
Olive Beetch: sometimes rather mostly we want much more thn we can take
Slash: so thats the same tht goes for me and my love for the fairer sex
Slash: lol
Olive Beetch: hmmm .. love?
Slash: oh aint that the way of a!! flesh? lol

Olive Beetch: a fatal attraction rather

Slash: what about love

Olive Beetch: love = nothing but a 'second hand emotion' .. pun intended

Slash: yeah it is if it's not the right thing lol

Slash: believe me sometimes having a bit more than lust for someone really spices up the sex life lol

Olive Beetch: yeah if its the right thing thn its both first n second hand .. [how lucky can one get]

Slash: oh I like to use both my hands. i believe thats the best way to keep a woman happy lol

Olive Beetch: oh .. i thot the stronger vessels think of it nothing more than some mild wrestling session

Slash: really

Slash: well i am not a strong vessel then

Olive Beetch: yeah thats sure handy

Slash: lol

Slash: girl you're fun

Slash: hey

Slash: bet you aint single

Olive Beetch: hmm pretty interesting .. i'm sure u've had 'exposure'

Olive Beetch: ouch

Slash: oh my god indecent one at that lol

Olive Beetch: i am

Olive Beetch: footloose n fancy-free

Slash: so whats your name lady

Olive Beetch: ivy

Slash: my god thats nice

Slash: hard to find such people

Slash: poison ivy?

Slash: where did ya get your cool sense of humour from

Olive Beetch: not exactly .. i believe there r quite a few leftovers

Slash: some hard experiences?

Slash: leftovers?

Slash: pray tell me why you think you are a leftover

Olive Beetch: experiences r always 'hard' .. u learn the hard way .. aint it so?

Slash: lol

Olive Beetch: i'm a living fossil

Slash: if we're talking of the same thing then you're bloody right

Olive Beetch: yes i think i am

Slash: lol

Olive Beetch: what abt u?

Olive Beetch: totally in the way of the world?

Slash: yeah

Slash: you got voice chat girl?

Olive Beetch: sorry no voice chat..

Olive Beetch: the mic isnt workin'

Slash: ok

Olive Beetch: wht did u say ur name was?

Slash: shumon

Olive Beetch: hmm .. i guess something to do with flowers.

Olive Beetch: right?

Slash: lol

Slash: hey you're a smart woman man

Olive Beetch: decide which

Slash: haha

Slash: i hope a woman

Slash: and even though i might never see it

Slash: a well endowed one at that heh

Olive Beetch: yeah .. we all take a chance ..u take a 'fair' chance there

Slash: you mean i guessed well about your gifts

Slash: lol

Olive Beetch: gifts? yeah ..now assets ..

Olive Beetch: fixed deposits

Olive Beetch: n good interest drawing

Slash: lol

Slash: it's like this line I had read somewhere

Slash: a man and a woman talking

Slash: and the woman talks about her virtues and being good

Slash: the man says it's not about whether you're good or not its about whether you have the goods or not lol

Olive Beetch: heh we r all goods

Olive Beetch: lol

Olive Beetch: i laughed at ur joke

Slash: yeah

Slash: thanks

Olive Beetch: gotta be good goods .. right

Olive Beetch: so wat do u do

Slash: yes not the ones that only have to be held up with strings lol

Slash: doing my doctoral in microbio

Olive Beetch: oh thts great

Olive Beetch: yeah right .. so if we gotta be without strings .. shud be light alight

Olive Beetch: oh so u make those slides n the likes?

Slash: no man i have seen some of that, even with the most demanding sizes, stand quite much on their own even after the strings are gone lol

Slash: really they look like German engineering

Slash: well for now also work on them .. the slides ..

Olive Beetch: haha

Olive Beetch: u have solid contempt or profound admiration for tht 'german engring'?

Slash: man nothing but just admiration

Slash: you cant have contempt for such beautifully crafted things

Olive Beetch: but then it's a rule of the game that strings r outta question

Slash: lol

Slash: it's like that saying

Olive Beetch: yeah it's a craft

Slash: in another context but relevant

Olive Beetch: agreed

Slash: a woman without a behind is like a village without a church

Olive Beetch: lol

Olive Beetch: blasphemous!

Slash: oh well it's only really erotic when it's blasphemous
Slash: i mean i am too old for a wham bam thank you ma'm
Olive Beetch: hmmm
Olive Beetch: but then as some ppl say 18 till i die ..
Olive Beetch: though i'm happily 20
Slash: lol
Slash: oh yeah
Slash: but what i meant was
Slash: i mean i am over that stage of excitement over just that
Slash: and now prefer things that are more exotic and adventurous
Slash: quite done with silly things with silly women lol
Olive Beetch: and wht i meant was some ppl have this prolonged adolescence
Olive Beetch: aaah .. silly women?
Olive Beetch: thot ur admiration for the womenfolk was universal
Olive Beetch: whn did u start being selective
Slash: it's that particular phase in their lives that i sort of don't fancy much anymore @adolescence heh
Olive Beetch: okay
Olive Beetch: grown up person speaketh there
Slash: in more ways than one hehe
Olive Beetch: lol
Olive Beetch: this internet is fun!
Olive Beetch: dont you think so?
Slash: yeah wht do you like most about it though
Olive Beetch: in more thn one way...
Slash: oh yeah i sure do
Olive Beetch: well .. the scope of meeting new ppl
Olive Beetch: thts the best thing
Olive Beetch: n its all in the mind..n the lines
Slash: yes and that too those who match your interests exactly
Slash: yeah i like it
Slash: and the other thing
Slash: is that if you have an interesting conversation you suddenly realize that

Olive Beetch: in fact u know ..like acc to ur profile u r a 28.m. wherever ..who knows u might be 60/f/ jhumritaliya

Slash: what turn-on good conversations used to be

Slash: lol

Slash: welll true

Slash: but i wouldn't be half as .....as i am

Slash: lol

Slash: and you tell me honestly

Slash: are you really a woman or a man

Olive Beetch: yeah..for me only a good *** can beat a good convo

Slash: did you omit the star for c

Slash: lol

Olive Beetch: very honestly..waddou think

Olive Beetch: no i didnot..omit anything

Olive Beetch: lol

Slash: very honestly i am past thinking lol

Slash: ok

Slash: so the stars were for fuck

Slash: or fck

Olive Beetch: i'm a female ..a proud one tht too

Olive Beetch: the stars were 4 sex

Olive Beetch: though i ve not really had it too often..

Olive Beetch: had chances ..but funnily didnot

Slash: ummm thats the word that makes the world go round doesn't it

Slash: so you're a proud woman

Olive Beetch: absolutely

Slash: hmmmm and are your things as proud without the strings or not lol

Olive Beetch: as i said .. i'm quite freedom-loving

Slash: wow thats goooood

Slash: ok so what do you mean had chances but funnily did nt

Olive Beetch: i believe in quality..

Olive Beetch: nd that test was tough

Olive Beetch: so...

Olive Beetch: not a test exactly .. can say 'circumstance'

Slash: hmmmm ok

Slash: so whats good sex according to you

Olive Beetch: very romantic old fashioned

Olive Beetch: very wild n passionate

Olive Beetch: filled with humorous interludes

Slash: yeah i like that

Slash: i hate it when its just like pull your panties down honey i just got to put it in

Slash: i love foreplay

Olive Beetch: n of course with some good appetite

Slash: and i think ones got to kiss and lick and nibble every inch of the woman's body

Olive Beetch: tht forms the appetite

Slash: of course

Slash: and also makes you remember more of the experience than just the humping n pumping lol

Olive Beetch: hmm true

Olive Beetch: but thn u r among the few leftovers

Olive Beetch: who like being ole fashioned

Slash: i think having good sex is like making a biryani

Slash: lol

Olive Beetch: biryani .. okay in wht way

Slash: yeah and tell me what do these new lads do

Slash: lol

Olive Beetch: yeah both r aromatic

Slash: as in like in a biryani you got to make sure that the rice and the meat are equal quantities

Slash: similarly, in sex, foreplay and the intercourse got to be in equal quantities

Olive Beetch: hmmm okay .. sounds good

Slash: oh yes

Slash: to me sex is fun when you get to do so much foreplay and kissing that the man's rock hard and the woman's dripping before you even think of putting it in

Slash: lol

Olive Beetch: polyandry n polygamy have disrupted the sexual pie-charts... but then thats the only way u can gather experience

Olive Beetch: alright i agree with u

Slash: on wht

Olive Beetch: on having fun while havin' sex

Slash: oh you mean sex aint fun in itself

Slash: lol

Olive Beetch: sometimes it's not

Slash: elaborate pls

Olive Beetch: it gets a drag .. whn ppl forget they rnt pumpin in n out of an automaton

Slash: true

Slash: lol

Slash: u r right

Slash: it's like this one irish woman i used to be seeing told me

Slash: she said

Olive Beetch: yeah

Olive Beetch: anyway..

Slash: sorry had been booted

Olive Beetch: life's all about knowing diff things .. sometimes repeating the same mistakes

Slash: did you get wht i said

Olive Beetch: never mind

Olive Beetch: guess not

Slash: Slash: it's not about the size of the moon it's about the motion of the ocean

Olive Beetch: yeah exactly

Olive Beetch: lol

Olive Beetch: yeah i got it this time

Slash: hi

Olive Beetch: yeah

Olive Beetch: u there?

Slash: hellllllllllo

Olive Beetch: hey

Olive Beetch: where r u?

Olive Beetch: hey

Olive Beetch: hey

Olive Beetch: u there

Olive Beetch: hi

Slash: helllllllllllllllllllllllllllo

Olive Beetch: yeah

Slash: sorry connection went for a toss

Slash: so where were we
Slash: did you get wht i was saying
Olive Beetch: moon n oceans
Olive Beetch: yep i did
Slash: yeah that one
Slash: oooh and do u believe in that
Olive Beetch: n thts true
Olive Beetch: yeah in fact it wud be interesting to record wht each man or woman says after a decent f*** n kinda compile a lexicon
Olive Beetch: hehe
Slash: hmmm yeah
Slash: what i find the most erotic after a decent fuck
Slash: is the way some women orgasm
Slash: while u r inside them
Slash: man if you do it right those pelvic bones will almost crush your tool lol
Olive Beetch: hmmm .. guess lubrication holds good there
Olive Beetch: easy way in n out
Slash: oh yeah
Slash: but wht i mean is that if a woman gets a good orgasm and she is tight
Slash: sometimes the pelvic bones can tighten around your dick so well that it feels like your shoved it into a vacuum cleaner lol
Olive Beetch: oh alright
Olive Beetch: there experience beats naivety
Slash: ok so can i ask you a mundane question
Slash: lol
Olive Beetch: shoot
Slash: i mean the numbers lol
Slash: wht are your assets like
Olive Beetch: they r fluctuating .. suits me fine too
Slash: there i am back again
Slash: did you get the question
Olive Beetch: yeah
Slash: ok
Olive Beetch: i said the numbers r fluctuating
Slash: hmmm never mind
Olive Beetch: do not stay in place

Slash: i like to speculate
Olive Beetch: unlike the assets
Slash: and there's no fun without fluctuation
Slash: so go on tellme
Olive Beetch: so i'll tell ya the outer limits
Slash: ok
Olive Beetch: 36/ 28/ 35
Slash: thats nice
Olive Beetch: thts the average
Slash: 36 a b c?
Olive Beetch: whts tht abc?
Olive Beetch: oh okay
Slash: well you ought to know what that is
Slash: lol
Olive Beetch: but i donot know
Olive Beetch: sorry
Slash: ok
Slash: lol
Slash: that's ok
Olive Beetch: yeah guess i gotta find tht out
Slash: hmmm yeah i guess so
Slash: people like to know such things you know lol
Olive Beetch: coz it creates a size problem for me sometimes
Slash: hmmmm
Slash: lol
Slash: welll if you ever need help with the fitting tell me i would be glad to help
Olive Beetch: lol
Olive Beetch: i do believe in fitness..
Olive Beetch: nevermind
Slash: poor me you rejected my offer
Slash: lol
Olive Beetch: rejected? rather saved it for future..
Slash: oh that dicey little word lol
Olive Beetch: lol
Slash: so tell me the most exciting *** ual experience you had
Slash: or the most satisfying one

Olive Beetch: the most satisfying one .. hmmmm .. the day i gave up the virgin tag

Olive Beetch: tht was my choice

Olive Beetch: coz i fixed it up

Olive Beetch: thn never met the guy again

Olive Beetch: lol

Slash: ok how did you do that

Olive Beetch: he was pursuing me for sometime .. so i just thot of putting him to such judicious use

Slash: lol

Slash: he was pursuing you in real or on the net

Olive Beetch: both

Olive Beetch: we'd met thru the net

Olive Beetch: but thn had met quite a few times

Slash: ok

Olive Beetch: so it had got real..

Slash: so how long ago was this momentous occasion of your losing your virginity

Olive Beetch: but thts the only time i d had good S**

Olive Beetch: some 4 months back

Slash: ok so you had good sex just once in your life you mean

Olive Beetch: in fact u know wht

Olive Beetch: i was very scared as to i wud remain a St Ivy all my life

Olive Beetch: i was 19 n still a virgin

Olive Beetch: it was the biggest regret of my life till thn

Slash: so you did it as a favour to the church lol

Olive Beetch: yeah .. as a blasphemy yes

Slash: lol

Slash: and after that y u put a stop to it

Olive Beetch: n i admire myself at times for tht

Slash: agenda achieved and that's it lol

Slash: i admire you too for that babe lol

Olive Beetch: lol

Olive Beetch: it's like i'm yet to find someone

Olive Beetch: or someone to find me

Slash: lol

Slash: well thats not hard you sound like a fun person to find

Olive Beetch: yeah a fun person but a tough nut
Olive Beetch: and a nut whatsoever
Slash: tough nut
Olive Beetch: lol
Slash: as in
Olive Beetch: i hate no-brains
Slash: you mean you hate men without brains
Olive Beetch: yeah n they populate this world like bacteria
Slash: lol i do agree with u
Slash: so how long was your session with this fellow
Olive Beetch: not exactly hate .. but pity thm
Olive Beetch: oh lord poor creatures .. wht they r missing out
Olive Beetch: lols
Slash: so was this felllow quite up to your good sex definition or not
Olive Beetch: the exact session >> two hrs
Olive Beetch: this fellow was not bad for a test-drive
Slash: start to finish or just the humping and pumping
Olive Beetch: no it was not bad, coz we both were first-timers
Olive Beetch: so even it had been bad, there's no one to know
Slash: true
Olive Beetch: yeah
Slash: you show maturity beyond your years milady lol
Olive Beetch: n i'm sure u dont rem ur first-time
Slash: of course i do
Slash: but i have better memories than that one
Slash: lol
Olive Beetch: maturity... if u mean playing with words .. yeah tht i do a bit
Olive Beetch: but otherwise i'm a moonstruck loony
Olive Beetch: yeah better memories .. hmmm
Slash: yep some that i think i'll cherish till i die lol
Olive Beetch: old wine i guess
Slash: and exotic bottles in exotic places
Olive Beetch: lol.. tht oughtta be pricy
Olive Beetch: u sure a rich fellow
Slash: no no
Slash: i got the money from somewhere

Slash: but it was worth it

Slash: i mean this one time i had sex with this catholic irish puritan babe

Slash: in the backroom of an antique little church she had taken me to see and feel holy .. it had a small window to let in the moon

Slash: and we just lay there doing it for the whole night

Slash: lol

Olive Beetch: alright .. man u go places!

Slash: well i have been lucky with sex and women lol

Olive Beetch: my goodness thts straight from the mills n boons

Slash: yes it is

Slash: and thats why it was sooooooooooo hot

Olive Beetch: very lucky i must say

Slash: but I aint a sex maniac tho I sound like one

Slash: for example i haven't yet tried out the trains

Slash: or ferries

Slash: or disco loos

Slash: lol

Olive Beetch: hmmmm

Olive Beetch: good good

Olive Beetch: u must be eager to try them out

Olive Beetch: but thn with ur kinda exposure .. either it gets slightly obsessive

Olive Beetch: or a li'l disillusioned

Olive Beetch: guess urs the first case

Slash: no i don't think its either reallly

Olive Beetch: really?

Slash: i mean i appreciate sex as much as the next person

Slash: but it never comes in the way of my appreciating a person

Olive Beetch: thts a wonderful attitude

Slash: yes of course

Olive Beetch: wow

Slash: i mean i am a very emotional and a sensitive person

Olive Beetch: but thn do u ever segregate the two

Slash: and i really respect that side of others as well

Slash: now just because i get a hard on when i see a lady with big tits

Slash: doesn't mean i got no heart
Slash: segregate what and wht
Olive Beetch: lol
Olive Beetch: of course
Olive Beetch: i mean do u know/have u experienced love ever..
Olive Beetch: its not possible somewhere ..
Slash: yes i have
Olive Beetch: whn u r meeting new faces everyday
Slash: it is
Olive Beetch: okay .. really
Slash: and sometimes only then do you realize the difference between really feeling love and just thinking that its love when it's nothing more then just a bad habit
Olive Beetch: hmmm true
Olive Beetch: but it's tough
Olive Beetch: like i keep fallin in n outta love everyday
Slash: wht exposure does
Olive Beetch: yet i act the tough-nut all the time
Slash: is to let you that the best way to know what something is
Slash: to wait and watch
Slash: and not just to already assume
Olive Beetch: yeah .. guess thts true
Olive Beetch: oh i have this awful habit of jumping into conclusions
Slash: so now i never think that its just sex or just love or just this or that
Olive Beetch: u just do it
Slash: well as long as you jump into bed with them it's good lol
Olive Beetch: lol
Olive Beetch: yeah
Olive Beetch: lol
Slash: yeah i just do it
Slash: but i find it far more fun to do it with someone who's really fun to talk to and all that
Olive Beetch: there's no end to it however...
Slash: cause the worst is when you done it and over and then you don't have nothing to say

Slash: lol
Olive Beetch: yeah definitely
Olive Beetch: yeah the only thing u can have to say is "mam can i have it out plz?"
Slash: lol
Olive Beetch: the vacuum cleaners
Olive Beetch: lol
Slash: or like hey shit i think there's someone on the door
Olive Beetch: hmmm thats scary
Olive Beetch: hehe
Slash: but i doubt that a person like you will experience that
Olive Beetch: but less than losing the tool[s] forever
Olive Beetch: yeah i know
Olive Beetch: i mean it's a dilemma
Olive Beetch: somewhere i'm extremely whacky
Olive Beetch: n somewhere oooof an emotional fool
Olive Beetch: such a schizophrenic i'm
Slash: well only fools
Slash: realize the world
Slash: everyone else already knows it
Slash: there's a saying
Slash: there are people who think they know everything
Olive Beetch: yeah, lol
Slash: but then that's all that they know lol
Olive Beetch: yeah
Olive Beetch: i do live in dreams ..a lot
Slash: thts good so do i
Olive Beetch: it's better
Olive Beetch: really?
Slash: yep
Olive Beetch: but thn u getto realize thm too
Slash: wanna see a dream i drew
Slash: about the irish woman and me
Olive Beetch: yeah sure
Slash: there it comes
Slash: you got to
Slash: accept the transfer gal
Olive Beetch: hey r u sending it as a file?

Slash: yes]
Olive Beetch: tht doesnt work in my system
Olive Beetch: u better mail it
Slash: hmmm
Slash: so how does one send it to you then
Slash: oh that takes ages
Slash: why doesnt it work
Olive Beetch: no i'll chek
Olive Beetch: donno
Olive Beetch: have to get my system checked once
Slash: ok
Slash: got msn?
Slash: i could send it through that
Olive Beetch: okay my email is
Olive Beetch: <psychotica@hotmail.com>
Olive Beetch: no msn sorry
Slash: yeah
Slash: got msn?
Olive Beetch: anyway
Olive Beetch: no sorry
Olive Beetch: no frnds on msn
Olive Beetch: thts y
Slash: ok
Olive Beetch: don wanna overload my system ..
Slash: anyway so let's forget it
Olive Beetch: okay..
Olive Beetch: some other time
Slash: yeah
Slash: hey i really am having great fun talking to you
Olive Beetch: yeah same here
Olive Beetch: definitely
Slash: so where in del are you from girl
Olive Beetch: in fact u r a kind tht appreciates the basic human attributes .. good sex n great intellect
Olive Beetch: i'm from south del
Olive Beetch: u?
Slash: yes and you seem to be that rare combination reallly
Slash: the other side of ur midnite

Slash: where in south del gal
Olive Beetch: lajpat nagar
Slash: hey
Slash: you there?
Olive Beetch: yeah
Olive Beetch: u?
Olive Beetch: where r u from?
Slash: there i am back again
Slash: yeah where in south delhi lady?
Olive Beetch: lajpat ngr
Olive Beetch: u?
Olive Beetch: u there
Olive Beetch: hi
Olive Beetch: u there
Slash: hey
Slash: you there
Olive Beetch: yeah
Olive Beetch: whts wrong
Slash: hey this thing's really fukking up
Olive Beetch: i know..
Slash: can we talk on the phone instead or is that a problem with you
Olive Beetch: no the thing is tht the phone isn't in my room
Olive Beetch: plus it's still early don't u think so?
Olive Beetch: hmmm?
Slash: that's ok
Slash: never mind then let's chat on this only
Slash: so wherein south delh are you
Olive Beetch: lajpat ngr
Olive Beetch: u?
Slash: your sexy intellect is proving einstein's theory of relativity for me lol
Olive Beetch: haha .. theory of relativity eh?
Olive Beetch: theres one joke i rem ..
Slash: yes
Slash: lol
Slash: so wht are you a punjabi a sardarni or wht

Olive Beetch: einstein having written all the goddamn equations on the board n still kinda saying "but i still dont understand wimmen!!"

Slash: but then i realized

Slash: of course thats the toughest

Olive Beetch: i'm a half bengali, half punjabi

Slash: you can never understand something that's constantly evolving

Olive Beetch: lol right

Slash: wow the horniest cocktail

Olive Beetch: u prove darwinsm once again

Slash: lol

Olive Beetch: horniest?

Olive Beetch: well guess u r again talking from exp

Slash: yeh punjabi and bengali women have the best sex appetite in this country

Olive Beetch: good 4 everyone

Olive Beetch: but ironically UP n bihar top the population charts

Slash: so you must be quite something then lol

Olive Beetch: i'm something yes .. i have matter as i occupy space

Slash: well they're just reproducing

Slash: hmmmmmm

Slash: lucky the man who gets to taste that matter lol

Olive Beetch: oh u never know ..

Olive Beetch: there cud be a lot of unwanted materials

Olive Beetch: the pollutants

Slash: lol

Slash: like

Slash: well why don't you elaborate

Olive Beetch: like a need to look around more n more

Olive Beetch: and an insatiable hunger for everything

Olive Beetch: that's a bit too much to take

Olive Beetch: so ppl avoid it

Olive Beetch: n so do i

Slash: welll if you insatiable then you're really my kinda woman lol

Slash: so wanna meet up sometime or is that taboo

Olive Beetch: no no nothing of the sort

Olive Beetch: jus tht my univ tests r impending

Olive Beetch: n i'm on a virtual cruise

Slash: oh ok

Slash: hmmmm ok

Slash: well if you can chat for so long you can surely meet for a cofffeee .. sometime .. when i'm there in del

Slash: lol

Olive Beetch: lol yeah point!

Olive Beetch: but thn as a free citizen of a funny nation ..

Slash: so how about saturday for a coffee or a drink whatever you prefer .. and whenever you prefer

Olive Beetch: hey may be .. but say in may

Olive Beetch: lol i have this shitty habit of postponing

Olive Beetch: which kills the charm

Slash: dont

Slash: exactly

Slash: so lets have a little coffee a quickie

Slash: if one may call it that

Slash: and then you go study

Olive Beetch: but thn i gotta

Slash: gotta wht

Olive Beetch: i ve promised my mom [yes i have]

Olive Beetch: tht i m not freaking out for at least a month

Olive Beetch: hehe

Olive Beetch: n now shes keepin a watch on me like anything

Slash: well you aint freaking out you're just taking a break for 30 minutes for a coffee

Slash: thts it

Olive Beetch: yeah

Olive Beetch: hmm

Olive Beetch: u got a point

Slash: yep i know i do

Olive Beetch: it's just tht i ve logged on to ward off my exam daymares .. generally it's rather my nocturnal trysts with unknown ppl that keeps me ticking

Slash: i find you far too much fun to talk to

Olive Beetch: whn do u hit the bed generally?
Slash: depends on who i am with lol
Olive Beetch: oh thts very diplomatic of u..
Slash: yes well thats part of growing up
Olive Beetch: but thts life
Olive Beetch: thts applicable with me as well
Slash: yeah
Slash: so tell me one thing
Olive Beetch: yeh
Slash: since you must have been on the internet for quite a bit now
Olive Beetch: yeah
Slash: have you ever had cyber with anyone
Olive Beetch: no
Olive Beetch: rather yes/no
Slash: did you or did you not
Olive Beetch: once i had a bit with an american guy
Olive Beetch: in fact i got a compliment too
Slash: ok
Slash: and wht all did you do with him
Olive Beetch: tht was it
Olive Beetch: generally i believe in real action .. but tht one was pure seduction
Slash: yeah
Olive Beetch: n guess wht i humbly let myself be seduced
Slash: tell me about it
Slash: tell you the truth you sound like a delight for seducing lol
Olive Beetch: nothing great .. but just that that guy kinda blabbered about being fascinated by indian women, n then generally started talking romantic
Olive Beetch: n since i was in a groping mood i let myself loose for a while
Slash: and then slowly you didn't realize when your panties went down
Slash: and where ur fingers suddenly went
Olive Beetch: thats the twist
Olive Beetch: u know wht i always keep a control there ..

Slash: yeah you mean you never touch yourself

Olive Beetch: no matter wht all i type .. n no matter my panties wetness, i never pull them down

Olive Beetch: i do ..

Olive Beetch: but on self-stimulation

Slash: so wht you wearing right now then

Olive Beetch: n ironically once again u touch me n i'm on fire

Olive Beetch: right now i'm fully clothed [very happily]

Slash: hmmmmmm

Slash: ok

Slash: and you mean youre on fire right now or were or would be in a hypothetical situation

Olive Beetch: in a hypothetical situation i'm always on fire

Slash: ok heh

Olive Beetch: n sometimes in real ..

Slash: sometimes

Slash: pity it's not now lol

Olive Beetch: but a cyber isn't my type

Slash: neither is it for me

Slash: but it definitely can be done with a woman as interesting as you lol

Olive Beetch: let's keep the interest on the hard way

Slash: oh yes hard it sure is lol

Olive Beetch: anyway

Olive Beetch: i'm kinda .. weary

Slash: but anyway i guess it's best to catch a good wink now .. it's morning already .. sound saturday morning siesta ahead

Olive Beetch: hmmm

Olive Beetch: yeah

Slash: otherwise you will be too much of a good thing!

Olive Beetch: huh .. hey hey hey plz I expect too much outta me [not tht I'm modest]

Olive Beetch: coz i'm jus a fun lovin gal

Olive Beetch: I bet it

Olive Beetch: n yeah highly nocturnal

Slash: hey

Slash: i am being nice

Slash: don't take it for granted lol

Olive Beetch: lol
Olive Beetch: yeah thnx .. u r courteous
Olive Beetch: lol
Slash: oh very much so
Olive Beetch: thts a gentlemanly attribute
Slash: true
Olive Beetch: thn i'm a lady too .. i'm honoured
Slash: anything you wish to be lol
Slash: i am sure you are
Olive Beetch: be sure ..
Olive Beetch: okay thn .. see ya some other smoother time
Slash: yes
Slash: message me on yahoo if you're planning to come online tomorrow
Slash: then may be we chat then ok
Slash: babe
Slash: take care then
Olive Beetch: adios thn
Olive Beetch: yeah u too
Slash: bye
Slash: take care

And I hate getting too close for comfort. Escape, escape.

******

-- You can map on the city the human form. You can catch the city measuring you with coffee spoons and formulated phrases.

Bono grins, his usual evening smile on his way to the Utopia, looking up at the last tinge of twilight red through the car window, exhaling the branded nicotine, sprinkling my evening with a dash of Eliot. He does that as a matter of habit. His left hand index and middle fingers tango on my skirt-wrapped, unwaxed uncreamed rough thighs (inviting? though his are smoother, perhaps because he has never run a razor on them, at least am not aware of it, in case he has, yeah thankfully am not, but I couldn't be sure whether I would like a thigh all too smooth for my comfort to rub mine with, at times I think I would though, just for a testmatch, a higher order of smoothness, surpassing Bono, a fancy smoothness, unobstructed, better than those foreign drive-through carwashes, yet perhaps may be a little bit bumpy too, just a bit, rocky here and there, just a bit, lubricated, just a bit, with a luscious growth of dark brown tendrils, yet inviting?), my keen kohl-smeared eyes dance around a bit with the faint east horizon moon. I toss the words for eternity.

Bono, have you ever wondered how easily you engender the city? As if it was meant to be a female every time! It could be anything from a male, female, to a hermaphrodite or even a transvestite! It has the curves, the pillars, the shafts, the domes.

Now he pierces his grey eyes right through me. A hint of a triumphant curve on my lips. Words and kisses have been our regular shuttlecocks. He smiles back.

-- Yeah, the city is opting for a sex-change every now and then. It has transformed itself into a sex-hopper.

I try not to seem satiated.

He adores her when she's livid, that non-friendly adoration when one's brimming with orgasmic verbosity, yet not gushing it all out right away.

I resist his gaze, look out again. The tease and tonight make something hot in me.

Just look at the way you say it. The city. Why, what do you mean by that? What exactly? An abstraction? A concept? The idea of the city! (She chuckles a bit now) You know you simply wipe out the sheer physicality in thinking that way. I mean what about the smell? The taste? The longing, the ache, those city frames? Where do you kick them off to? It's a city. It breathes. It entices, like a wanton enchantress! It fills you with a tragic aura, like those victims in Arthur Miller or Tennessee Williams. Or it pumps into your circulation a beat of life, a new life. That invigorates. At times makes you shrink back with pious horror, you feel guilty to be alive. It has a new story to tell every time. Take a second look and it's not the same anymore. Is it?

-- Words, words, words. You aren't out of your fantasia yet. Wake up, you've long logged out of your virtual Eden, time for some reality check.

So he doesn't feel it? Or perhaps doesn't want to reveal. Bono too is wearing a mask and I act as if I wasn't aware of it.

Bono and I belong to the no-roots creed, happily severed our connections with the past, living in a timeless present. We're mild pretenders to having histories. We know that. Like everyone else we're fighting in a puppet-show, fortunately our weapons are stringed and we're glad we don't have the responsibility to pull them.

A would-be pedagogue. A would-be journalist. Brittle bricks of the fourth estate. Serving the errant knaves called words.

Bullets and kisses are the only things that confirm you're alive.

We pass from the long empty streets of Lodhi Colony to the brilliantly lit Rajpath crossing the India Gate. He loves cruising around before bumming in at Utopia. Cars swish past like raging beasts. Painted Aishwarya Rais glimmer in the neon lights, the streets look sensually orange. From Cannes to Cancun, misrepresentation all through. Global doll games.

******

On Saturday evenings, the Utopia teems with the press fraternity. Almost everyone seems to take a dive into the pool of liquor and cocktail the night away. I recognize a few faces from my father's clan and wave back. The others become a part of the crowd.

Two of Bono's dad's friends are here too. I know of them, Shekhar Sehgal, Evening Newsline. Bono introduces the other, kind of stumpy and mild-looking, with a receding hairline. That's Pratham Mahey, Star India. We feel obliged to join them, after their terribly keen handshakes. Mahey pulls out a chair for the lady.

They order chilled beer, Kingfisher. I wonder for a while and settle for a Limca. What do they sing when three chain-smokers get together? Smoke on the Water, Fire in the Sky.

Sipping from his glass, Sehgal emits,

-- So Mahey, your Vikram Luthra left Star One, eh? Wonder what he's going to do on his own. Who can give up the best TRPs for something that hardly can be called to be a TV News Channel?

-- Yeah, it's a loss for sure, Mahey sighs. May be wanted to move beyond fame you know. It's difficult to understand this lot but perhaps they would eventually make a difference.

-- Such an all-rounder boss, Sehgal replies lightly knocking the table twice. Reporting, anchoring, to moderating, heck everything's a cakewalk for this dude. But still working under a big banner does a world of difference.

Bono butts in,

-- He's a gladiator, he'll survive it. He needs kicks and that's a good sign for he dares to dare. He'll bring some relief from the flux of shit soundbites they sell for news.

Mahey rides high on decibels,

-- Don't give me that shit news crap of yours, young man. Boy, we sell what sells. So if the PM pees in his pants that's the scoop guaranteeing glued audience. And just because your dad's World-view leans leftward there's no reason why it only should claim to be journalizing: more like senile communists desperately penpushing for a living. And who really reads them, eh? Ask your dad! News is what you pass off as news.

Bono bites back,

-- It's far better than your pretty faces airing the Miss India's latest lingerie, or the supermodel's bizarre hairdo.

-- Bizarre for you, but some do like it.

-- Yeah, they do. Says precisely why they watch your so-called news-channel.

******

Transcending the virtual for the real. But why? At least in that make-believe world there were a couple of real poetic moments. Odd spasms of sudden thrills. Pure spontaneity.

What do they quibble about? Numbers, facts, bylines.

I know Bono would simply go off to sleep once we get back. The night's serene with a frowning moon upset with the prose of life.

I pick up the pieces. The scrapes of Nowhere.

THIRTEEN

Fuchsia

What's the colour of disdain? Or indulgence? Or a disdainful indulgence? The colour he was wearing today? A crumpled oversized jacket of a dirty pinkish shade. Bright, but dirty. And grey denims.

Almost never been washed.

He had met her in the morning to show the latest scribbles but she was in a hurry. Could hardly say meet me after the classes. He had looked a bit lost in thought, in a world of his own. Distant. Good, he must have been thinking things through and through. Cooking up verses. Or sketching. She hadn't yet had a glimpse of the pencilled world he kept in his folders.

They had had five sessions already. The last working day before the December break was supposed to hold another. However, the attendance as usual was atrociously thin. So they had called it off. Now each one to his own or her own. Capricious little drafts, penned first impressions struck off.

There were the new arrivals piled up on the adjacent cushioned chair. The last library update Bishakha had asked the faculty to compile. If only there was another soul in the staffroom. The brand new books almost plaintively demanded her vigilance. Most of them had fancy covers, in artistic black and white or a splash of too many at once. She didn't feel like opening and seeing what they held within. It was three in the afternoon, no one else would come in at that late an hour. All she could do was stash them in her personal locker and phone up Bishakha to let her know that they were safe. Almost a dozen of them were there. Her locker was full when all were in, looking like an overcrowded orphanage. She keyed it and let out a breath. The peon was out of sight again. She looked around for a minute and then came out, huddling herself close inside the grey overcoat, scrounging for meagre warmth.

Outside it had the ashened face of grey, the colour of gloom. And there she was tiptoeing towards an orangey pink, the colour of scorn. She had just decided the colour scheme of her somersaulting moods, she had attributed fuchsia to scorn. She wanted to scorn the day just as it scorned her, piercing prickly needles of contempt right through her over-cushioned flesh.

Not many years back remember, when you still weren't Roy, how you wanted to get out of that pigeonhole of a room, without even a camp-bed, how you slept on the bloody cold December floor without even a mattress or a blanket, just to hear the stupid sound on your YM, --Knock, Knock, Knock! Who's there? Beelzebub? Aah, no, never Beelzebub. The little box merely said at 3:33 a.m.s or 4:44 a.m.s, Ash is now online. Then almost instantly, the awful sound, the door being flung open and someone stepping out of it as if running away from her, frantically, Ash is now offline. Even scorn so often scorned, even a fake indulgence made still more fake by simply refusing to acknowledge its existence. And all that show of living on, waiting endlessly for a two-second cacophony, three pistol shots in the orchestra of her soundless monotone, three back to back declarations of her being less than an insect in the world of arachnophobes and disinfectant-maniacs.

And all that was purposeful after all. Something to fall back on. Some kind of a sensation in her desensitized orb, a swing of difference, a vibration of bruise. An occasion to finger the keys on the board, to insert odd snippets of futile images of fertility in her impotent globe. She didn't remember their first meeting of course, she retained no memory of the fateful rendezvous, didn't know which was the moment she was supposed to regret so thoroughly. Just that the so-called 'real' had stopped making much sense for her, she was sucked into this weird world of wired souls. They called it the web and Ash the king spider had her in his grip. She was the willing victim, she needed to be devoured. A slow death as an alternative life.

She was reading about the latest disorder to hit the charts: addiction to the Internet. So after heroin, gambling, alcohol, cigarettes, sexual deviancy, or eating Milky Way bars it was the world wide web that was the warp.

People who become addicted often do so because their lives are not fulfilling. They can't seem to find passion, enjoyment, adventure, or pleasure from life itself, so they have to invent these experiences in other ways. Whether such feelings come to them through gambling, getting 'high', 'tuning out', or becoming over-involved with the Internet, their work, their hobbies, or anything else, there is often a lack of other pleasures that drive people (at least in part) to crave pleasure from their addictive behaviours... people who become addicted to alcohol and other drugs usually have serious deficiencies in their life management, stress management, and interpersonal skills. Early on in life, they experience a great deal of pain and personal suffering that they can't figure out how to deal with effectively. This drives them to seek external relief and comfort in the form of alcohol or other substances. As this pattern of behaviour gets repeated over time, their bodies become physically addicted to the chemical substance, and the addiction then becomes even more difficult to end.

Was she an addict? She took the test they had made freely available to help unwitting victims.

1. Do you spend more time than you think you should surfing the 'Net?

   Yes No

2. Do you feel you have a problem limiting the time you spend on the 'Net?

   Yes No

3. Have any of your friends or family members complained about the time you spend at your computer?

   Yes **No**

4. Do you find it hard to stay away from the 'Net for several days at a time?

   Yes No

5. Has either your work output or your personal relationships suffered as a result of spending too much time on the 'Net?

   Yes **No**

6. Are there particular areas of the 'Net, or types of files, you find hard to resist?

   Yes No

7. Do you have trouble controlling your impulses to purchase items, products, or services on the 'Net?

   Yes **No**

8. Have you tried, unsuccessfully, to curtail your use of the 'Net?

Yes No

9. Do you derive much of your pleasure and satisfaction in life from being on the 'Net?

Yes No

Three years back she would marvel why the fair-faced Bono wouldn't make her lose her wits the way that strange triple knock would. Why would she stay up night after night harking to their silence, stay logged in, hopping from Gazebo to Kolkata Online to meet that stranger of the dark. Always behind the veils. Always leaving her high and dry. They said the only way to make a connection was through a wound. And she was digging deeper into the relentless churn of consciousness, ever fuelling that chemical reaction that flamed from her flesh leaping at the forbidden drum. She would turn off the private messaging, the message alert, and would sit in the consummate unquiet of fleeting images and senseless nonsequiters. Ophelia, wassup gurl? //smiley .. yawn yawn//depressed .. glurg glurg let's do something unusual tonite folks .. let's get loud // music //beer … shit biting cold this side//coffee wud be better .. oh the kiwis will have it hot now//watercooler .. humidity coupled with heat can be killing//graph-sinks .. hicc hicc //beer let the toad turn into the prince now .. frogs have ruled for long//hammer .. operation time-kill n looking 4//ideas .. any1 got a date tonite//happycomp .. yawn .. //cigarette .. yawn//trash

It wasn't too different yesterday.

"I'm getting a ticket for Boston for the 29th. I'll be flying to Dallas for a coupla days to meet Richa Arora and do the courtesy stuff. Will be visiting her grave too. Hope all that's fine with you."

"I wasn't informed of anything of the sort."

"Well yeah, I was corresponding with Richa over mails. I think it's best if I visit her personally. There're things she has told me about, and I guess I got to go and do my duties there."

"Duties?"

"Yeah, well, you can call it so. I can't go on with a guilty conscience forever."

"Oh, so what we have here is another of your remorse-feats, eh?"

"I don't really want to have a tiff over nothing right now. I'm tired if you don't mind."

"Tiff over nothing? Nothing is it, eh? Nothing? Oh really? Nothing indeed! Who the fuck you think I am, a bloody hired skank?"

"Right, I'm going to hit the bed. Good night.'

"Excuse me? No good nights anymore okay? I've been mum all this while but that doesn't mean you're forever going to get away with your goddamned 'decisions'. Look we need to talk. I need to know what's going on. I need to know what the heck Richa or some other bitch has been spewing in your mind that you suddenly decide to take the next flight to Boston!"

"Not suddenly. I've been talking to her for about a coupla months now. And the decision wasn't hasty either. You know I don't make hasty decisions."

"All right! So all this while you've been hatching plans to slip off without bothering to let me know even for once?"

"Change your vocabulary. It really sucks."

"Let's not get into linguistics, alright?"

"Fine! For starters, I haven't been 'hatching plans' of any kind. I've been talking to Richa like two mournful adults and since I'm in a state of belated shock, I have all the reasons to go and seek clarifications and get my conscience appropriately cleansed. I'm sure there have been misunderstandings. I could have helped Irene survive longer had I been there. She had simply refused any kind of transfusion or chemotherapy. It was a frenzied death she had chosen for herself, all too betrayed by her fellow believers and to some extent me. I owe three years of my JHU life to her. I have my obligations."

"But what about me? Your lawfully wedded wife for godsake! You've no obligations towards me?"

"Listen, let me come back, we'll talk everything out. We'll sort it out, okay?"

"Sort out what? Sort out the still more effective ways of imposing your decisions on me? Sort out the still easier ways of settling scores with your late girlfriends? Hmm? What? Tell me, the list never seems to end! How many skeletons you got in that closet of yours, huh? How many more?"

"Why are you hell bent on exaggerating things? I had a past like everyone else. A past in which you had no role to play. Now, if that makes you jealous I can't help it. Have I ever asked you what all you did before tying the knot with me? And who was more eager to get married? You or me?"

"Right! Now you're talking. So, say it clearly. You wanna get rid of me, don't you? This Boston thing is a bloody gimmick you're hiding behind. Perhaps you regretted it from the very first day of our marriage. Ugh? No? Oh nice friend Ophelia for a wife? No way! Then why? Why didn't you resist it then, when it was still resistible? 'Cause you wanted something to kill time with! A wife, a milkmaid of a girlfriend, or the damned projects of yours. Everything was equally substitutable. Albeit you found out that you've had a sad bargain there. You got a no-good wife, who was a faceless good fun when hidden behind the screen, securely tucked 10 thousand miles away. But face-to-face, you sadly discovered to your great annoyance, that she was a complete stranger and a bore! Why? 'cause you! had nothing much to share with her, nor did you have the intention of getting to know her inner world! You never even tried violating her and dirtying your hands with the scum you thought she harboured in herself! Huh, you hypocrite, tell me on my face that you aren't going to come back, tell me if you've finally sucked up to them and bagged an assignment of eugenics! Tell me, c'mon, to fuck off and believe me, I will!!"

The words were enough to bear the consequent hush. A deaf and dumb world. Spastic in its mute ways. Convulsive in its stillness.

******

The foggy afternoon was soaking up the last remnants of heat. As she ambled through the empty corridors of Arts Block, she felt the chill. The walk to the Science Block wasn't much, she decided to take a peep at the sagging mercury in the fancy thermometer they had put up just outside the physics lab. 11°C, it read. The lab assistant was packing the apparatus back into the drawers and shelves. Looked a bit irritated at her intrusion.

"Can you tell me where they hold the Zoology Honors third year classes?" she asked, timidly.

"Over there, to the right, the second last room."

"Thanks a lot."

"But it's empty now. Nobody's there."

"That's alright. I just wanted to look around a bit."

"Looking for a student?"

"Yeah, in fact, I was looking for Ashish Acharya, Zoo third year."

"Okay the tall boy? He must be in his hostel now."

"You know him?"

"Yes, they had their subsidiary physics practicals with us until last year."

"Okay."

"Yes, you can ask for him at the hostel reception counter. There will be somebody there for sure."

"Okay. Thanks a lot!"

"Mention not."

The rites of passage. The emptied follow-noon hour. The lull all around. The walls doing the noiseless lounge-act, loafing around her as she tried muffling the sound of her heels. She came out, trod through the narrow lane flanked by eucalypti and other leafless trees. After the fall. The shed leaves had been burnt in heaps and nature's clutter undone.

The boys' hostel was a medium building of red and white paints alternating to produce a disciplinarian air. Just beside the cafeteria and common canteen. Usually during the full sessions, there would be thundering volumes of rock or pop music deafening the ears of passers by. The principal was lenient at times, and didn't fuss around with the smallest defiances in the college premises. The pronounced accent of strictness would be reserved for end of semester, especially during the approaching annual examinations. Usually, there were very few students in the hostel during the preparation leaves or winter breaks. Ashish Acharya apparently was one of them.

There was a young chap at the reception: a rickety desk with a fat register and two black telephones. The placard at one side read: BOYS' HOSTEL MHC. The boy at the desk was on the phone; engrossed in himself. Didn't notice her coming until she tapped on the table.

"Just a second. Yes?"

"I'm looking for Ashish Acharya."

"Room number?"

"Err, I'm not really sure of that."

"Well, let me see. Oh you mean the one who sings?"

"Umm.. well he's in Zoology third year."

Okay, yeah, the same guy. Tall, pony-tailed?"

"Yes, yes!"

"Yes, room number 69."

"Which is the way?"

"Take the stairs, second floor, end of the left corridor."

"Thank you very much."

"Welcome. One moment, please write down your name, class, and purpose of visit."

"Oh, I'm a teacher here."

"Really, oh am sorry then, didn't notice you were a teacher. Ma'am, you've to fill up the details anyway. Just put in the particulars you'd like to provide. And yes, phone number. That's a must. See there's column for that as well."

"Yes, I can see that. Alright, there."

"Thanks. Please take the stairs and turn left."

"Thanks a lot."

The door to the room number 69 was spooky. And embellished. The panes in the wooden grids were covered with posters in raging red, bathetic blue, violent violets to say the least. They turned out to be the singing sensations U2, Megadeth, Dream Theater, Pearl Jam, Coldplay and Pink Floyd. She mused what was stored inside.

It was slightly ajar, so she pushed it a bit instead of knocking. He was there, lying in his full length on the single bed they provide to the third year students. Single room. He sat up, visibly baffled.

"Oh Ma'am, it's you!?"

"Yeah, I just thought of peeking into your world a bit." She knew she was sounding cheeky. Why? To bridge the age gulf? To cross the official relationship: teacher-student one way traffic?

"Oh cool. I mean what a surprise! Wow!"

He was smiling, and by now had got down from the bed looking like a lamp-post. His pony wavered to his movements, an escort of sort, a cheeky one.

"What's so wow about my visiting your room once in a while?" *Good, keep probing.*

"Nothing, just that it's so unexpected and so great!"

"Well thanks. May I sit down?"

Poor chap. Embarrassed young man before a postlapsarian Eve.

"I'm sso sorry! Please ma'am."

Pulled a plastic chair that housed some crumpled jackets and sweaters. A pair of dirty brown socks as well.

"Thanks."

He sat on the bed facing her, trying not to look anxious about her alien presence in his abode. Intruding was becoming her favourite pastime.

"So what were you reading?" she finally shot the suspense-diluter of a question.

"*Disgrace*, by J.M. Coetzee."

"Oh that's a helluva book to read. Did you know it won the Booker in 1999? We have it in our new MA syllabus."

"Yeah, I know. I got it from a senior."

"Alright. How far have you reached?"

"Well, about nine chapters."

"Oh so through with the Melanie-Lurie episode?"

"Err well, I guess, yeah. He's with his daughter Lucy now."

"Okay, may be we'll discuss it later, over a cup of coffee, alright?"

"Sounds cool."

That dirty pink he was donning in the morning was hung from a hook on the wall. In fact the room was quite a poster gallery. A broken badminton racket at an angle to a big snakey S of old shuttlecocks, a series of posters including Sex, Sins and Sensibility, Sex and the City with Sarah Jessica Parker in a skimpy black outfit, lifesized black and white posters of Kurt Cobain, Ozzy Osbourne, Joe Satriani, and Sofia Loren. Several newspaper snippets cut and pasted on a cardboard hung from the bedside wall. A number of photographs on the thermocol right above the study-table. A small board saying Armchair Casanovas Just Play At It. Under a switched off light green lampshade.

Something was playing on the small Sony CD Man kept on the edge of the bed. The volume was minimized. *The Best of Nirvana.* Cobain kohl-rimmed on the cover.

"I see, *Nirvana*?" Break the ice, break the ice dammit.

"Yeah, a rare collection in fact. Not mine of course. Borrowed it from a friend. You see, most of the CDs there, on the table, they aren't really mine. But in a way they belong to me. They love being with me. I make them feel special. They come alive when I play them."

"Hmm, can't see the speakers."

"Over there, above the shelves."

"Alright, yeah. Nice!"

Something wasn't quite right. What exactly? No flashback for god-sake!

"You want to listen to it?"

"Not *grunge* right now. Something else may be."

"Okay I got this *Guns and Roses' Live Era 87 to 93*. How about it?"

"Great! Does it have *November Rain*?"

"One of its best versions. Almost 12 and half minutes long."

"Heh. Okay! Lets have it then."

The song played for a good 13 minutes, or so she thought. Was it the best? Err, she preferred the ones she had heard before. Let's not think aloud right now.

She got up and stood by the table. Looked closely at the photographs.

"These seem to be from a series. Something like a theme-album?"

"The theme was 'In Bloom'."

He was watching her two-inch brown heels under the blue denim long-skirt she was wearing under her overcoat.

"I have a series on high-heels as well." He declared, his mouth curving in a crooked smile.

"Really?" She arched her brows in fake surprise. "Let's see them."

"Just a minute."

He shot up on his feet and opened the last drawer of his desk. Took out a red-bordered black folder with a stark red stiletto pasted on the front.

"Scissored from the *Vogue*. The rest is mine."

Young men's fetish mustn't really affect you now. Have a grip.

The pictures were in colour, in a red and black combination. The first one, a cross. The arms in black, the trunk in red. The shoes upturned, their soles with the heels jutting out making a weird effect. The background wasn't too clear.

"Soles, ehm?"

"Yeah, I like the ventral side of everything better."

"Okay what's the backdrop like?"

"Well it's world map I had got from CP. It hasn't come out fine."

There were more of the likes. One had a naked foot at right angle with the ankle and placed in unison with a high-heeled red gumboot to resemble similar angles of two congruent triangles. There were the respective reflections on a puddle of water giving the inverted images of the pair, deliberately hazed.

"Hmm, well, what's the idea behind these snaps?"

"I'm a foot-lover. A pedophile of sorts." A calm-faced reply. Perhaps the comfort level had shot up exponentially.

There was a different one in the end. A black pair of gumboots kept perpendicularly over a newspaper headline: WHO'LL FIT INTO THEIR SHOES? Two snaps below the line: Bush and Saddam.

"This one makes a relevant statement." She remarked, smiling.

"Yeah, it fetched me the second prize at St. Stephen's."

"Impressive. You're a regular then?"

"I try to be, but it's an expensive thing. Each album costs me about 600 bucks roughly. So I kind of restrict myself to two-three albums a semester."

"Those are the latest?" She pointed towards the ones on the thermocol hanging from the wall.

"Yeah, they are."

She rose and stood by the table once again.

"I guess I'll put on my specs for a better view." She added.

Twigs of six-petalled white flowers, one or two in sharp focus. A blurred image of a woman's back. Hints of a white translucent garment.

"What flower is that?' she inquired.

"I'm not sure. It grows in our ramshackle of a house in Jamshedpur. I took the pictures there, this autumn break."

"Is it really white?"

"Umm, well, some have traces of pink. But basically white, yeah. A very bright white in fact. I tried looking them up in the Botany field atlases but couldn't really locate the genus."

"I see. And the woman?' she was a little reticent this time.

"Oh she's a distant aunt. In fact, a widow. Stays with my grandparents and looks after them in a way. The best thing about her is her shape. I haven't seen a better curve than hers. Although I haven't seen much I know."

"I see. The petals look a little dull in this one. No?" she wasn't sure herself.

Hope he's not very touchy.

"Cool, you noticed that. Well it's the same twig I have used throughout the series. It looks fresh on the first day. The second day of course it shows signs of wilting. It took me two days to pull off the whole thing."

"Almost bare back I see. A great shape indeed." She grinned.

"Heh, yeah, I'd told you." Grinned back, the crooked one.

"Then why do you call it 'In Bloom' when the flowers are actually wilting during the shoot?"

"Well, depends on what you're looking at, the flowers or the woman's back. And anti-chronologically it's in bloom anyway."

"Aah, yeah I guess."

The Flower woman. She knew her story. The woman dressed in white, dishevelled hair, singing crazy jingles for the lost one. White lilies, snake lilies, tulips, bougainvilleas, shiuli. She too had collected them.

> Now that lilacs are in bloom
> She has a bowl of lilacs in her room
> And twists one in his fingers while she talks.
> "Ah, my friend, you do not know, you do not know
> What life is, you who hold it in your hands;"
> (Slowly twisting the lilac stalks)
> "You let it flow from you, you let it flow,
> And youth is cruel, and has no remorse
> And smiles at situations which it cannot see."
> I smile, of course,
> And go on drinking tea.

The flower woman. Now frozen. Coffin-bound. Framed. Scratching the wall in pain, trying to disappear, trying hard to become a zero. The flower woman, her flesh invisible under the garment of blossoms, white blossoms. The trickle of sweat on her back soaked up by the spongy buds. The deserted one. The document of madness, the flowery sheet to write the script of madness. She's mute. She's frail. She's lack. She's O.

The hole in my bathroom window that I've plugged in with a newspaper ball. I've shut out the world there, before it rolled me up into a crumpled ball and tossed me around. Said I was their globe. I was their apple.

"These aren't the best ones actually." He declared, after a while.

"Sorry, I was a bit lost. Come again." She recollected herself, and fixed her stare on him.

"I said those aren't the best of the series." He repeated, endlessly weighing the words in the air inside his throat.

"Really? Then where are the best?" She had puckered her brows in a sly smile.

You're milking the young Satan you know. And you're too old for an Eve.

"I'm not really sure I can show them to you." He was callously reticent. *Boy, learn to fake innocence first, you're too innocent to fake.*

"And why not?" she demanded, a bit irked.

"Well she's nude in them." *Revelatory, isn't it?*

"I see. Show me anyway. Nudity doesn't intimidate me." *Dig deeper. There's a sign you can see. Or have stopped believing in signs as well?*

He took out another folder from the drawer. This one wasn't ornamented at all. Secret mine there. No drawing attention of any kind towards it. He gave it to her and sat down on the bed glumly, moving his fingers through the abundant crop of black mane.

The same white flowers. The woman's breasts, torso, legs at different angles and degrees of blur. No focus on the face.

"Is she a shade darker than you?" She asked, for purely aesthetic purposes.

"Yeah, in fact quite a few shades darker than me. I call her the Black Venus."

"Oh, there's a fascinating story by the same name, written by Angela Carter. You must read it." She chuckled.

"I guess I will then. Since you recommend it." *Laconic?*

"I seriously do. It's a pity you aren't in English. You've a definite inclination to be literary, although you yourself aren't quite aware of it."

"I could have been but the cut-off for our college was 85. I had a 79 only. But I kinda like doing Zoology too. I like seeing those different species of animals, insects, microbes. In a way, when I take a snap, I do what the biologists do to the dead specimens they store in formaldehyde solutions. They too freeze death. I freeze the moment, an expression, at times, a thought."

"Can I ask you something personal?" she was decidedly jittery.

"Go ahead, I'll see if I could provide an answer but ask anyway."

"How did you make her agree to pose for you?" *You're kidding a kiddo? A kiddo? Not quite. Not yet a man though. The Amorph.*

"Oh, that's alright. Well, it's nothing. We used to have it whenever we could. The afternoons at my grandparents' are too languid. Nobody hears a sound when they take the post-luncheon nap. It's almost eerily quiet. And the attic, they don't even bother looking into. Both suffer from rheumatism, grandma has gout as well. They can't really climb the stairs. So, we never really had any problem. There wouldn't be any maids around during those ungodly hours. You can walk away with murder really, it's that sleepy a place."

"So one fine day you just decided to capture her in your lens?"

"No, in fact I always nursed the idea of shooting her. She has a marvellous body. And there isn't much she can do otherwise. Just doing the household chores that she does everyday. She can read English so I gift her little storybooks at times, often comic books. She likes Tin Tin a lot."

"Hmm. I see."

"Yeah, you know, that was the least I could do for her. You know how a widow's life could be in the interiors. It's really sad. She was married off at 13. She hailed from somewhere deep inside Bihar, not Jamshedpur of course. It's such a well-developed city. But she discovered that her hubby was an old impotent bastard who fortunately soon popped off and left her at the mercy of his sisters. She fled and begged refuge and my grandparents kept her ever since. She must be thirsty-sevenish now, but she looks younger. Perhaps that's 'cause she works all day long and hasn't had a chance to bear a kid so far."

"And you think you'd give her the chance?"

"What chance?"

"Of bearing a kid?"

"What crap! Of course not! Anyway she's hardly those matronly type. She's strong and has a booming voice."

"I see."

"Yeah."

A macabre lull for a while. Is there anything else to fall back on, she wondered. Wondered what he was pondering on.

"So have you written something lately?" She lets out, finally.

"Well, yeah. I had come in the morning to give you the scrap."

"You can give it to me now." She was patronizing.

"Yeah, just a moment."

He took out a page from the notebook lying on the table and gave it to her. She read it quietly, pausing during moments that promised hidden meanings, hinted at a past.

A Snap of Sometime

Sometime winks at me
Sod off
Damn you
Thou shall not
Getdefukkouttahere
Yet in secret sometime puts other things in my lap
Her camera-friendly eyes
The girls' wanderlust
A mouthful of sky
Corridors of the sky at Arts Block, MHC
Sometime has filled my dawns with zooms of haze
Opened the plaits of her dusks, spread it all over
Brushed the languid ageless arms of her bloom
Almost making love to me
Loving, yet not revealing that loving
Should I be mad about her?
Should I keep standing like an imbecile clinging on to her ghostwhite stole
As does a sentimental faggot?
Push me but I won't budge
Is it only she, who can love, can't I?
Looking like frail digits in years
She suits herself
I have never known those musty eyes, sonnet-like
At those lips, that chin, those hands and fingers

I have never cast a glance but to make a little point of overt dissidence
Afternoons, nights, even midnights have been dormant rebellions
Thinking whensoever, I can do to them, whatsoever I like
Make them stay up at nights
And store them in an album of indulgence
Towards this methinks, the less than thirty you
Glanced quite a many times, but didn't say a word
When I almost turned to thin air, then just
You sprang from your seat and fetched me a notice
That said romance of the manuscript was a thing of the past
But I had waited, in case you wrote something
Said nothing
Harked hard to hear the silence
Even then nothing
Why?
Shouldn't one love after the first doom?

******

"For her?" She asked finally.

"For you." He replied.

FOURTEEN

Tides

slashes, dots and other sporadic nonsenses
till your breath rises with the churning seas
and falls back, still restless, freezes
as if searching, through portholes
for an answer, anything, letters,
even that inadvertent "deus ex machina,"
i think i'll come suspended as it were ...
on the neoprene backing of a mercurial wire,
keeping company on long dark nights,
when luminous hugs of screens suffice for lights ..

Wetting her feet in the wanton sands wetted by the distended belly of the Arabian Sea, she was gazing into the unknown. There in the hungry pit lay capricious desires, unfulfilled or fructified, without a beginning or an end. She was reaching out for the endlessly proliferating darkness, and the ceaselessly multiplying depths of seas, that were paying their obeisance at her feet. There the inverted black lid of a sky sitting like a dome on a vast concavity, paying no heed to her solitary fears, giving no special reference to her witnessing the universal soul. She was drifting into soliloquies again, into the tortuous maze of words, into stillness and timelessness of her own making, an escape from ennui.

The surge, the splash, the retraction. The incessant cycle of being. The evaporation, condensation, precipitation. Circling heat of organism, circling matter and soul, cycling desire. Black deluge of the night, the crescent moon like the sly whorish id of a smirk.

She was here to be benumbed to submission, to feel comatose and insensate, to plunge in the warmish winter of the Western Ghat.

And standing at the extreme right end of Chaupatti, at midnight, she was filled with a chilling sensation of inconsequence. She felt small. She remembered the microbes he studied under high-resolution microscopes. They all mattered. There were scores of fat books dedicated to them. They caused countless physico-chemical reactions in the body, spliced enzymes, triggered bad hormones, upset the pH balance, raised or lowered the temperature. They were not insignificant. Both the infinitely great and the infinitely small had roles to play in the cosmic scheme. Only mediocres like her had to cope with irrelevance. And the entanglements of mediocrity, of storylessness created the chaos of nonsense, the undifferentiated body of haphazard moments leading up to a nothing. A ticking clock that didn't show the time, and hanging by the minute-hand the sad corpse of sensibility.

She turned from her monochromatic world of black to the tingling bells of the steamy stalls she had left far behind. She had strolled out alone for quite a bit now, and was beginning to feel the fatigue. The sheer physicality of the feeling baffled her. If there were mental coordinates contributing to the overall sensation, she couldn't feel much. All she knew was that her limbs wanted a respite. The journey needed a halt.

She sat down a little away from the waves, on the dry sand and began watching the tides come and go. The slowly heaving bosom of the sea beckoned her like a nursing mother spilling over the excess of her maternity. The foaming whites were the trickling milk from the taut nipples of the lactating breasts. What would it be like to have a pair of suckling lips at her breast? How did it feel to hold a miniature human being, to feel its saliva drenching her buds?

An experiment in disconnection. A trial of absurd futility of solipsism, a test of poetry without a listener. That age was long over; now every atom had links with the rest of the world. Every bit was accountable in the enormous circuit of information; every ion in the electrolyte solution was under observation. The roving eye of technology had impossibly digitized them, and she was a deviant unit in the electronic dustbins of space and time. Scrounging for self in the dumpyard of cognition, she cursed her myopia and threw senseless expletives at the matrix.

I'm not Ophelia nor was meant to be. Then why, why did I ever pretend to be what I was not? Why? A Redemption? Could I ever stoop so low as to seek a redemption? For whom? To redeem him? The big H? Prince Hamlet beating his much documented breast in my watery grave? I know I'll drown; when I'd drowned once I'll drown yet again. And he'll declare,

Your silly silent outcry Ophelia
Is a footnote to my epic disdain.

He'll mock me again, from his slant gaze he'll laugh at me, while kissing my dilapidated swollen corpse with the mouth that feigned madness.

My anti-self, my Ophelia. I owe you as much as I do to the womb that generated me. You are her, aren't you? But you've dried up, you've been shed. You're a dead womb, a closed wound. In the lowest depths, you and me will tinkle our bones to make watery music. We will leap from C-minor to teevra Ni, riding underwater currents; we will be the Solitaries mounting our destructive imagination.

Diabolic Ophelia, daughter of a rat
Under a gravestone forever spat.

You're a ride Ophelia, nothing but a take-off, a petulant Pegasus for the flighty me. I'm the rider, so beware. Though you would make me think otherwise. But I'm your dark-double, I'm in the light and you're wasted. I'm the shadow, though I'm the speaker and you're nothing but a mute chaser. I'm a bosom and you a flame. I'll drown you to douse you and let you be at peace in your nemesis.

******

When she woke up all groggy the next morning, she was in bed in room number 22 of MCI guest house, Colaba, South Mumbai. They had found her asleep on the sand after getting panicky about her vanishing act and conducted an elaborate rescue operation. She was suitably chided by Shoili who almost imagined her being swept away by a gushing wave, while Kanu tried pacifying the enraged elder sister. The couple Shikha and Pradeep had slipped out for a morning stroll by the sea. The group was here to attend the week long World Social Forum '04 and all except her could feel the general excitement in the air. And she was here on unpaid leave for the winter break was long over.

"Ayeee you must give yourself a break. It's high time you get out of your home and start looking around. Take stock of the world babes. Forget about that man for a while and start doing things for yourself. Get a grip dammit!"

A furious Shoiiii venting lava of transferred sentiments.

"C'mon, let him sod off to Boston or wheresoever he wants to sod off to. Just let him. You come with me to Bombay for the WSF and have fun for a while. There's lot like you, and you won't have problems gelling with our herd. We'll stay in a nice guest house and you can share my room. You'll refresh your memories of Bombay and will be helping us with the organizing. We'll cruise around the whole city like we did last time together and ride the local train. We'll run on the beach and lose a bit of weight. At nights we'll gulp in cans of beer and vodka and gain back the weight. We'll go to Elephanta island and I'll try hooking you up with a *phirang* so that you can kiss and tell the tale later. We'll light bonfire on the beach at two in the night and get smashed. Before that we'll shout slogans and march in all the rallies and wear ourselves out for dreamless sleeps. In a nutshell we'll have a gala time, so why don't you get your lazy butt moving and pack some summery clothes to enjoy the sultry Bombay winter?"

The sun was peeping in through the golden yellow curtained windows. They were slightly pulled apart and one of the panes opened. The rays formed a zigzagging parallelogram partly on the floor and partly on the big sofa by the wall. Kanu was stretched out on it, her elbows balanced on the cushiony sofa-arm, her eyes twinkling with a naughty good morning aimed at her. Her drowsy eyes tried best at responding back.

She moved her legs and let a bottle of Aquafina mineral water fall on the floor. Shoili galloped and reached for it before water could spill out. The tea was already there on the bed, the stainless steel tray showed signs of sprinkled sugar, Marie biscuits, breadcrumbs.

"We had already ordered." Shoili tried familiarizing her with the things around.

"Yeah, good. Is there some tea left?" She asked, gratefully.

"No we finished it off 'coz it was getting cold. Hang on, I'll call the room service."

Shoili got busy with the telephone while she staggered towards the bathroom. Her face was visibly puffed up, ostensibly it was more than a nine hour snooze. She splashed cold water on her face to let go the oiliness and wiped it dry. Brushed her teeth with Pepsodent and felt adequately freshened up.

Star News was covering a report on United Liberation Front of Asom and its willingness to go ahead with talks with the Indian Government. Mention of a certain Paresh Barua, their demand for sovereignty and reluctance to have an external mediator came to her ears as she came out of the bath and sat square-legged on the bed. To her great relief, the tea had already arrived.

"I wonder how many NGOs from the North-East they'd have at the forum. I was going through the stall registration site and I found quite a few." Kanu remarked, flipping the channels restlessly and settling on MTV for a while. A surge of high-pitched Hindi remix songs boomed out from the screen with a spectral display of colours. It was the A.R. Rehman–Andrew Lloyd Webber joint-venture Bombay Dreams played on the music channel. A hottie on the billboards.

"I'm not sure," Shoili answered, sipping a mango drink she had ordered for herself. "But it has surely a gargantuan turn out. They're saying that the youth camp is already teeming with folks from everywhere. That's good news for sure."

"Yeah, true." Kanu lighted a Wills Classic from the twenties' pack lying on the round centre-table with glass top.

"Pass me the packet." Shoili said, putting her emptied Mangola back on the tray. Missed the catch and spurted the f word out.

"Dude you never get the thing right." Kanu dropped a little gay smile and switched over to CNN. Christina Amanpour on the war and captured Hussein, yet again.

"This is one woman I admire for her guts but wonder at her affiliations." Kanu gagged on the cigarette and together they made a smoke-joint of the room.

"She's a damn popular face you know. Quite like our Barkha Dutt. Heh, it's almost the other way round." Shoili was fast on her way to light the second fag, and regarded her sister briefly as if to say you damned teetotaler.

"...a day before Christmas, three American soldiers were killed in the town of Samarra, a hotbed of the resistance. The Americans have decreed that no pro-Saddam demonstrations will be allowed, even if they are peaceful. Immediately after Saddam's pictures were shown on television, there were bombings in the Husseiniya and Amariya districts of Baghdad, killing six people. A suicide bomber attacked a police station in Khaldiya, around 100 km north of Baghdad, killing 17 people, many of them policemen. Saddam's supporters were angry after a newspaper owned by Ahmad Chalabi published a picture of a dishevelled Saddam talking to a nattily dressed Chalabi in a prison cell…" Amanpour poured on.

"You think the forum can pose challenges of strategy and tactics to the goddamned circus going on in the name of war? They are saying it's nothing but a talk n fuck show, with too many slogan-mongerers gathered for a political dumb-charade." Kanu arched back, looking up at the ceiling, exhaling nebulous rings of smoke, twiddling her big toes together.

"Let's see how much of free speech is allowed in the name of socialism." Shoili said.

"Am sure bandwagoning for political advocacy will have a field's day."

"Like these geeks from World Bank and other pro-LPGs were ranting that it's not growing in influence, albeit the size was unprecedented. Heh, poor unwanted guests."

"But it does portray an image of no discrimination. I just hope it's not all rhetoric and no action."

"You know it's like this long tiff the theoreticians and grassroots activists have been having over line of action. Both say the other is useless and parasitic on the other."

"I wonder how it's going to be at the youth camp. Shall we stay there for a coupla days?"

"We might. But as a warning must tell you that a luxurious bath, a comfortable mattress, beer cans and AC are but some of the endless things you aren't gonna get there! So think again!"

"Heh, you little hypocrite. But I can always find a sexy Mexican in the next camp, or a bunch of French bombshell-groupies high on marijuana. What about you Ivy, you too don't wanna stay a night there, like your sis?"

She was almost jolted out of her wits at the question thrown at her. For a while she wondered what exactly the words meant, then speculated what the expected answer ought to be. Finally she let out vaguely, "I dunno. This room is fine. Whatever you guys say."

"Listen to this," Shoili, squinting at a column on the opinion page of an English daily, started reading out. "The principal vice of the WSF in the perception of the MR 2004 is its alleged captivity to the NGO bureaucracies. 'NGOization' as a pejorative has been tossed about a great deal in recent debates on the relevance of the WSF. Allegations that the forum is becoming the fief of a small coterie of powerful non-governmental organizations (NGOs) that dispose off massive budgets, are in part because they are disbursement channels for official development assistance from the industrialized world. An alternate forum was announced last November, explicitly crafted to be all that the WSF failed to be. Under the banner of 'Mumbai Resistance' (MR 2004), this coalition of some 250 organizations seeks to go 'beyond the limits of WSF' and forge an 'organized resistance' that is continuous with the 'militant traditions of the recent anti-globalization and anti-war movements'. Mumbai Resistance, according to its website (www.mumbairesistance.org) , opposes its quest for 'a concretely defined alternative socio-economic structure' to the 'amorphous' slogan of the WSF, that 'another world is possible'. Building on a 'basis of self-reliance', the programme, it claims, would move 'towards a genuine socialist order.'"

Kanu breathed out deeply, "I just hope they don't bash us up for putting up a stall there. But know what, I'm excited about where Madam Arundhati is gonna be. Here or there!"

"Politics is good sport for her; she's one of the smartest of the lot, 'em commentators."

"Hey, she bats just as well. The Narmada has got every *nar* and *mada* in the valley swooning for respite from her onslaughts. Wish there had been a few more like her."

They laughed a hearty one and became quiet. She felt lost again.

"When are these guys gonna come back? I thought we would look around the city today." Kanu looked out from the window for a godsend answer.

MTV was spoofing high art on their show *Fully Faltoo*. This time it was Mona Lisa Gets Funky. The Lady Gioconda lashing her tongue out, pulling her own cheeks to almost a meter on each side, flapping her suddenly elephantine ears, serenading Da Vinci on the rocks, exposing herself to a high voltage shock and sporting the hedgehog hairdo, and finally doing a flashing her 32 at once toothy thank you for not changing the channel act.

******

They took a cab to the Gateway of India and reached there within 10 minutes. Scores of shops, latest models of sedans, and human beings with modern bodies breezed past them like a sequence in a dream. She felt like a Peter Pan in search of Neverland. There were humongous banners of the latest Hindi flicks, with Shahrukh Khan's massive face painted on every second board. Banners of the Hollywood production *Love Actually* had hit the halls which was doing pretty well. Hugh Grant too was granted an audience amongst the Bombaywallahs. The city was different. For one, the sea made the difference. That was enough in itself. A redeemer Delhi would give anything for.

They were feeling hot inside the taxi. The three of them had ventured out; the couple never bothered to return on time. Shoili wagged her tongue like a clairvoyant Cassandra, "Don't worry, we'd catch 'em snuggled close in the backseat of the hall, watching Hugh in action, and following it up themselves."

She was sandwiched between the duo. Her sister and her sister's lover.

"Mumbai has improved since you visited last time, eh Ivy?" A concerned Kanu wanted to make her speak desperately.

"Err, well, I guess so. The last time we were in a different place, I think not far off from here. It was the MTNL guest house." She said lamely.

"Yeah, it's pretty close by. You can take a peek again in case you get nostalgic about the MTNL loos." Kanu in a light mood, trying to make it still fluffier, cottonier for her. It's just a smooth glide to the Gateway, she seemed to say. Then we'd glide over the sea, she seemed to say.

Shoili staring out from the window and swallowing Bombay in. Shoili pressing her snub-nose onto the tinted pane and spotting Mercs. Indulgent Shoili lost in herself humming along with Kishore Kumar on Radio Mirchi, "*Yeh Bombay sheher haadson ka sheher hai, yehan zindagi haadson ka safar hai…*"

She, too, was meandering into a world of her own. The signboards everywhere screamed out a 'Mumbai' at her, while she painstakingly held on to the older, comfortable Bombay still. Were there explanations beyond a stubborn egotism? The harbingers of criticisms would label her variously: un-decolonized, essentialist, pseudo-elitist, still harping on the ex-masters. What she couldn't explain was the strange emotional bond she had with the names Bombay and Calcutta; her nascent consciousness had always known them so, spotted them on political maps of India during geography tests. Why the two-mindedness? Why always a double bind, manifesting paradoxically in taller buildings but shorter tempers, wider freeways, but narrower viewpoints. We spend more, but have less, we buy more, but enjoy less. Where were the happy families lost in bigger houses, precious little time for a song in the heaps of more and more electronic beats and remixed jarring noise of the times? She wondered if more degrees meant less sense, more knowledge and information meant less of wisdom and judgment, more experts and specialists led up to more specific problems, more medicine and drugs ensured less wellbeing. Their likes were drinking too much, smoking too much, becoming gallant spendthrifts but silencing the innocent clowns within, rash-driving and living on the fast lane, losing wits at nothing, getting angry at nothing, staying up too late, waking up too tired, televisioning like thoughtless morons, and praying to monsters for gods. There were endless possessions and properties to take care of, but less than a cynic's value to bother about. Talking too loud for effect or clarity, loving as often as peeing and hardly ever managing to love at all, hating whatever was out of reach, whatever meant a self-deterioration. Making a living was easy, but not a life. Adding years to life and not life to years. Everyone seemed to have been all the way to the moon and back, but have trouble crossing the street to meet a new neighbour. The spiritual healers were railing at space-scientists: But what about the freaking inner space? What's that now? Bigger things, but not better things. Conquered the atom, but not prejudice. Writing more, learning less. Planning more, achieving less. Having learned to rush, but not to wait. Building more computers to hold more information, yet where's communication in this age of digital reproduction. These are the times of fast foods and slow digestion, big names and small character, steep profits and shallow relationships.

These are the days of two incomes but more divorce, fancier houses but broken homes. These are days of quick trips, disposable diapers, throwaway morality, one-night stands, overweight bodies, and pills that do everything from cheer, to quiet, to kill.

******

The torrential Arabian at the Gateway made her come back to terra firma. The entire Bombay had come down to the Ghats, there were too many people for her comfort. Too close for her not to feel claustrophobic, as if trapped in a shut room, something she had been doing almost all her life. There were hawkers on the pavements selling hot tea, milky coffee, *mitha paans*, Mother Dairy ice-cream, Kwality Walls ice-cream, candy floss, fancy *golas*, and quite a few *panipuri*-wallas selling yummy fried dough balls dripping with chili-tamarind juice. At a slightly secluded corner, they stood at the edge of the brick railing and looked down, into the splashing waves of the enormous watery grave, promising eternal suction.

The steamer-ride to the Elephanta Caves was an hour-long journey, one-way. However, the tickets for the next ride were all sold out. They purchased the single-decker ferry coupons for 80 bucks each. They still had three hours to kill until two-thirty in the afternoon. They decided to see the Prince of Wales Museum first, followed by a brief visit to Jehangir Art Gallery and wrapping it up by a quickie at the McDonalds.

Shoili picked up a tiny brochure from a street-seller headed Mumbai Tourist Attractions. It read:

Welcum to Mumbai, a gret place of histrical intrest.

ART AND MUSEUMS: Shhatrapathi Shivaji Mahar (Prince of Wales Museum)

Tip rating: *****

After visiting Elephenta caves & Gateway of India, its just 5 min walking distance, you can see Chhatrapathi Shivaji Maharaj Vastu Sangrahalaya", *aha one more name change*; *they changed the name recently from Prince of Wales Museum to this long one*. The bilding itself old Victorian Gothic style bilding,supposed to be gr8 front view, but it has beautiful garden, and tall trees hiding the building from outiside. So my font view pic ,you can see only trees hahahaha Pic i kept at travalogue. During World war I,the bilding was used as hospital between 1904-1914. I never realise that,the Museum visit will be Enjoyable.:). As I had been there when i was in school,I really forget how it looks. They renovated recentely part of front wing,so it looks like morden interior.Good lighting arrangement too.The entrance of the bilding,you can get Audio guide,in English,Spanish,other few languages. If you like to have glance,before entering ,buy booklet of Museum, at Museum shop. Its not free,Rs10. Ground floor has ,Terricota figures collection(Karnataka state),Indian sculptur,and natural history. First floor, huge collection of miniature painting,from 15th to 16 century.They have Napal&Tibet section.Can see beautiful lamps from Napal.I took few pic of Museum,just have a look at my travaloge pic,to see what am talking:)) I really liked Museum visit,and photography is allowed,without flash.For using camara, you have to get the admisson ticket Rs 30 extra. I suggest whoever visit Bombay ,This place is must must see place :)). Timing:10.15am-6pm Admission fees Rs10, Foreigners Rs300. Monday closed.

Turning the page didn't make much of a difference.

ART AND MUSEUMS: The Jehangir Art Gallery(1952)

Tip Rating: *****

This pic is photgraph displayd at The Jehangir Art Gallery,Gallery is near to Museum bilding.End of the road corner building.Before leaving to Mumbai i read in magazine,Mr Uddav Thackery, going to exhibit his photo collection of Maharashtra FORTS,more than 28 forts,its all Ariel view photos. Awwwww i can't imagin,our India has beautiful old forts!!So beautiful&amaging:)). Really it was good collection ,I really enjoied my visit there.One thing I noticed, its free admisson,when i went inside there was not much crowed,but when i comeout later,people were stading in queu for entering the gallery .But onething Mumbai ppl are very nice,they wait in queue in bus stop,or anyhwere,they follow the rules.heheehehh cant say same thing to Delhi,so u can imagin my surprise of ppl standing in queue:)). The pic here you can see example of photos,its Kolaba fort,near Alibagh,Mumbai. This gallery other halls,they gave rent to artish for low rates to brief periods. It is managed by Bombay Art Society.Inside they have one coffee shop, i dintgoinside.

Address: M.G.Road,Mumbai-400023

Directions: Near Wales Museum .

"What the efff is this?" Shoili was aghast.

"A computer print out. Must be from one of those personal message boards. At one rupee per page on Xerox and five rupees for the leaflet this guy is surely making some money." Kanu was cool enough.

"Whoa! I'm gonna sue the jerk." Shoili crumpled the paper into a little ball and threw it into the incessant traffic of M.G. Road. It landed under the wheels of a deep blue Tata Indica and found its way finally into a streetside drain.

"Damn, you shouldn't have done that. Why did you throw that marvellous evidence of syntactical evolution into a dirty drain of South Mumbai?" Kanu almost on the verge of tears. Shoili on the verge of plucking the chap's eyeballs out.

They had Chicken Burgers and French fries at McDonalds. Gulped down quite a few cans of Coke and finally sweet-dished on the cheapest stuff on the menu: the Mc Ice-Cream cone worth seven rupees. Halted for a few minutes to glance around the surfeit of cheap clothes and junk jewellery sold at the Fashion Street, right outside McDonalds. The glitzy smalltime street-malls allured them with fake denims on sale at unbelievable rates, garish make-up sets made them go nuts and try out the starkest red lipstick on the inner side of their wrists; they lost their sense of time amid the ornamented vermilion holders, the colourful bangles, bracelets, silver earrings, enormous plastic and black metal loops and rings, the beaded necklaces decked with semi-precious stones, the tinkling trinkets, the dangling charms, talismans with inscriptions in Urdu or Sanskrit, the pendants with faces of Hindu deities, anklets and silver toe-rings to embellish painted feet. Caught a few sly vendors cozening the *phirangs*, and gave them knowing winks of fellowship.

******

"Omigosh! Dan! Dan Benedict! What the hell you're doing here?"

Kanupriya Sehgal at her shell-shocked best, suddenly out of the blue.

She was trying to balance her steps so as not to tumble into the muddy depths of the Arabian while boarding the steamer to the

Elephanta Island. She glanced up to see a strikingly handsome white man grinning back at Kanu indicating a past acquaintance.

"Khanou, hey girl! I knew I would catch you one of these days." The grin had widened by now.

"Wait a minute! The forum?" Kanu emphatic, jumped into the boat with the ease of a nimble-pawed cat. The two of them followed.

"Yeah, what else?" He helped them find seats.

"Damn you man! Why didn't you gimme a call before?"

"Hey girl I tried your number. A sexy voice said it was out of service now."

"Oh, okay you had my old number still. Alright, meet my partner Shoili Sengupta, and her sister Ivy. Girls, this is Dan Benedict, I know him since my Leeds days. He was the sexy senior the girls used to drool on and used to envy me, coz Dan was all pally with me trying to quote straighten unquote me out! And once both of us had hots for the same girl, damn remember Bianca Shepherd?"

Same old long-time-no-see crap. She felt mildly distressed. Moved away and sat in the extreme corner which had the red tube tiers dangling from the painted rods above.

Next to her a middle-aged, dark lady in a peach coloured saree. South Indian but she couldn't tell which zone exactly. She never could.

Another Bengali family on board. Chatterings in bong. *Okhane jash na, chup kore bosh, ekta chaati khabi lafalafi korle*. Don't go there, sit quietly, will get a slap if you jump around.

Otherwise, different inflections of the national language. *Hum Hindustani*. Occasionally some English, mostly fragments, tidbits interspersed between imperfect potpourri of Marathi, Mumbaiya Hindi.

The steamer was moving, cutting across the belly of the sea like a hungry shark. She was the observer once again. They were sharing a Leeds-time anecdote probably. Why the hysterical mouth-twistings equally executed by that Dan and Kanu? Her sister seemed a bit reticent. Formally yours.

It's bloody too deep to jump. Fancy a water-grave. Where's the copy of Don Juan by the way. Death by water. In the wasteland.

The huge grey sea lashing its tongue at the boat's gush. A thousand fangs before I foam, a 100 leaps before I drown.

The receding Bombay skyline. Obscure patterns in the sky. What's that called, *nimbus*?

A line of legs. In pairs. Covered in sarees legs, exposed below the skirts legs, thin-flanked legs, strong-kneed legs, fat-calved legs, white in grey trousers legs, waxed smooth honey-complexioned legs of Kanupriya Sehgal, exposed from below her knees where her khaki capri-pants end.

A chorus of swaying legs. A nymph dance of a sort.

Snaps beside the lion at the Caves. All four blessed by Shiva.

"What exactly does the Shivalinga represent?" *Phirang's* scavenging on the tropes of Indologist act.

"The male virility. The prowess."

"I see."

"Say it. Just the penis." Goodbye metaphors.

Snaps beside the canon, under Shiva-Parvati, the unidentified deity, the pillars, the big-boobed rocky virgin, the monkeys.

"Come with us to the guest house. We'll book you a room" Kanu to a tired Dan back at the Gateways. "Can't believe the ride's over!"

"Yeah, it was fascinating. I loved the big horned cows near those potters' shops. And no, I can't stay at the guest house. Thanks, but I seriously want to be at the Youth camp."

"Man you're obsessed with your youth."

"Heh, guess I am. Another world is possible and it's an all-young world. No oldies allowed."

"Whoa! Discriminating at the very base?"

"Selectively, yeah!"

******

Faces. By the day, endless faces. Days in room 22 were January delights. A small foot-long in height fridge to store the vodkas and Mangolas. Gorging on MTV, 70s Prem Chopra-Jeetendra flicks at 12 noon while the lovers were away putting up the stall and expanding contacts, selling pamphlets. Sensitization. Women need more working space. Employment for rural women. Safe sex in the interiors. Workshops to create AIDS awareness amongst village women. Area of work—remote regions of south-eastern Maharashtra, central parts of M.P. near Bhopal. No not the gas-victims. Greenpeace taking care of them. Other women. And men too, but of course. Awareness for all and sundry. Even educated folks. Click. Here by the poster. Click. By Mr. Toby Temple, Director of Women's Call, from New Jersey. Oh glad to meet you sir. Click. One more. Click. Thanks a lot! Have a nice day looking around Sir. Heh, yeah it's an ocean of people. From all over the world, yes. Very true. Indian food, yeah Maharashtrian food Sir. Toby, call you simply Toby? Sounds great! Sure, she'll escort you to the food stalls. Bon appetite Toby.

The bathroom was teeming with balloons as big as side-pillows filled with water. On closer inspection, Shoili discovered they were originally the condoms their group was distributing for free.

One of the days, they drove to Marine Drive and kept sitting there till midnight.

At the Hukka Bar. At Mocha. Kanupriya Sehgal looking like a tall Egyptian queen seated on a burnished throne, and high on Smokey India.

Shoili showing the middle-finger while posing for a snap.

Pillow snatching at nights. After the nth vodka and slight vomiting. Shoili's love-handles pinched by an excited knickerless Kanu. Her strawberry bra all too conspicuous under the thin white negligee.

An apologetic Shoili all too embarrassed at her rocking love-life.

******

She contributed an article to the Mainstream within a week of her coming back.

World Social Forum '04:

A Theatre of Hope in Diversity

Another World is Possible.

And did you notice that she was bluffing all through? Not the facts moron, she faked the orgasm itself.

FIFTEEN

Track

mononucleosis.

the kissing disease.

the curse of Valentine. the fall out of the scorn.

I don't remember which one, however. which of the curse-hurlers is responsible for the burning body and splitting forehead. it's difficult to figure out.

who had the infected mouth .. but I can't afford questions

I'm not into punctuated remarks .. I know there's hardly any scope for punctuation when the epstein-barr virus is doing havoc in my tortured cells .. I can't get up .. I'm waiting for maa to help me with the potty .. oh she'll merely accompany me to the loo .. that's all .. nothing more .. I'll beat the shit outta my system myself.. I'll try to at least

Who was it I wonder .. mini mouse or the fat-arsed nurse I've forgotten what the fuck she's called now .. who cares .. she won't come and make me move my butt now.

minnie mouse my grimy li'l wifey who's all too happy to have me not at home .. now she can have her x-s and y-s with pleasure at leisure .. without my ghost hovering on the ceiling or perched on the window grill .. no wonder she hasn't messaged .. I don't blame her .. I would have erased them then and there had she dared

maa hurry up .. my bladder is full .. I told you it's potty to denote the urgency .. why can't you hasten things up a li'l .. your babla will get a li'l late for his school .. goodness maa he's only four .. how much would that matter .. perhaps he would get the hang of the letter C a trifle later than his peers .. C for cock and he's already learnt that and in case he hasn't he's gonna grow up to become a dumbfuck just like his kaku who kissed lips and arses of nuns and witches without discriminating and is suffering the consequences now .. tell him nuns don't often have clean disinfected lips .. ask him to wash the lips and arses with dettol or savlon before embarking on any goddamned project .. tell him that maa .. don't forget .. infections are crazy .. tell him that .. contagions make you feel like a rat .. no you're back to the *Blatta* .. you're back to the drain .. no matter how much you tried climbing out you're BACK TO THE DRAIN

maa I'm waiting ..

hurry up .. she's supposed to come and meet me .. she called up and talked to you respectfully didn't she .. all the respect one can have for a non-english speaking aging granny .. that's you maa .. did Richa hurt you maa .. coz she spoke in English first .. coz she asked for me in English after reading the voicemail I sent her on her cell phone finding it switched off for whatsoever reason I don't care contemplating on .. you had to answer back in English and you couldn't do that .. reason why boudi gets irked with you .. reason why babla yells get out of my way granny or you're so weird granny and you kiss him on his cheeks in return .. boudi in her tight capris and spaghetti top screams at babla in Boston benglish bob leave granny alone don't bug her porte bosho .. granny's happy bouma wants the child to porte bosho .. bouma screams from the kitchen putting the glass bowl of a Mexican i-dunno-what into the microwave bobby I can't hear you reading you li'l urchin wait I'm gonna report everything to daddy and no cartoon network tonight .. bobby sets the volume up .. granny wonders .. granny receives the phone .. it's a girl asking for her younger son who's come to visit her for the first time after his wedding .. shuntu as she calls him has taken ill almost as soon as he hit the Boston airport .. something's in the air .. she doesn't quite make out .. she can't comprehend .. senses are failing her .. babla could have compensated but bouma doesn't let him speak much in baangla .. she has to help him clean himself up .. they took him to the doctor day before .. some mononukis he said .. they didn't tell her anything else .. she and babla haven't been informed .. they belong to the same category .. just that they grudge in different languages .. the girl's asking again .. she can understand the word shumonto .. she says in the hindi that she learnt in Benares .. woh to bimar hai .. bouma is devastated .. what the hell is she blabbering away now .. amay phone ta din maa .. snatches the cordless from maa .. yeah .. oh Dr. Roy has taken ill but hold on I'll just hand over the cordless to him .. wait a jiffy .. maa's bewildered .. bouma to maa in hushed tone

.. what if she wasn't Indian maa .. but bouma it's mostly yours and runtu's Indian friends who call up and they know me by now ..

my bladder is full .. it's Richa on phone

-- Good Morning. I heard you're ill.

Yeah struck down by mononucleosis. Picked it up some two months back. Now it has surfaced.

-- Oh that's awful!

YEAH

-- I'm so sorry to hear that!

YEAH

-- Are you feeling alright now?

NOPE

--I can understand.

HMM.

-- Then I'm afraid we can't meet up. Unless I fly to Boston which I might.

HMM

--Well I'm in Chicago now. Might be coming next week. Not sure yet.

Take my address from my sister-in-law. It's difficult to talk. Let me know in case you come here. Bye.

-- Er, sure. Bye and get well soon. Take care.

maa comes in finally .. eto deri .. so late .. shuntu ke chhilo baba .. who was it dear .. a person I'm supposed to meet .. she gives me some dried plums to eat .. good nutrition she says .. Sunsweet Dried Plums better than the other fruits .. package nutrition .. the smart snack .. naturally very low in sugar and fat cholesterol-free .. beta carotene precursor to vitamin A .. essential for vision, growth, reproduction and a healthy immune system .. dietary fiber potassium to normalize the soaring blood pressure and improve muscle contraction .. pitted California dried plums inside .. refrigerate after opening .. store in a cold place .. store in a cold place .. store in a cold place ..

boudi's suitcases could possibly be cold too .. as cold as her .. when she takes cans of plums, tang, cashews, peanuts, shampoos, soaps, perfumes to flaunt at her ballygunge place baaper bari in Calcutta they don't always get sour .. boudi sports the jamdani or baluchori then during the pujas of course .. that too during alternate years .. to take a break from AadiBoston Shaarbojonin Durga Puja Samiti

.. so every two years 452/R ballygunge place sees Flex shampoos, Camay International soaps, Revlon International [not the cheap made in India ones] lipsticks on the racks .. then boudi remembers her shantiniketan days and her double BA in music and geography and sings the fashionable cassettized CD-ised robindrosongeets to make her clan happy .. in return they let babla play in the huge teak bed with the sandalwood paste and doi on his forehead to ward off dangers of falling down on the red tiled floor and colouring it redder by a generous offering of infant blood.

I never tried copying others' games .. but Irene Scott is not going to leave me alone .. those mails must have carried her digitized saliva .. something like an electronic version of it .. mononucleosis.jpg .. scan and see and suffer .. fever fatigue sore throat enlarged tonsils swollen lymph nodes in the neck swollen spleen enlarged liver rashes headaches .. torn in the USA

the telecast goes on .. FOX NEWS .. family killed in Dallas shooting .. sergeant Frederickson in charge of investigation .. 15 minutes on history of shooting .. five minutes on America's gun-culture [leave out Detroit] .. two minutes on the right to bear arms .. one and half on the profile of National Rifles Association .. four minutes on politics and gun control .. half an hour on the sons of guns who gunned them down ..

[I'm watching the TV carefully .. flipping channels at times .. the remote in my hands .. the volume is set at low .. babla aka bob needn't be woken up from his afternoon siesta .. what's minnie mouse doing now .. she's watching NDTV Night Out if she's with her firebrand sister or a silly chickflick on HBO India if she's alone]

dada will be coming back late .. the polymer physicist at Boston Petrochem Inc. has little time for the yodellings of his wife or son .. I idolize him in more ways than one .. Sondeep Roy likes having vodka with lime however .. to beat the Boston bite .. I need to ask him if he could talk to head of department of microbiology at JHU today .. they know each other .. I doubt if he had the time though ..

I'm waiting for his black Chevrolet Optra to park in the garage of their pretty bungalow in this green suburb .. he cares for the car as much as he does for maa .. a garage outside and a garage inside .. for parking .. to shelter during troublesome nights of snowfalls ..

more of FOX NEWS .. America's elite academy under clutches of religious intolerance .. sexual abuse scandal .. coffee-cookies supper stuff .. 108 people given him examples of abuse. Only eight of them were Jewish .. the rest were Catholics, Baptist, Lutheran, Episcopal, Presbyterian, Methodist ..

I think I'm sleepy ..

Gun son church lurch health stealth meter Peter chant rant bomb aplomb prick stick lick click bush push benedict convict potter butter WTC ecstasy madness sadness resuscitate enervate gyrate pirate suicide homicide squad ward nauseous precious tanks ranks oil spoil land grand feticide aside beside deride joyride

shuntu phone

maa's deep voice from the dining room .. she's cleaning the refrigerator with soap water and scotchbrite ..

-- Dr. Roy

yeah

-- Richa this side

yeah Richa temme

-- I don't think I can make it to Boston next week .. I called up my office and they said a strict no .. I've to get back to Dallas ASAP .. I'm sorry

that's alright .. thanks for calling ..

--I have hardly anything else to say about Irene, Dr Roy. There's nothing new. You know about the pain she underwent. But that's history now. I spoke to her father in Wicklow a few days back. I don't think he wants you to visit her uncles in Dallas. I don't think he likes the idea.

hmm

-- Dr. Roy I can't do much about it I don't really think I can.

hmm yeah

-- I tried though.

I know you did

--Yeah. I hope you understand. Am sorry the American air didn't suit your health.

no need to be sorry.. it's nothing to do with America .. I picked it up in Delhi .. I kissed an infected mouth .. that's all

--Well, unfortunate nevertheless

yeah that's true

-- Get well soon!

could you please tell me to get the hell out of here soon, instead, Miss Arora?

-- Er, goodbye Dr. Roy. May be I'd call again from Dallas. Take care.

you too. . thanks

I'm still waiting for dada to return .. it's a rough night .. boudi's on phone .. ballygunge on the other side .. babla is watching Mowgli on cartoon network .. not with me of course .. I'm in the guest room watching the After Dark Friday series .. this room stinks of dettol so babla has been ordered to keep distance by his parents .. I don't know where maa is .. I don't want to know .. she makes me sulk inside .. minnie mouse must be squeaking before her batch of mice .. let her .. she makes me feel like hulk hogan .. I feel like putting her in a mousetrap and watch her day and night .. under observation .. pinkplumpkin is somersaulting in her grave .. or having casual sex with fellow Catholic skeletons .. something like that .. I don't care much .. I never did .. she never did .. she never does .. it's a rough night .. am not gonna tell anyone how rough the night is .. an unabridged rough night

maa please get me the laptop I need to check my mails

Ash enters Kolkata Online

Buddy Ophelia is offline

it's a rough night ..

SIXTEEN

Ride

The twin wheels of the Atlas Goldline were gyrating with his Sony automatic CD Man, almost beat to beat. Cycling on the wet lanes of campus was something he had cherished ever since he came to Delhi. There was something about the early February air, still a bit chilly, though the nippy days were over. Almost three weeks since the college had started after the winter breaks. Almost five weeks since he had last been with her, there in his tiny hostel room.

There brother, draw the line, draw the line. His moving knees touched the metallic front rod of the antediluvian tandem and fell into an alien shiver. Cover yourself well, told you.

The Atlas Goldline. A father's legacy to a son. And the carrier at the back still had the fragrance of his mother mingled with the smell of rot iron. And yes, stains of sticky sweat that trickled down her fretting back, that biconcave lens of a back he had set his primitive eyes on; his Black Venus. His Pentax had come alive then, and that falling drop frozen forever on the rolling Kodak reels.

No more of those mellifluous menacing western disturbances, those innocuous winter drizzles to dampen the streets. Just the long winding garden pipe with water overflowing into the asphalt tracks. Hazardous for reckless cyclists.

A two-horned emaciated bison in the name of a vehicle. Good for an on-campus excursion, all by himself, and his Pentax 4870.

The ridge was of course there, but cycling was not allowed within its premises. A tree-shaded patch of green occupying quite a few square miles. The snake-lake and the bloody lake. *Khuni Jheel.* The dibbling ducks. The marauding monkeys. The loafing dogs.

Reflecting watery streets, an alternate mirror for the sleepy little island of a place. A little hermitage now, safe from the deafening sounds of the madly honking traffic. Sporadically cars rushing past with Save the Black Buck painted on its rear. Generally it's Rocky Loves All or Jai Mata Di.

The time students faced their tests head on. Not even two months to go. Mugging up almanacs to crack the expected riddles. Hardly a crosschecking ever. MPD Guides *zindabaad*. And Graduation Made Easy: Champion rapid readers to breeze you through the ordeal of examinations.

> Mapping the city on human frames
> its caressing, copulating domes and shafts, its mating pillars and vaults
> we print on its backyard, bricklane barbwired bitch
> awaiting her territorial cur,
> pass that blackhorned bull and his variegated she poised in hormonal harmony.
> Discover lyrical magic lying idle in the dirt
> and in certain dewsoaked woodland walks,
> while coupling words and pauses entwine with subsequent blackforest spells,
> and hold a charming eternity in numb palms.
> At times on gilded afternoons
> I smell soft sunlight on sunlit you, dreamily catching your photons here and there
> beneath shivering peepal leaves, collecting camelfoot under veiled skies
> at times admiring poppies, at times pink roses,
> wondering where were the pollens dropped.
> Afterwards, at the cafeteria, I try listening to A Sensitive Plant
> and Shelley's dramatic intensifier plays havoc with our filtercoffee fumes
> as you point out the rivulets of invisible Styx flowing down our touching knees
> engrossed in their secret rendezvous
> usurping us.

Where was she?

He had caught her scrubbing the floor once in that crumbling Jamshedpur house. The solitary Eve was gazing at her winking shadow on the soap water in the bucket. On all fours, a bit of a lethal black bitch in heat. Her buttocks arched up, big toes pressed together. Tinkling toe-rings making music for the eager ears.

Not a blank slate there. And his chalks weren't white. They were brown. Did they write well on the inky body just carved out from blackest clay? An early dusk there, but the outlines of twilight had impossible scripts in store. Play well.

In that murky matchbox of an attic, there was hardly any space to lie down. She had to clean up the years of dust to get a decent breather. She almost sprained her bare ankles as she tripped on the broken leg of the discarded chair. Household debris. The remainders of a family that's chucked out from the archives. Dumped in the seedy alleys for slow death in time.

There were cats, rats, mice, pigeons, sparrows, crows, cuckoos, roaches, bugs and numerous other co-habitants sharing the attic. Scrounging for a space of its own. A history of mating games.

melanie,
here, forever in the dark, in the bathing blue light
here in the lightlessness, in the soft blue time
here under a suckled sky, here in the dark
come to me you insinuating black mist
and color my senses green

beside a darkling thrush, slithering hands
snakelimbed interdigitation
rebuking coordinates of cartesian schemes
here's the amorphous, delight in itself
here's a coveted hallucination
delusion cherished

foaming release in the body of black
dotting whites, doting dashes
long dead gods resurrected in the pause
like a sudden meaning

A stunted David Lurie there. An aging Melanie. Ripe for disgrace.

Women; a sincere request! START RAPING MEN!

It's the most underrepresented activity isn't it, and every man ought to be raped once for the innumerable mental rapes each of them has shrugged off his shoulders.

Gay man raping gay man: still a man raping!

Lesbian fem raping another: still a woman getting raped!

Reverse the equation! *But why blindly emulate us*?

You don't quite know what rape is all about, do you? A pathetic "The Rape Must Go On" under your breath after watching Bunuel's

The Exterminating Angel wouldn't suffice. It's more than an aesthetic plea, to capture the male howls on a sound recorder. The raging desire to put the male before the hungry caverns of the fanged feminine and document the sighs, the groans, the fierce cries of mutilation.

Ghettoized with the bugs and chumps, ghoulish cats, giant red ants. Tough calls for a naked body, indistinguishable from the ebony cloak of sultry summer nights. Wrap the white around to make the curves stand out. Click.

Now put the tulip on the navel. Click. Night flash.

******

She watched him as he entered through the main gates of the college. She was on her way back. Back home. Or whatever it's called. He was riding an old black bicycle, the one that's still common in dingy lanes of West and East Delhi.

He hadn't yet noticed her. There in the front-casket his camera holder tucked safely in. Rephrase, his eyes tucked safely in.

He honked once. A small boy in winter rags moved away from the centre of the gate. Son of a daily labourer working on the construction site. Photogenic with the watery nose and dusty bare feet. Special feature: eating a brittle cake of mud dug out from the cement heap.

He saw her walking towards him. He waved at her, exclaimed a mild surprise, corrected himself: he was seeing her walking towards the gate, and not towards him.

"Long time!" He was the first to speak.

"Yeah, I was away for a while. Had gone to Bombay." Matter-of-factly.

"I know that."

"Really?"

"Yeah, had gone inquiring about the club meets. Tried having one even. But a sad turn up. So wound up in an hour."

"Okay. Never mind. At least you tried."

"I did. Anyway."

"Written anything new since then?"

"Idle scraps. Nothing substantial."

"Hmm. Yeah don't force yourself unnecessarily. But be alert. You never know when a line hits you."

"Yeah. You're leaving?"

"I am in fact."

"In a hurry?"

"Not really. Why?"

"Would have liked to talk a bit."

"Okay. Let's go to D-School."

"Great. Be back in a jiffy. Will put the cycle in the shade."

They were walking the university lane on that calm February afternoon trying to see the mythical, the magical, the transformative in its familiar terrains. That green-painted irongate at the entry, the little haven of the word-soaked bibliophiles to vent out the magma within. Vestiges of the monumental city, its essence filtered out to sparkle from the wayside stalls, with the sprawling Kamla Nagar market just a rickshaw-ride away. Fragment of a city, a tiny piece of the urban pie, the hub of its ineffectual angels.

There was the old thick-rimmed bespectacled man selling the cane baskets he'd made himself. The fellow was such a story-teller. An erstwhile *satyagrahi*, ardent believer in the talisman of Mahatma Gandhi. Still sporting the Nehruvian white cap. Angry at the fast changing city, clenching his non-existent teeth at the gritty, hopeless, beleaguered metropolis so impressive though a garish resplendent debauchee at times.

Capitalizing on their circling walks and D-School special filter coffee, they drew the contours of the dipping hour. Amused by each other, amused at the thoughtful perambulation, amused at discovering a co-wanderer in the Neverland. Amused at the wicked silence perching on the invisible tendrils that crept out from their parted limbs. Sallying forth on a jaunt accosting the known unknowns, those everyday faces one never bothers saying hello to.

Signatures of the daily verse that languish in the bins of time. Underlining the barren fertility of overcopulating city that had forgotten its libraries. Turn the page, sang Bob Seger.

Room 69 offered dual sinks to drain out a quivering part of the selves; mutual sinks to receive and mutual sources to offer. Twin mouths, twin limbs in pairs. Currents exchanged, offguard.

She was under an intense obligation to unburden herself, her weight must be discharged into this recipient of grim exhilaration, this novice soul thirsty for experience. To paint ever new fictions of the centrifugal plots and centripetal sympathies generated from the city's heart. An entire Chandni Chowk to seduce the Pentax. Old Fort to romance the shutters. Clearing out the jungles of conurbation to create a little pastoral to be viewed through the tiny aperture. There, through that hole, everything was suitably gay, at its poorest best.

Dissociated sensibility indeed. The shrewd voyeur. The sensationalist.

The two non-participants. Insatiable appetite for theories of sex, food, citylights, movement, change, transformation, stalemate.

Cultivated arrogance to keep feelings at bay. Sentimental faggots.

Cynicism as a garb to get ahead, all for self-defense.

Sprezzatura, Castiglione's emphatic old advice.

"Did you always want to teach?" He shot the first arrow, after a while.

"I always wanted to write, and hear my own voice echoing in a room. I wanted others to hear and respond to my voice."

"You should have been on the stage then. Dramatics."

Her naked hands were wearing the gloves again; it would soon get dark and they would get numb.

"I got chucked out once. Pretty early. They said my voice was not fit for the stage. Not good enough without a mike."

Yeah, those squeals in the centre of the huge dais where you had to somersault to the arrogant Tushar Prasad's whims. Never more! Pined and lashed and crazed at the rejection. But wouldn't suck up to the brash male ever again. Would put up a little theater every hour, within minutes of packing up the previous, would shift from class to class with the ease of a mountebank.

"Can't believe it could be you. Had heard you reciting the Kamala Das poem during Harmony." He said quizzically, all set to refute a point of phonetics.

"Without a mike it's different." She cut it short. Let's not dig up rotten graves okay?

The strings are lost. No regaining the semblance of ties, no harping on pale metaphors to strew up a patchy life. Let the senses go haywire, they'd always been that way. Too many tardy indecipherable moments, too many days spent in seclusion, too many names frothing all around to let alone a single soul.

The slight oooh of a pinprick. Otherwise, no more to be heard or felt. Line them up, those endless chat-nicks with a hidden history to parade before a mesmerized pair of eyes. That was all reality had come to signify to her.

There was scope for everything. There was always a listener, a contributor.

She had been grafting faces. Plucked the real out of the imaginary and planted it there, whatever was couched before her sipping coffee, on the plastic red chair carrying the logo Pepsi.

She did not wish it away, the weariness. Perhaps a beginning to another little self-ode. Cultivated and nursed the fickleness, lost in incipient inertia. The twin strings of life: fear and fatigue, wariness and weariness.

.... She woke up all shaken till bones. Out of her reverie. To find herself perspiring mildly. Even in such cold. Dusk invading. Cigarettes lit in several hands. Neon lights that blanketed this insidious city, conscience of ill-illuminated streets, impatient, restless to declare their heart-wrenching stories. And the tiny specks of light emitted from burnt ends of ashened nicotine. Million fireflies swimming in the air headed towards chaotic salvation. All belying their bravado, witnesses to their masks within.

> Dusty by-lanes, our citywalks under neon lamps that make a gilded aquarium of life
> We watersnakes glide in and out, coming back for infested waters
> Our El Dorado swims in orange incandescence of portent myths
> We sink deeper every day like mad seadivers looking for pearls called eyes
> Shuddering with January lightenings, wrapping coldsweat in flesh-blankets
> Or musing under March skies expecting roadside epithalamions anytime
> Marigold beds rise in the airs of zero-gravity, rocketing times of crashes incumbent
> Expanding like a silly fat balloon of heat and disappearing like winking satyrs in no time
> Our heteroglossal love, our copious love of erstwhile loves of people hitherto in love
> Our gossips of fascist poets and communist gaolers, or advocators of

philandering hotbods
Our dispassionate faces before other pleasing faces during those endless coffee-chats
Are but rolls in unfinished reels that wheel and churn us in a cyclotron
We're unplagued lovers, unblighted by Jerusalem's breast or Persian metaphors
Not worried by Yellowstone geysers' flunkey threats or bushy monster's dovetailing lies
And the only ram that matters being Rammohun, we're the 'happy few' snubbing the world for its coarse mischief
We're not puppets, nor mimics, we've escaped it all now in a serene lawn guarded by university palms
We're the neolovers moonstruck once again, bad lunatics out of cells, bringers of rain
Store inflections of the exquisite feeling as definitions accrue in private worlds
Bombarded with worlds we toss them all in amorous games of wicked hobnobs
We're sexual freemasons with sworn allegiances for many moments to come
Dilettantish in all but love we're atypical in a glorious way known to us
We can speak through a kiss or line, self-created, and we toil for them
Looking for 'henceforths' and 'what-about-nows' during fresh forenoon hubris
Poaching the entire globe's weight for rusty measures of uncertainties
We trade in hysteria that's showcased on glittering flashlights of cityscape
Searching endless archives to hide figs of these daily miracles
And after theories, themes, romance let's be apotheosized in a webbed kiss

"Scraps of wetted history of silences personalized over a coffee. How's the line?" He was smiling with a malevolent glee, recklessly curving his thin brown lips to dissolve the last traces of awkwardness.

The two were playing a Beckettian endgame, trying to find the respective barrels to hide themselves. Scramble for stage-grottos.

"Hmm."

I want comfort. I don't want volition. I don't even want seduction.

I just want to be passive in a dignified way

I don't know what exactly is the dignified way

We're on the verge of an exchange, but am afraid.

Haven't you had enough? She gave you your quota of experience in a packet. You wanted sensation. You had it.

And you? Didn't you want too? A passive osmosis? Didn't you offer imaginative inputs into my narration with your spellbinding gaze on my talking mouth?

I can't handle it. There's a surplus of torture every time.

I want to disappear. I'm emptied of everything.

But falling back on silence is the refuge in mediocrity.

As long as she was absent, mute, I was gutsy; now in its intimidating presence I'm just another urban coward. Without my lens I'm a nothing.

Verse is the password for inner circle intimacy. I always had the chance to get ahead. But there's something private about my using of it. I couldn't make it my trump card.

Its dignity always overwhelmed me. I shrunk from its abuse. I couldn't rape the lens. I raped her instead. With a click.

I was horrified by its native squalor. My homeland's.

I was negated in their presence, especially in Kolkata where mother tongue isn't art. It's reality. An alienating one. Never had I written a verse in my tongue. Too afraid. Too insecure.

So I tried making love instead. In my tongue. Got a jarring monotone back.

"Let's check out Bookland before it gets too dark."

SEVENTEEN

Spill

Smoothen the frizz. Let your dry hair relax. Specially tested for Indian hair texture, the Gentle shampoo from Garnier Ultra Doux, enriched with walnut oil and peach leaf, leaves your hair light and shiny. The nourishing conditioner, with its rich melting texture, smoothens and detangles the frizz, making hair soft and manageable. Proven results in just three weeks.

The backcover of a leading Sunday mag donning a picture of a pink-foundationed, wigged (long, shiny, healthy, burgundy-streaked) woman with a settled salved mood on her face.

That morning was a bleak one. It took off with a bang: NO WATER in the taps. Pray why? Not even the stipulated three hours in the morning? Notwithstanding that winters were still on, that summers were still an impossible month and a half away. She had gone down in her nightie to look into the matter. Hadn't bothered wiping off the kohl sticking out from her eyes. Yesterday's thin-lined application now lumped up into a little black globule at the corners. But of course you aren't romancing the plumber are you? The hubby's away. For how long, only he knew. You can afford to miss the bath in fact. There's no water in the flush however. You can't afford to err… shit. Or the better way out would be to shit and … flush it off as and when the water comes. If it gets too stinky, spray the room-freshener.

The generator had burst at a depot. No supply until evening. Pretty little February famine, with the Valentine's Day just a week away. South Delhi's perpetual water crisis made the headlines everywhere. As its ultramod inhabitants did too. Smooth-bodied, frizz-free haired, botoxed betrimmed booties. Never mind the waterless bathrooms. They must be in possession of a secret solution to the mammoth citywide problem. But of course they wouldn't reveal.

At least the net was on. The computer was working. Early at 8:30 in the morning on a lazy slumberous Sunday that was more than enough! Especially when he was not there to lounge around with his menacing eyes criticizing every little bit of her careless existence. He had been gone more than a month now and after the initial days of terrible loneliness she was now beginning to enjoy her re-entry into temporary spinsterhood. Back to her days of girlishness, her swimming in the heap of unwashed clothes piled up on the bed, with herself sprawled somewhere amid all that crumpled fabric. Her diving deep into the 500-gram bottle of Kissan mixed fruit jam without his prancing eyes. He was not there to sniff around if the room was suitably detoxified. There must be some rodent friends of hers, living with her ever since he left. And the balcony had become a splendid potty-pan collecting pigeon poops. She would have to call the *jamadarni* to do the clean-up. For now, the door was tightly shut to close off the foul air.

She had accomplished quite a few feats already, that too by 9:12 a.m. that Sunday morning. She had changed the skin colour of her Yahoo Messenger from a pale lavender to a glittering maverick blue. Her desktop theme was made appropriately animal-friendly by selecting a jumbo-sized shot of an eagle-head with its predatory optical organs beating all escape plans of hapless victims. King of birds there. Though the Miss India among them was the peacock still. Er, there's a miscalculation somewhere. A cock can't be a miss. But then .. well anyway. Cocks can be missed, nevertheless.

From Friday's horrendously pensive disposition, she had evidently bettered. A palpable change of heart there, triggered by what exactly she couldn't figure. Couldn't bother less. All she was feeling was a sharp sense of gastric hunger; the libidinal call had taken a backseat. Yesterday was spent in self-lubrication and self-pampering in the bath. That too with the meagre three-bucket water stored for day round use. Duly cooled, she let herself recline on their doublebed with a newly changed bedsheet all for a wondrous self-satisfaction. And it did work. She woke up at five in the evening, noted the missed calls, got back in the line wherever she wanted to, ordered chicken tikka, chicken mixed chowmein, and shammi kebabs for the dinner. Also asked in for a two-litre bottle of Lehar Pepsi, a big packet of rusk biscuits, and Bikaneri special mixture. Now it made her doubly happy to imagine that such a feast would be anathema to the pink-foundationed girl on the backcover of the Sunday mag.

There was still some food left in the fridge. She took it out, unfinished chowmein, a few pieces of kebabs, all cold, unsavoury to the palate. The half-eaten Bikaneri was lying on the table; she hadn't bothered putting the packet back in the cupboard where they kept stored bakery stuff. She considered breakfasting on the leftover mixture for a while, then junked the idea for good old tea, biscuit, bread-jam. Realized she was glutting since yesterday. Comfort eating? Yeah, Bridget, you made it all hip. Comfort eating rules coz it's still better than binge boozing. No way. Look at those Italian wines, alright their pictures on the Lifestyle page. Some can even beat their French kins. So they say. The gourmets. Paid for eating and drinking. Whoa! That's all what's still good in life. Eating n drinking, n shitting n pissing once overstuffed. The basic natural cycle. Follow mother nature my soul. Rest in her lap. And remember comfort copulation of those early days when nothing really mattered. No partner fixation, no set priorities, no looking back or forth. Just a frothy present, just lots of words and intertwined friendly caresses. But like a fool you desired that your blood stream should boil while fucking, that you must be experiencing nirvana every time you open your doors. Those guides to enhanced sex drive didn't help, that deep tail of the y in your name that supposedly signified a powerful libido didn't help either. Kids today are doubly cynical than they were a few decades ago. Obviously, all knowledge is a step forward in degeneration. Curse yourself for cursing Wordsworth. Curse yourself for making fun of the Child. For mocking innocence. Cut the crap and sip the tea. And don't, don't break that long noodle strand. It's a beauty. Admire its length. Its resilience to the shearing forces of the fork. There, cooked flour standing tall against forked steel.

The computer speaker volume was turned at the max. So that she could hear the 'Knock, Knock, Knock, Ash is online' sitting in the drawing room with the cold grub spread on the centre table and watch *A Streetcar Named Desire* on Zee MGM. Marlon Brando in action. Elia Kazan behind those breath-taking scenes with Vivian Leigh. Her father's choicest movie ever. It was more of an emotional preference for sure. A fantasy fiction of homoerotic idolatry so many males were ushered into at the mere sight of the ravishing Brando. The sixties' men were more full-blooded, more Genet-ic in the boldness of their beliefs. Assertive, believers in redemption. Looking for redemption in their own little way. The bell-bottoms her father was wearing in those dusty photo-albums were personal statements of purpose, notwithstanding his countless bylines in the economic and financial pages of those various Times. Of India, Financial, Economic, Hindustan. Quite a life there, from one-table offices to gigantic media houses with endless cubicles with a computer each. That's progression. But wonder why he left all that and settled for the small weekly eco-political review printed from Kolkata. Finally, they were staying in Salt Lake, finally Maa had a roof-top garden. The cat family too had grown considerably. And Buri, the oldest one was still alive, Maa's most loving companion for almost 10 years now. There were days when Buri and other female cats would get sick, gyrate on the floor due to a throbbing ache in the hind. Just above the anus. Mating calls and desperation would creep through her senile frail body. Buri wasn't allowed to mix with the rest; she was of a terribly jealous nature and had a scarred history of biting a visitor once. A strange life of dual seclusion and company, Buri and Maa. And Baba editing those thin editions of *Viewpoint* from his personal study-room, before the old computer she had known for years. It was still doing fairly well, Baba used to get it checked periodically by the hardware specialist recommended by a friend of his. At times Baba would give her an article to write for him. She would do it at the quickest possible pace and email him. He still didn't know how to sms. Or how to check for the received calls on the cell phone. He still had problems doing an internet search, or typing out difficult URLs on the address bar of the internet explorer. She'd call up and instruct him many times. A sweet role reversal there. She was the far-off secretary her father banked on. The dependable daughter. But only to her father. She had been harsh to a rather soft-souled mother quite often. Those usual quibbles before one decides that it was time to leave the mother's domain and set sail in the big bad world but a world promising a future instead of domestic stagnancy. But of course such resolutions were blown away in time; by the next morning a hot cup of Maa's superb Red Label tea was enough to make the yesterday disappear. Now the warmth was missing. Now she was the one always looking for explanations to defend herself before a sarcastic eye. Often an indifferent eye. Earlier, she would speak like a little snob in the house. Crosstalk at her mother. 'Converse' with Baba. Or manage to interject if Shoili was present.

She would plug in her ears at times in cold rebuke to escape the ceaseless motherly banter Maa showered over her. But there were so many things to talk about. There was always a dialogue happening in their family. Always a debate, always a minor dispute to forget the stalemate. She wondered how her father amassed so much of knowledge without resorting to the Internet. She was baffled at how he ever managed to communicate so much without being able to type a simple message on the cell phone. Mental blocks, the psychology columns would clarify. Break with the old typewriter which now was sentenced to a lifetime of captivity in the Godrej steel almirah they had in their bedroom. Buri, Maa, the typewriter—inmates of the same dungeon of confinement. Dis-use. Detention, incarceration, perpetually in custody. Suffering a mute sentence of internment for nothing beyond ever featured as a possibility. The never been mated Buri if let out in the streets would be ravaged by the curs almost instantly. The old typewriter was unable to bear the load of the excess work the computer could do. And almost no need of discarding a rough sheet there. Just the flawless printouts of the final draft. The first and the last, with no traces of striking off faulty sentences, grammatical errors, syntactical mistakes or a twisted logic in the sequence of points for and against the issue. In-built digital editing, machine-enabled, ubiquitous. Wordiness was an error too, it got the green underline. British spellings too were mistakes; they were underlined red. Sadly Baba never could enable the UK auto-dictionary to decide on the verbiage. He had to bear the wounded blood-spilling words always. On a sea of red they would float as little islands of mutiny. On a screen that had co-opted even red, the notorious colour of dissent, the words would stand out like insurgents before a guillotine of the spell-check bathed in red. The next time she would go to visit him she'd quickly do the needful. All the mending required to make it better. Anything to keep her Baba happy, even living with the facade of a perfect marriage.

The Arnold Anthology of Post-Colonial Literatures in English was lying on the big sofa. She had issued the rather voluminous book on Friday. There, the certified experiences passed off as minority literature. Suitably exotic, some suitably 'diasporic'. She liked the word, Diaspora. Everyone had something to contribute in the expanding meaning of that word. He too dealt with 'spores' at times. Those were encapsulated male or female germ cells to tide over unfavourable periods while ensuring widespread dissemination at the same time. Spreading out. Expanding. Breaking barriers. On the dais of the world a well-marketed popularized self-enactment. Look at me. I'm suitably ethnic, ain't I? With this baggage of inflections, intonations, this skin, this strange nose, these small feet, these broken nails, this frizzy, dry hair that your Garnier Ultra Doux can do nothing about. And see, how well encapsulated I exist! Summer or no summer, I hibernate like a stunted grisly bear in the cave of fear. What would he say? Damn, what if he feels I'm being heedless. No, he wouldn't like that. No I mustn't call up Bono in Mumbai. So what if he's an old friend? Of course, I know he wouldn't ever ask. But you know him, he likes undiluted attention. And under no circumstances would I ever let him have an opportunity to think I'm neglecting him for another. And how can I, I'm incapable of that. He wouldn't express it, he'd swallow all the hurt inside. He's not dispassionate, only a lot reserved. And you love him for precisely that right? See how he has managed to reserve your existence for himself. Congratulations on winning the life of a sweet satellite. Long live the revolution.

Do you really know what exactly are you grunting about?

Not really, eh?

Knew it.

Ariadne Unbound?

Out of your rough Greek hedges
Walking into Ophelia's grave, walking into aphasia
Through eons, through long black tunnels
Without words, unscripted
Now trotting hallucinatory banks, sandbars on Indian beaches
Leave your footprints behind
Abandoned white flesh that singed way back
Tanning at ease, for another's myth
In her white flowing robes she switches on desire
Ringtones make up her sounds, mystic aural metaphors
Of steel, cellophane sheets, other modern details
She has her notepad full
She enters the keys
Picks up old headgear of her lost lover
Perseus, who bended like pipes in history
To transmit alien waters through her
Such museums of love, aches, stylized to fit in

She walks the ramp of history now
Making a washbasin of a helmet
After an epithet from a cached play

******

10:35 am by the computer timer. 10:34 by the cell phone. The rude eagle staring back from the desktop, the palm tree and the sun scorning from the Nokia screen saver.

******

Meetu Suri's StyleFile on Sunday Lounge:

You can wear short skirts with long boots to cover your rather long and thin legs—but in a stylish way to let no one know it's a cover-up.

You shouldn't look top-heavy so go for dark solid colours [black/green/maroon/blue/brown] with a velvet finish. Go for fabric that has a free fall to avoid looking too busty.

Colour and streak your hair to complement your complexion. Burgundy doesn't suit all.

Bask in Sun-deep on Sunday Nexus:

I'm in an illicit relationship with a married woman who's in control of my office life. She dominates me socially and professionally and has been pestering me to help in her husband's promotion. I'm married with two kids and though I have a loving wife at home, I don't gel with her for ours was an arranged marriage. I like to be in the company of my secretary but I hate her dominatrix mode. Also, if she loves me why's she bothered about her husband's promotion. I need help. Please advise.

Cook with Calra on Sunday Lunch:

Nutty ways: Almonds, peanuts, walnuts, pistachios and cashews can really put the spunk back into your life with selective dosage. These are loaded with vitamins and minerals, help run the digestive system and smoothen the tracts, lower blood cholesterol and fight coronary disease. Get nutty and fruity to bring back your salad days.

Keep your cool with the colourful all-season light drinks: Choco Shake, Heavenly Mocha, Coffee Mexicano, Grape Delight, Coconut Colada, French Kiss, Italian Smooch.

The animated world that percolated into her consciousness through the endless columns and write-ups on flashy magazines confirmed one thing about herself: she wasn't a part of all that was happening around. Neither the wild Singaporean luncheons with lions, nor the temple-storming at Ayodhya or remote cases of sati and child marriages in Rajasthan. He was not excluded from his engineered world of biotechnical revolution; Shoili too was engrossed in fighting for battered women in her own way. Baba had always been the committed journalist; Maa had Buri and gang. Where was she?

Her regular doses of irregular India were not extracted from authentic journeys into the hinterlands but from IndoAsians.com's weekly updates on Incredible India. A Sikh holding an enormous black umbrella helping a lungi-clad man to cross a rocky stream with a grayish torrent of water from a gargantuan cataract in the backdrop; an old sandstone house by twilight donning a ghostly bluish-white hue with two red-turbaned gorkhas playing chess on a tiled platform and a veiled woman refilling the hukka; a man rowing a boat in the belly of a calm river on an orange dusk, nature's watercoloured brooklife painted by the divine brush; a close-up of two uniformed pantry-workers leaning out from adjacent bogies on a moving train and exchanging a breakfast tray; a quiet dawn at an obscure railway platform with the coolies reclined on the stone-slabs barely having opened their lids, a few early passengers catching the morning news on All India Radio FM, sipping tea from clay-cups called *bhars*, with the first rays of sun peeping from the peepal canopies shading the drowsy podium. Snapshots of the Indian mosaic, obtained in the blandest possible way, whether in India or Etats Unis d'Amerique. The images were suitably without a caption or addendum, left the imagination to a freewheeling ride of its own. A curious test of geography there; 'spot the indiosyncrasy' session during a break from the online game of TextTwist with the machine. [You needed a real opponent for Literati which originally was the scrabble.] All that could be called Indian about her gaze was the instant response elicited from somewhere within her to those mesmerizing pictures of her beautiful country that was perpetually seeking validation of her suitability from the rest of the world. She was as familiar with those images as she would be with a photograph of a cherished comb or dress or even a book with her signature on the second page. That man in the last snap clad in clothes used to make gunnybags that hold a quintal of rice, that man warming his hands beside a small fire he has managed to light with twigs collected in that jungle, that man living in the huge hole in the banyan tree, his refuse for the one-night-stand, does he really live there, in that obscure forest ostensibly located somewhere in India? What was the proof besides the rags he has on, that it was really shot in India? How to know if those snaps weren't fabricated, a trick of the video-graphics revolution, to mix and merge and forge a saleable India? Why would these breathtaking snaps do the rounds on the net? Why wouldn't she get an Inscrutable America or Indecipherable Britain instead? Why the exclamation mark had to follow a much-typified India always? And who was she to beat her breast lolling on the drawing room sofa for more than seven hours on a breezy Sunday afternoon shuttling between the boobtube and the computer monitor expecting the YM to go knocking anytime?

The pleasures of the self-exiled. The incessant interviews with oneself. The little girl about to be married at the Kalighat temple in Kolkata, her dark face painted with sandalwood paste, her quaint eyes with endless suspended questions all too known to the rest of the world and all too impregnable to her, that little girl now staring at her, from the screen on the BBC News site, that little painted face could say, "I made a soul cry."

******

She was running in an open field. She was heaving, sweating. There were too many masks around her. They had the IDs written on their faces.

A white hand gripped hers strongly and pulled her into a tricoloured tent. The colours were red, white and green.

The white man was Dan. He said, "Let's realize your collective dream of merging into the White. Let me do you a favour."

He was kissing her full on her mouth. She wasn't resisting a bit. She was sucking his insides into hers. She was realizing what she always wanted to be. The dominatrix.

I inspected the red hole some time back
Its mucous lines had all turned black
Used and left off, unattended in caprice

No surreptitious tickles to give it smiles
Only plastic opening and closing of valves…
Here put your hand in mine. What do you see?
A white hand and a yellow hand.
Heh I see a man's and a woman's.
Hmm
See, it's just perspective.
Yeah, it is.
Then?

Then? Then nothing but your selective amnesia, that is what it comes to then.

Okay tell me, what am I forgetting?

Oh you don't need to be told of that now! You can choose to ignore the colour! I can't.

And why can't you?

Coz there's a history of difference and violence associated with them.

And is that all? Still harping on history are we?

Aren't we?

But why? Our relationship without these external markers means nothing to you?

Of course it does. That's why I'm with you right now.

Then why don't you simply come out of your colour paranoia?

Colour paranoia? Oh yeah? Now you're going to tell ME what colour paranoia is? *You*'re going to define what *I*'m going through? Who the hell gave you a right to? And go ahead, I don't quite give a damn you know.

Right. So what're we arguing about when you aren't even going to give a damn.

Arguing? Heh. You see the difference? Don't pretend that you don't. You come here on a pretty little scholarship to do research on the oppressed and marginalized of Indians. Actually in your head you love to nurse the notion that Indians are oppressed and marginalized. You come here as a little white knight, a research scholar bent on discovering the truth, the real state of the temple sex-workers in this remote little patch of oriental idyll. Suitably criticizable, exposable. Blank enough to serve as your guinea pig of theoretical labwork, to be museumized in a slick book of definitions. You come here for a little while, see the dark sides of it, then run for light again, gasping in the experiments of the dark and with a story to tell and grab your share of the cake. Whoa! And, and it's you who doesn't see the difference! Doesn't see the whiteness of your skin and the non-whiteness of mine!

Alright, I'm white. Heck, is that a crime? Does that make me a pest you can't but demonize?

Who's demonizing you? I'm merely telling you what you choose not to see, coz it hurts.

No, it doesn't hurt me. I like you and I'm here with you. The now matters to me and the now I am sharing with you.

Hah, but when you go back to Leeds, this now will be a little speck in your cumulative history, a speck you can tinker around with, present whichever way you want.

It's not me but it's you who's making a lab-exp of our relationship. Tell me honestly, aren't you sleeping with me just because your husband had it with a white woman?

To some extent, but surely that's not all. Your colour ain't your best bait. Unfortunately, you have better things stored in your repertory.

Then why are you hell bent on understanding our relationship simply on that basis?

No, that's not the only basis. But it's there and I'll not hide it.

How does it matter?

Oh it does!

Really? So who's endorsing the inferiority complex now? Who's getting gooseflesh at the mere look of the skin? You or me?

When I look at our skins I don't feel inferior. But I shudder at the bloodshed and self-hatred the difference has caused. And don't forget who created that difference in the first place.

Hey, are you trying to hold me responsible for what happened a century ago?

A century ago? Hah! Take a look around and you'll find innumerable instances of it happening now.

I just don't understand your kinds you know. You folks have a problem with everything. You never seem to look for solutions but are ever searching for more and more problems.

Yeah, coz all solutions are temporary.

Sure, they are, but at least embracing them can lead to a bit of temporary peace of mind.

Peace of mind, indeed!

I never used to believe it but now I'm sure, it's you Indians who are much more racist than we whites are. And look at you, spawning problems like eggs as if there never has been an iota of development anywhere.

You know what, when I and Shumonto used to be chat-friends, there used to be this hoard of chatters we were friends with, scattered all over the world. During those virtual crusades, I had discovered what exactly is meant by what you just said.

Yeah, and you still never felt any ounce of discomfort while talking to your so-called racist brethren. You still never ventured beyond your fixed territories, Kolkata Online and Gazebo.

I did, occasionally, but not out of real interest I admit. Anyway I had friends in these two rooms only. But elsewhere there were things that forbade me from venturing further. I didn't know a foreign language. I still don't. That's a big deterrent.

Then what are you trying to arrive at? A big show of lamenting your racist fraternity's double-standards?

I'm not arriving at anything. There are certain things we just have to live with. For instance, I'd have to live with the fact that for him Irene Scott was the epitome of feminine sexuality, why, coz she was white and buxom. The other faculties that she possessed never attracted him, neither was he bothered to unravel Irene Scott. He desired her, had her, forgot her, resurrected her for precisely the same reason. His white woman.

And aren't you doing the same with me?

Yes and no.

Oh please! I'm nothing more than a white rat for you. You want to see how my white skin gets stained by the intrusion of your yellow. You are only concerned if there's a chemical reaction in your body at the sight and touch of white flesh. You are just experimenting in a controlled set up. And you need a problem to harp on so you create the colour divide while the basic premise doesn't change: you just can't forget that even in this ultramodern world and with your educational qualities your man is in love with your competitor, the white woman. That your man chooses the ghost of a white woman over your live yellow flesh is an out and out insult to your theoretically exalted ego. And therefore you've set out to conquer whiteness, to reclaim yourself by emerging victorious in a resilience test. "I'm not tempted by white skin!"

I'm not. It might produce curiosity but it cannot tempt me. That's a bigger word. Much bigger. And I've not placed Irene as a competitor. You have. And he has. Say something new.

Sure, you love her ghost. There look she comes.

Irene! What are you doing here?

I'm here for the WSF '04.

But aren't you dead? They don't give the badges to ghosts anymore.

Hey, I need to attend it. Get me a badge please.

But you tried drowning me in the loo.

Sorry I did. But this is important. They're dying of AIDS there. I must do something about it. I must sensitize people.

Go back to Dallas. Go away.

They need me here.

No one needs you here.

He needs me here.

He's NOT here! You've snatched him away.

Click!

Who's there?

The Cameraman!

What do you want?

A sensuous clip. Of you two interlocked.

We can't. We are opponents.

Here, take the L'Oreal Hair Color, and here's the Fem Fairness Bleach. Now there would be no difference.

Give me a cherry brown instead. I'll polish her face brown.

Quick, quick, we're running out of time here.

But where's the Black Venus? We want her black back as the backdrop to create the contrast.

We've no time for that! Hurry up!

There!

Knock, Knock, Knock. Ash is Online.

The door to the tent is the YM?

Yeah, didn't you notice? The curtains are maverick blue. You changed them this morning.

But no music?

Yeahhhhhhhhhhhhhhhhhhhhhh. That's what I say when I'm relieved after peeing after a long time!!

Hmmmmmmmmmmmmmmmmmmmmmmm!

Don't dare hmm! Your hmms suck!

Everything sucks as a rule!

You know what sucks the most? That I'm not the son of a stinking rich business tycoon! I mean what the fuck! If I had been a bum, I would have understood. But my only problem is that I can't get anything smoothly in life. I am made to crawl and scrape and bruise myself before I finally get it. Why is the design of life so fucked up? There are millions of people who get things free of cost with the minimum of effort. I know I can screw a 100 at a time. But I never get a level playing ground. You don't know how deeply draining it is to wake up every morning. And get reminded of the fact how fucking insecure your whole fucking life is. It's like living in a fucking bunker for days on together during a nuclear war! I mean what the fuck...

Yeah, these insecurities eat up a person ....

Nothing can eat me up. Absolutely nothing. If anything could have, I wouldn't have survived these 31 years. Yeah! Ha-ha! If I had let anything stop me, I would have been nowhere today. Everything is in the mind. Your fucking hunger is in the mind! Or u can go without food for days! Haha! I won't die so easily. And I am not talking about what people do and what they don't! I am talking about what they can and what they can't.

Yeah, if people think they can, then they can.

Of course! And they do! But the question is whether it's worth it or not. That's all. The first day I came here, I meet this dick in my lab. He's from some MEC somewhere in India. Asks me, so where did you graduate from? I say AIIMS. He asks which year? I say 1996. Then he says didn't you apply in 1996? I said I did. But I got bumps from everywhere. He says "arrey yaar how come?? u are from AIIMS and u got bumps from everywhere!" He was almost talking as if *pata nahi* I was talking to some fucking stud or someone! You know what, I don't have anything against anyone. But somehow it's difficult to rationalize what happens to yourself. You just know you are gonna fuck the whole fucking world when you can someday. Yeah, teach every motherfucker a lesson. No big deal. Just a satisfaction that you fucked the same world which screwed you someday. May be it's difficult for you to understand what I am talking about. May be you are thinking on the same lines as everyone else. That I am a big arrogant thickhead!

I can very well relate to you. In fact, I have indeed gone through similar phases in my life too. And I didn't have practically anyone to turn to. Not even my own family.

Yeah, actually I generally do not turn to anybody when I am in a fix. Coz in the past I haven't found too many people to help me. So I have groomed myself to face my problems alone.

It was bad. But those times taught me to turn to stone for a while. I dunno how those periods passed. I know. I thought the same. In fact, that habit still persists and I know that it gets doubly difficult to communicate to anyone during such a phase. People don't understand you and you can't explain things.

I don't try to explain my problems to anybody unless I am extremely hard-pressed or I feel the person can help.

Yeah, but sometimes you are answerable to people who can't help you out of the situation and they make sure your life is fucking screwed to the max. Such people ask the maximum questions. They just make sure it's turned out the worst for you. They turn your fucking life into living hell.

Yeah so they do. Sometimes being totally oblivious to the fact that they are screwing up your damned life. To be honest, no one else had appreciated my move except for you. It's not easy, I can't mechanically forget things, though I do not voluntarily recollect things. Don't dig up old graves. I found it quite astonishing when you didn't react like the rest. I was very jittery. Thought you'd think I'm an intemperate moron to have done such a thing.

Anybody with a sane frame of mind would have reacted the way I did, though you keep saying I am not sane enough!!

Not really!!! You are crazy enough to have actually understood!!!! Not understanding is the normal situation!

I don't think I want a sanity that cuts off a person from another. It's so difficult for two sane individuals to connect. Perhaps everyone ought to be a little mad, a little innocent, not hard and calculating all the time. Yet a wish is merely a wish. You are the only MCP I adore! Now what do you object at?? To be adored or to be called an MCP?

Nothing. I like calling a spade a spade. A jade a jade. A maid a laid.

You're nuts! Haha!

You did understand me. So I must tell you my problem as well.

Shoot.

My ex-girlfriend was a white-witch. My wife is a skank. I'm sick of both of them. I'm sick of the economic slump that pulls me down. I'm sick of the bumps I got here at every step. I'm sick of the blasts and the terrorist-tag being an Asian puts on my sleeves. Anyway, what's your problem?

I'm obsessed with a man who's a sentimental faggot. Incapable of a single positive emotion. He's wooden. Sing a song of disconnection please. I want to commemorate my misery.

Alright. This is Bad Religion. Music now. Bass! Guitar! Drums!

Can you feel I'm not life anymore
I can't see, I can't breathe
See you quiver like the dogs on the streets
Looking down on as I beat you
It's bad religion, from a broken nation

******

The cell phone. It's ringing. She was awake. Once again with a heavy head. No more afternoon siestas. Take the call.

"Goddammit why do you always take so late to attend my calls? I just gotta say I'm coming back day after." Snap.

EIGHTEEN

Breach

In the softbright golden light of a 60 watt bulb a southpaw was steadying his unruly crop of thick black mane. To the soft notes of John Coltrane a pair of drinking eyes was relishing the scene. The brush in his left hand, greywhite, greyknobbed white bristled, sparkled with a sudden strategic incident ray, drinking eyes drank a bit more, swam in the sea of light and shade, ocean of hallucinatory delight.

Fortyish-fiftyish cinema stuff. With that lightgrey checked shirt and those steelgrey khaki trousers, with that tidal wave of frontal hair and glassless now bare eyes peering into the yellowed washbasin mirror, with those day-old stubbles and tinge of pink on the cheeks, there stood a beauty half aware of itself in the postcoital hour. Bliss was it to be alive and young, or not old enough, and to be gazing was very heaven.

He turned. He saw. Saw her seeing. Watching. Gazing the way she used to. The old way. The comfortable way.

"Still quite the pretty boy."

He heard the words like the way he used to.

"Yeah?" That's like getting an Order of Merit, to be called so, a Legion of Honour, a great something meaningful, a chestful of heart.

"Yes." An unfeigned yes, a truly yessy yes, *Instinctive*, in italics, capital I. Comes out as smooth as breath exhaled, unobstructed, as water gushing out.

"Really, *Madame*?"

He was smiling, wickedly, knowingly. After all these months, enough to make three perilous years, he could still smile in the old way, the comfortable way. Best love friends?

"And to think that you never bothered all these years!"

Not bothered? Who wasn't bothered? What all did botheration imply, entail? Hadn't they been in touch? Those monthly exchanges on Orkut, occasional mails, six-monthly birthday e-cards, featuring on others' lines, getting bitched/dogged about quite often, wondered about, contemplated on, distant-advised at times. These then didn't count? She understood what he understood by botheration. She had different account to give of that aspect of botheration. Physical proximity and its dubious etcetera.

Sure he had the right to complain, to be carping a little, and be nitpickingly sniffy, to transform three to all these and get away unscathed, uncontradicted. It was his time to accrue few real apologies, sincere ones.

He let out a sigh, the old way, the known way, like a Gregory Peck would, or a Gin Kelly.

She could see him scrounging for light, clearing cobwebs of linklessness with his extended left hand. He was trying his best, she could see, with a drop of whine enough to tell her what lay beneath that utterance.

She didn't try forging the non-existent link, didn't try building the broken bridge of correspondence, like the way old lovers do after an unwarranted collision with an ex. Isn't that the way they say it? Old wine, old flame, old heart.

In stead she acted catty.

"And to think that you still bothered, after all these years."

"Guess someone just had to. In this case, this someone is invariably me: me then, me now, me always, idiotically enough."

The grudge-balloon was billowing up, she could see. So she smiled wickedly to prick it. Hot air bubbled out.

"Thank you." She said, meant.

Physical proximity had one day made her want to twist that neck as she had seen in the film *Raat*. The neck's turned around a precise 180 degree getting the back of head on the ventral side. She thought it made a pretty sight, to have a mass of hair instead of the face on the front. She wanted to do it herself, on him. His neck was so handy on that six-by-seven bed in her parents' bedroom, with the gigantic teakwood-carved mirror giving her a beautiful rearview of what could have happened. Wrenching a thing out of existence. Or recasting it, like she would recast Fanon. Give it another mould, do a contrapuntal reading, read against the grain. Reshaping was always fun. Then it sank into her that perhaps she merely wanted it destroyed, merely destroyed. Like one wants to see a lovely painting destroyed, a canvas torn, throw a mugful of blueblackred paint on it. Like one wants to break a statue in a museum, a statue all too preserved and protected, behind glasswalls. Like she had wished the Grecian urn shattered, smashed to minutest shards of his Keatsian imagination. Like one simply wants to rape, at times as a mild hobby, as a bit of self-indulgence, like stoning a crow or kicking a cat.

His neck was a work of art. Someone in his mother's line must have been quite a sculptor of neckgenes, a connoisseur of those AT/GC sequences, how else can one obtain such a perfect neck? Not endlessly long and thin and tapering like that of a swan, but a human neck. Humanly beautiful, humanly destroyable. And what had induced such destructive feelings in her, what had made her realize the destructive feelings in her, what had made her more familiar with her affiliation with a casual rapist? Physical proximity, merely that.

How often does one feel that way? To kill, to twist, to gun down, to stab, to wrench, just like that?

Just like that she had traced the contours of his neck, devising all the while how to break it, rather imaging the broken neck. She saw no blood coming out. That recast it was to have, had got to have the absolute finish. Finesse. Fineness. To have blood guzzling out would look messy, like the work of an amateur painter who has taken a nascent delight in gore. Finesse. Neat and clean and pretty, a twisted neck.

She had kissed it most obsessively, making a pool of hot saliva at the points where the jugular vein made its skin ridge. Where she could feel it running underneath. Where she could feel something throbbing. Or was that the cranial artery, she mused, that made itself so conspicuous, so vulnerable to a merciless thumbrape, so beaten a beat of gullible physiognomy. She marvelled at the sheer fragility of that human frame, how easy was it to demolish it, such strategic points abound in that familiar body, such familiar points inviting incisions, dreams of such tender incisions of little deaths, shy bruises accompanying nailscars, deadening for a moment, or deadening forever. Mere impulse and strategy.

Yet when that neck was too far to touch and bruise, she caressed it lovingly. A thicker neck was girdling hers up then, she would snakelimb around it as interdigitations would grow, invisible tendrils would grow. Handling two of them she would draw herself out into a straightened rope and then coil around both of them. Physically around one, mentally around the other. Thus the set up resembled a pulley of sort, a rope tied to two poles endlessly pulled from both ends. A gymnast circling from pole to pole. A pole dancer in the nude. Imbalancing polarities.

Paradoxes are seldom not strange, brooding with one in all uncanniness. Living a lifetime with her until they announce themselves. That what was, now is not though once it might have been. Like those dead stars that one finds up there. Keeping the illusion going somehow long after they have been burnt to cinders. Eons too late, light-years too far. Old brown papers with maudlin scribbles made musty over the long drawn years, discovered only now, crazy portals!

What had caused that 'him' of yonder time to reflect such moods by lamplights or dark? 'Us' sounds pretty absurd now, like two atoms whose valenceis failed the molecule.

"Freedom bounce hurts."

Her voice was shaky, though she was declamatory.

He still didn't know what to say to her, lost in her calm listlessness, her unmoved storms. She was testing him again, yet again, as if he was a little frog she could examine at will. He knew she had a spate of specimens hidden somewhere: toads, cockroaches, rats, pigeons, moths.

"You didn't have to," he said at last.

"Oh I had to, just had to!" She was unsteady and firm. Driven by a great impulse and strategy she was all that and more.

"I just had to Mitakshara Thakur. What would you know of the sheer thrill of this? Zero! Nothing, you know absogoddamnlutely nothing about my present situation. Not that I ever expected you to know, not that either. But then you called so suddenly and after so long that I think I owe you a little briefing on my state. Yes I am free, *free* in that magnificent sense of it, free with all the encumbrances unremoved, still *free*. Free for the time being. No job, lovely. Resignation when premature and voluntary is very precious. And liberating. In all sense of it. No hang ups. Money? Oh he'll gimme money! He'll feed me. Keep me. Oh am such a little brat. It gives me so much of fun to think of me as a spoilt little wifey. I might keep a little doggy you know, one of those fancy breeds. What do you call 'em? Chihuahua Taco Bell dog? Ala Paris Hilton. I'll go in for nosejobs, hair-streaks, bikini waxes and all of that. Then this arty little smarty will head for exhibitions of all kinds, exhibiting herself, if you please. Hey I'll work on this freaking frame of body, make it as doll-like as possible, as sculpted, as automatic and ordered, until, my love, until honeyball, I give up all that for a peculiar crabbiness of a kind. And that's when he finally gets the JHU post, there I'll fly along with him. Destination EnnuiSea. That whole big place is that. Just that. An ocean of concocted visions. Where I'll contribute one of my own.

Livecam. EnnuiSea. LondonUranus. Splendour. Consumption. Placid beaches. Florida. Tall towers. Seattle. Casino royal. Vegas. Intrepid. Moscow. Tokyo.

Where's Iraq? Where's Guantanamo? *Crazyy? Earthcams to be wasted on them deserts*?

Never!

Stealthy mails of raped women screaming. Soldiers laughing, putting it in and out. Rhythmically.

Then a voice:

You filthy bitch. Porn for your kinds, eh?

Makes you feel radical, makes you feel fucked, awesome!

Space floats serene and frenetic ..

Space maddens. Whole world's a screen. Whole time a click, a beep, or a blast.

"But you know what? Before all that commences, I'd have had my revenge."

He stared at her glaring face, unable to gauge what her rhetoric implied.

"No, not in the future. I have had my revenge. Today. Imagine my pleasure when he gets to smell your cologne on my breasts! Bliss, pure bliss! Just a few hours away. Just with a plane landing."

City, City, my murderess, my saviour! Haven't I fought all my life for you? To be with you, in you, inside you? City, haven't I resisted pressures to leave your wasted breast and neon lights for laps of distant alien greens? For orchards and lawns and grasslands and rural sweetness of a very rich land? All the lures of ecological beneficence and economic-munificence, haven't I stayed clear of all of them until this moment? But now I'll make an epic entry into all that I stood against and you will watch it, City. Oh yes, you will.

Earthcam with its autoreferential pretty images of livable life, throbbing and on a virtual platter. Exported visions of life. That is all life is and ever can be. LondonUranus EnnuiSea different from all imagination of all History. Each to his or her own, big images of big history, big men, big women, big cars, big apartments, big flats, big televisions, big washing machines, big tanks, big MiGs, big bucks.

"You were never this broken Ivy. I've never seen you this broken."

"Shut up, silly. Who's broken? Honey, I'm about to begin my real life, at last. The Real Life that unfolds in parentheses, love. In brackets, between words. With unheard knockknocks, Unanswered who'stheres?. We generally have the status: Invisible to All. We disappear like smoke. Leave no ashes if we're smart enough."

She didn't know what she was saying. All she knew was that her life of conscious infidelity had begun, commenced. Now she was really virtual. Authentically so. For it was now that physical proximity has been given its due. Breach has been committed in the name of distance, as an ode to distance, as an excuse to substantiate distance. This time, she was happy to realize, the breach was from her side…

And that was the beginning of poetry…